Many Savage Moons

A Novel

I0678890

Ben Spencer

KNOCK-KNEE BOOKS

About the Author

Ben Spencer lives in Concord, NC, with his wife and daughter. Please visit benspencerwrites.com and/or benspencer.substack.com for information on Ben's latest writing projects.

ALSO BY BEN SPENCER

THE DEER KING (Novellas)

The Deer King

The Sundering

Last of the Baronites

For You

Part I

2008

She looked like gothic architecture, like a nineties indie movie, like the night after Christmas. He had spotted her in the bookstore and considered approaching, but she was leafing through *Birds of America* and he was embarrassed that he hadn't read Lorrie Moore's work. But now here she stood, one of the front-of-the-mall folk, smoking a cigarette. He angled her way, the swirling smoke from her cigarette beckoning him closer like witch's fingers. Tasty in the nostrils. She saw him and bit.

"What do you want?"

"A smoke?" he chanced, eyes moon-pie wide.

"No." She ashed a nuclear winter. Spotted the Borders plastic. "Not unless…what's in the bag?"

"*Shalimar the Clown.* Rushdie."

She eyed him, a sprite's mischief therein. "Trade you, straight up."

Fuuuuuuuck, he thought. He loved Rushdie, and sixteen bucks was sixteen bucks. Still, the thought of where a grand gesture might lead intrigued him, so he handed over the goods. "All right," he said, "but I'm issuing a fatwah on you to get it back."

She laughed, surrendered a Camel Light. The twining ivy of her neck tattoo showed as she leaned in with the lighter, the plant ravenous, wanting to strangle. Black hair, possibly dyed, flowed like the River Styx. Pearlescent skin. She wore jeans surprisingly free of holes and a thin, cheese-rind–red jacket over a sloganed black T-shirt. Nathaniel couldn't read the words.

"What's your name?"

She leaned into the next inhalation, sending the smoke into the catacombs of her lungs. "Winter," she said as the smoke rolled out, fog on a glassy sea. "Winter York. And you?"

"Nathaniel Pilot."

She cocked an eyebrow. "Pilot?"

"Like the light, not the guy flying the plane."

She grinned, peered at him through mail-slot eyelids. Took another drag. Ashed a flurry. "Okay, then. What do you want? A drink? My phone number?"

"Your phone number. But that's only because I'm going to need a book review when you're done," he said, nodding at the bag in her possession.

He thought she meant to laugh, but her eyes snagged on someone in the far parking lot. He followed her line of vision, found a linebacker waiting, sandy blond hair atop a Lego-brick body and closing fast. She dropped her cigarette, now all cherry, and stamped it out. "How about we fast-forward to a date? Are you parked nearby?"

He pointed to a blue Civic in a second-row spot to their right, readily accessible.

"Okay," she said, nervy. "Let's go."

*

He sped out of the parking lot, their hapless pursuer a pinprick in the rearview mirror. Nathaniel wasn't worried about being followed—it was the greater Charlotte area, there was an interstate; Captain Muscles couldn't catch them if he flagged down a jinn and wished for a carpet. As they sped away, she tapped her fingernails on her teeth, the nervous heartbeat of a tiny marching band.

"Let me guess. Problems with organized crime."

The tapping stopped. "What?"

"The guy in the mall parking lot. He's from the mob, right? This being North Carolina, I'm going with the Pepper Flake Gang. Crazy bastards. They caught you eating...no, *selling* vinegar-based BBQ. Shit. That's it. You're the owner of a vinegar-based barbeque joint trying to open up shop in western NC and the Pepper Flake Gang contracted Joe Hoss back there to put a hit on you."

He was hoping for another smile, but instead she gave him a look of dull amusement, possibly ironic. "Do you eat a lot of barbeque?" she asked. She tapped out another Camel as she spoke, eyebrows trampolining into an arch, a silent request for permission to roll down the passenger-side power window and light up. He wasn't thrilled with the idea, but he gave his assent nonetheless by way of a quick head nod.

"I wouldn't say a lot. A normal amount. Four, five times a week, tops." He didn't usually make this many jokes, but now that he'd started, he was having a difficult time striking a balance. *Dial it back a bit, Chuckles,* he chided himself.

"Seems reasonable," she said, granting him a generous smile. "Actually, I'm vegan. Kind of. I'm on my fifth go-around, but I'm optimistic that this time I'll make it stick."

"A vegan, huh? Cool. What was your Achilles Heel the first four times around?"

They were roaring like rapids toward the city proper, south on I-77 in the direction of uptown, which was what the good people of Charlotte called downtown. Noise barriers parted the pavement like the hands of an urban god. "Dairy. Specifically cheese. I can behave at my place, but then I'll go out with my friends to a pizza joint and the mozza-fuckin-rella will get the best of me. It's difficult being a vegan and having a social life at the same time."

"I bet. Me, I couldn't do it. The ice cream withdrawals alone would send me into shock."

He glanced and saw that she was smiling again, but it was a distracted grin, a watch face covering grinding gears. Whoever linebacker Bob was back there, he had his hooks in her thoughts. Nathaniel was undeterred. He knew that he wanted to win her affection. His initial attraction to her had been instinctual, strong to the point of being disconcerting, and charged by the tension that he didn't belong in her realm—meaning the tattooed, red-leather, cigarette-smoking demesne.

"So where are you taking me?" she asked.

"Did you get your tattoo in Charlotte?" he replied, answering a question with a question.

"I suppose that depends on which tattoo we're talking about." Her eyebrows flirted with him, or maybe he imagined it.

"I've always wanted a tattoo," he claimed. "An anchor, perhaps. Or a pale, frosty moon."

"A moon?" she questioned, as if the suggestion had caught her unexpected.

"Yes, a moon."

She smiled, brushing aside whatever it was about the idea of a tattooed moon that bothered her. "Are you asking me to point you in the direction of a tattoo parlor?"

There were days in life like this, Nathaniel knew, but they were rare; days when the humdrum fractured and possibilities seeped in, possibilities that required a certain impulsivity and recklessness to be capitalized upon, days that called upon *yeses* to questions heretofore unconsidered. One tattoo was worth drinking long and hard from such a day's cup. "Yeah. Sure. You point me toward a tattoo parlor where they won't misspell *mom*, and I'm game."

He was watching the road but he felt her gaze on him, piercing and curious. He risked a glance and their eyes met with a spark; her striated greens kicked up a kind of helter-skelter pulse in his body, and, for the briefest of moments, he felt as if she was inside of his skin, wreaking havoc with the wiring.

"I know a place," she said. Her voice was earnest, like green tea. He thought he must have struck a chord in the very soul of her, but she quickly brought him back to earth. "Then, after you get your tattoo, you can take me back to the mall." He must have looked confused, because she said, "My car is still there, you know."

He hadn't given the first thought to her car. "Yes, of course. Back with the hit man from the Pepper Flake Gang."

As soon as he said it, he knew that he had mentioned parking lot guy one time too many. She didn't say a word, simply stared ahead, allowing the silence and the cigarette smoke to hang in the air like bad humors. *Idiot,* he thought, chastising himself. Not wanting to let the bad mood fester, he changed the subject back to their impending adventure.

"So, which way to the tattoo parlor?"

*

Other than its underground location beneath a bevy of street-front consignment shops, the tattoo parlor was the opposite of what Nathaniel had expected: it had the feel of a pristine cave, the sort of abode where cultured fairies and nymphs might dwell. Its subterranean polish was tempered by the kitschy furniture and the sandalwood incense drifting through the air; combined, they blunted what might otherwise have been too severe an aesthetic. Nathaniel's attention was immediately drawn to the paintings on the walls, a fairly cohesive collection that struck Nathaniel as playfully dark. There were blue-black bats weaving through the gloaming, a midnight island on a tempestuous sea, and a trio of red and silver abstracts dissected by a thread of yellow and black—the coil of bumblebee colors plunged into the heart of the first two abstracts before unraveling into chaos on the third. Nathaniel was taken in by the abstracts immediately. He thought they looked like Rothkos transforming into Pollocks.

"She's good, isn't she?" asked Winter.

"Yes. Clearly."

"Wait until you see what she can do with a tattoo."

Nearby, but out of sight, the dental buzz of a tattoo gun short-circuited into silence. The tattoo artist and her client were hidden behind a Shoji panel, a pair of gentle silhouettes and a reclining chair. The artist peeked around the paper screen. Seeing Winter, she broke out the pearly whites.

"It's you!" she exclaimed.

"It's *you*!" Winter replied in turn, effervescent. Nathaniel watched with interest as the artist broke away from her work to give Winter a more personal greeting, a would-be hug that, owing to tattoo gloves, turned into an Eskimo kiss of sorts, noses not quite brushing but coming close. They laughed at the awkward intimacy of it. When the tattoo artist turned to Nathaniel, he half-expected a rebuff for infringing where he didn't belong, but no, she gifted him the same show of teeth and a countenance so bright, it bordered on expectant. For a moment he felt as if he was seeing an old friend but embarrassingly had forgotten who they were.

"Name, please?" the tattoo artist asked with an affected formality. Whether she was teasing him or teasing Winter, Nathaniel wasn't sure.

"Oh, this is Nathaniel," Winter answered for him, laying a proprietary hand on his arm. He leaned into the touch a little, attempting to signal, as new romantic interests do, all manner of unspoken desire through this first kiss of skin. "He's looking to get inked."

"Today?" The artist crinkled her nose.

"It's an impulse tat!" Winter said, making it sound like a positive. "Something small. He was thinking of an anchor, maybe, or"—she turned to Nathaniel—"what else did you have in mind?"

"A pale, frosty moon."

The tattoo artist smirked sweetly. Nathaniel glanced at her arms. What looked like a billowing storm cloud of ink erupted out of the armholes of her simple gray T-shirt, fragmenting into birds that flew up both forearms all the way to her wrists. She caught Nathaniel in the act. "We could do the phases of the moon," she said, eyes alight with mischief. She turned her forearms vertical so that the birds soared toward the heavens. "Run it up your arm like so. We'll be twins. My birds can fly to your moons." She must have seen the fear in his eyes, because she laughed, a proper guffaw. "Or we can put it on your deltoid. I assume that was your first choice?"

"Yes," he responded, too out of sorts to say anything clever. He feared that if he feigned nonchalance, he might leave the parlor with a full sleeve.

"Okay then," the tattoo artist said, giving Winter an only-because-it's-you look before returning her attention to Nathaniel. "My name is Kelly Anne. First let me finish up with my client. I should be done in about thirty minutes. Then we'll see about that moon." As she walked away, she made eyes at Winter once more, adolescent peepers voicing noiseless opinions about the boy in the room. Winter flipped her off. Kelly Anne laughed, a schoolgirl in spirit.

Nathaniel and Winter retreated to the couch, a pinstriped red and white that looked like it had sprung from the imagination of a Soda Jerk. They settled into the rather firm cushions with a touch of self-awareness. Nathaniel had been slightly embarrassed by the tattoo artist's eyeball insinuations, but all in all he supposed it was for the best. For the first time that evening, it felt like they were on a legitimate date. When he looked at Winter, she failed to meet his gaze for a sheepish moment. A positive sign, he thought. His eyes descended, as men's eyes are prone to do, and, among other things, he was able to decipher the slogan on her shirt.

"You're a plagiarist? Who did you plagiarize?"

She verified the emblazoned white lettering on her shirt with a quick glance, **plagiarist** in a playful, lowercase font. She mused for a moment over her reply. "Hmm. My mother, for one, more times than I'd care to admit. Eleanor Roosevelt, on my college application. Richard Ashcroft—"

"The singer for the Verve?"

"Oh, yes! I've been known to stare off into the middle distance and recite Verve lyrics like poetry, claim them as my own. You can get away with it on this side of the Atlantic, unless you slip up and start in on 'Bittersweet Symphony.'"

Nathaniel laughed. "Tell me more."

"Okay. When my first serious boyfriend was on the verge of breaking up with me, I tried to stop him by channeling Tom Cruise in *Jerry Maguire*."

"You said 'You complete me'? Really?"

"Uh-huh. On his parents' porch with tears streaming down my face. I'm not sure if it counts as plagiarism, though, because in the moment I truly believed it."

She was wry from top to bottom. He laughed in spite of himself. She reached over and took one of his hands with both of her own, a smile like a cracked egg spreading across her lips, there and then gone again. Her droll mien reassumed, she raised concerned-counselor eyebrows. "Now, you."

"Now, me what?"

"Share. Something. Anything. Just make it real."

Her hands felt like chilled rose petals, papery-soft and lovely. He searched for something genuine to say, but everything real about him seemed tied up with who he had been with his former girlfriend, Angelica, and he didn't want to tarnish this new beginning by invoking the specter of the past. Time ticked. A couple of lame jokes crept to his tongue, but he held them in, sensing that by giving in to the temptation, he'd be copping out. He began to feel embarrassed. Maybe even a flicker of anger. But then it surfaced, a great gray whale of authenticity propelling out of the depths to present itself to his conscious mind. *Fuck,* he thought when he thought of it, but it was a call-to-arms *fuck,* the sort of don't-give-a-fuck-*fuck* that begged to be played like a trump card against one's better judgment. Based on his impressions of Winter, he thought she might appreciate it.

"I saw a ghost once."

"You're kidding," she said, intrigued.

"No. It happened during spring break when I was in college."

Quizzical eyes, a sly grin just short of a smirk. "That's...an uncommon time to see a ghost."

Nathaniel gestured "hold up" with his hands. "It's not what you think. A group of buddies and I had rented a cabin up in the mountains. We were playing poker one night and I lost first, so I decided to go outside and enjoy the night air. And yes...I was inebriated. There was a clearing behind the cabin, and I walked out into the middle of it to have a better look at the stars. I was standing there when a woman appeared from out of the woods. She was dressed in a simple white cotton dress and she walked right toward me. I remember genuinely thinking that she was real. But the closer she came, she started to dematerialize, until, when she was about seven or eight feet away, she vanished altogether."

"Did she say anything?"

"She raised her hand and opened her mouth just before she disappeared, but no sound came out."

Winter ruminated on the specter's soundless O the way a sleuth might on a clue. "Did you tell your friends?"

"No. I never told anyone. Wait, I take that back—I told my brother once, after a long night of drinking, but it made him uncomfortable, so I dropped it, and never brought it up again."

She pulled her hands away from his startlingly quick, small creatures evading a snare. He felt the loss of them, and for a moment wondered if he'd done something wrong, but when he looked up at her wandering-planet eyes, he knew it wasn't anything he had done that had caused the hiccup. She started to speak, but then bit the words into her bottom lip. She smiled and said something else.

"A ghost. Do you believe in ghosts, now that you've seen one?"

"That's a good question. Funny enough, I'm not sure. I've lost the sense of certainty that I had back then. All I know now is that at the time, I didn't have a doubt."

She appeared content with his answer. "I feel that way myself, sometimes. About the past." All at once she looked uneasily into the middle distance, as if she was trying to find the right vantage point from which to view her own secret history. "Looking back, I sometimes find it hard to tell the difference between what was real and what wasn't real. And then at other times I can't help but think: what if the ghosts of the past come back?"

He couldn't tell if she was speaking metaphorically or literally, but the look on her face unnerved him. He started to ask her if she had ever had an experience with ghosts, but before he could, she stood up and gestured at a water cooler in the corner of the parlor. "I'm thirsty," she said. "Would you like a cup of water?" He shook his head. She walked away.

He stole a look at her as she left, trying not to gawk but appreciating the sway of her ass in denim. Reeling in his eyes, he used the spare moment to put his thoughts in order. There was no doubt that he was falling for her, no doubt at all, and all the signs suggested that she was, at the very least, enjoying their time together. Having reached the age of twenty-seven, he had too much experience with relationships to believe in falling in love at first sight, but he did believe that two people could make an initial connection that suggested other forces were at play. He had experienced it years ago with Angelica: a voice, distant but unmistakably clear, had whispered in his mind, *She's the one.* No voice had spoken this time, but from the moment he met Winter, he felt as if he were being pulled into her orbit by the mystery of her personality. He was taken with what he'd seen on the surface, but, like the twining ivy diving down her neck, he sensed that she was rooted to deeper layers, and that if he did her the honor of waiting patiently, she would show him a truer version of herself.

She returned chewing on a thought. "I nearly mentioned this earlier, when you said that you had seen a ghost…"

She was interrupted by the opening of the tattoo parlor's front door. A draft of early autumn wind came kicking in, playfully assaulting the room with its cooler temperatures. Nathaniel hoped to hold Winter's attention, but the spell of the conversation was broken; with feline alertness her eyes went to the door, ascertaining the threat level of whoever had walked in. He watched as her face relaxed and her eyes contracted into mellow pools, and only then did he turn, expecting to see some innocuous character but instead laying eyes on one of the largest human beings he had ever seen, a colossal demigod of a man wearing a sleeveless T-shirt and cargo shorts while sporting a beard that called to mind Kris Kringle if the jolly old elf had survived a stint in a Siberian gulag. Covering the man's right arm was a brilliant orange and blue octopus. The blue underside of the tentacles licked at the man's elbows and upper shoulder, while the bright orange body floated in a brachial sea of flesh. The octopus looked stunningly alive, even more so, perhaps, than the man, who, if his expression was any indication, had recently been either drugged or sainted.

"Hello, O," Winter said to the giant.

"Oh. Hello, Winter," the big man replied in turn. The oddly-named O cocked his head at Winter like a perplexed parrot. "Funny seeing you in here today."

"Why is that?"

"There was a man in here earlier today? Looked like a surfer dude who had grown up and gotten a job at a bank? Big guy, muscles, but with a professorial air? He was asking about you. He said…"

Kelly Anne's voice sang out from behind the Shoji panel. "Shuuuuut uuuup, Ooooo," she crooned, in the singsong register people use when they don't have a means for speaking in code.

O looked stumped for a moment. Then, comprehension dawning, he backtracked and made things worse. "I mean, there was a guy, he said he maybe knew you? But it wasn't anything… I don't think…wait, that's it!—he said that you recommended the tattoo parlor to him. That's all." The big man shifted his gaze to Nathaniel and repeated himself for emphasis. "Yeah. That was it."

Another ditty from behind the wood-framed paper door. "Thaaaat diiiiidn't heeelp, Ooooo."

The big man dropped his chin and brought two fingers to the spot where his bindi would have been, were he Hindu.

Winter intervened. "O, Nathaniel. Nathaniel, O." Nathaniel glanced at Winter before he stepped forward to offer O his hand, and saw, to his concern, that she looked unsettled rather than embarrassed, the same as she had in the mall parking lot. He assumed that the man in question was the same one that he had seen at the mall.

"Hello," O said, wrapping his ham-sandwich paw around Nathaniel's.

"Nice to meet you," Nathaniel replied. "O? Is it short for something?"

O, grimacing, mumbled, "Yes."

"A taboo topic here in the tattoo parlor," Winter explained, stepping in to steer the subject once again. "O is Kelly Anne's business partner. And the parlor's other tattoo artist."

"Gotcha," said Nathaniel. He wondered if he should mention his impending tattoo, but O figured it out quickly enough.

"Are you waiting on Kelly Anne for a tattoo?"

"Yes."

"Is this a walk-in?" he asked, loud enough for the entire parlor to hear.

"He walked in with Winter, if that's what you mean," Kelly Anne called from the back. Nathaniel could hear both Kelly Anne and Kelly Anne's client snickering.

Nathaniel looked at Winter, who rolled her eyes. Before turning away, she blessed Nathaniel with a flirtatious *fuck them* wink, a strong enough sacrament to make him feel immune to the ribbings.

"What type of tattoo are you looking to get?" O asked, seemingly oblivious to the minor drama surrounding him.

"A moon, I think."

O nodded, suddenly very present. "And where do you want it?"

"On my upper arm."

"All right. If you have your heart set on Kelly Anne, I understand, but I'll be more than happy to sketch a design for you if you would like to see what I can come up with. Your call."

Nathaniel looked to Winter. "He did the birds on Kelly Anne's forearms," she said. The softness in her eyes suggested that going with O wasn't a bad choice, only a different one.

He turned back to O. "Sure."

*

Nathaniel was deep into the tattoo, trying to settle into the bones of the pain, when O leaned in and jarred him out of his zen-like trance. "Hey man," the tattooist said in a thick, furtive whisper, his breath smelling an oniony pong. "Listen, I don't know how you know Winter, but I would tread carefully if I were you."

Nathaniel opened his eyes. Winter and Kelly Anne, who had been standing close by moments ago, had wandered off and were out of earshot. O, poised with the needle, looked a bit the mad King Triton, the octopus flexing into view.

"What's that supposed to mean?"

O huffed, but he kept his voice down. He clearly didn't want the women to hear. "I don't know if you've noticed, but Winter is…different. And it's not just a put-on. The otherworldly vibe she gives off is earned. It's like she lives two lives. One here, and another in a dark dream. Listen," O continued, leaning in even closer, "I've eavesdropped on enough of her conversations with Kelly Anne to know that she's got some weird shit in her past. Maybe even in her present."

Nathaniel gave an uncertain chuckle. "Thanks for the warning, but I—"

O plowed through Nathaniel's response. "And the guy I mentioned earlier? I don't know if he's an ex-boyfriend or what, but you could tell by the way he was talking about Winter that he is a very possessive sort of guy. He was all nervous and jittery, and he kept saying that he had to see Winter or his life was over. Weird, stalkery shit like that. He was real…um…handsy, too. He must have touched me on the shoulder ten or fifteen times. He even left his phone number, told me to call if she showed up. Not that I'm going to…"

Nathaniel tried to digest this information as best as he could, but Winter and Kelly Anne were returning, engaged in their own whisper duel. Winter wore a sour apple expression, while Kelly Anne seemed to be making some final point. The unsettling nature of what O had told him suddenly cast Winter in a new light, and Nathaniel, for the first time that evening, saw her for the stranger that she was, and not as the tattooed earth goddess that he had conjured in his mind. But then she dropped the sour apple face and turned to look at him, and he lost his purchase on the insight.

"It's coming along really nice," she assured him as she approached, looking at the tattoo. O had added a few artistic flourishes to Nathaniel's straightforward concept, overlaying the moon with clouds and including an impression of a faint nighttime sky. Nathaniel had been pleased when he saw the sketch—it was undoubtedly superior to the prosaic satellite he had envisioned in his mind's eye. Of course, he hadn't seen it since the real work began; for all he knew, O had butchered the original and was now tattooing a Rorschach blob.

"Why wouldn't it be?" O said, sounding peevish. He looked like he was nursing an unspoken grudge.

Kelly Anne reached over, and, waiting until O was in-between ink strokes, strummed the harpsichord of hair at the base of his skull. "Now O," she said, "that's not how we talk to friends."

O grunted, but didn't respond. Winter eyed him curiously for a moment, a rejoinder on the tip of her tongue, but, after a moment's consideration, turned to Nathaniel instead.

"There's a pizza place up the road if you want to get a bite to eat after your tattoo's finished," she said.

"Yeah. Of course. But wait…what about your car?"

"It can wait." She graced him with another smile. He had more to say, but the two tattooists were taking up too much space in the room. Tattoo parlors, he decided, weren't the best place to take first dates: it was hard to make a connection with an eccentric friend and a grumpy octopus-man in the way.

O continued tattooing, but beneath the buzz, Nathaniel could hear him breathing big-bad-wolf breaths, huffing and puffing, working himself up to speak. At last, he let fly. "So, Winter, did you know the guy who stopped by earlier today?"

She turned stone-faced. She seemingly hadn't minded the subject of parking lot man so long as he was alluded to in passing, but, faced with a direct question like this one and the one Nathaniel had asked her in the car, her strategy appeared to be ignoring the matter entirely.

O pressed on. "Look, I'm not trying to make things uncomfortable for you or...your new boyfriend here"—Nathaniel felt a blush blooming in his cheeks—"but this guy was really intense, and he seemed determined to find you one way or the other. If he comes back again, I'm going to..."

"Look. She knows, okay?" Kelly Anne interrupted. "God, O, just relax for once. What did you think we were talking about over there?"

"He's not an old boyfriend," Winter interjected, her voice sounding like chipped ice. Nathaniel met her eyes and she met his. She was speaking to him, apparently. "He was my professor back in college. Creative Writing. He developed a strange obsession with me at the time. There was never anything...between us. Not on my end, anyway. For whatever reason, he's trying to make contact with me again. It started a few days ago. I thought ignoring him would do the trick, but I guess not. Still, it's no big deal. I've dealt with him before and I know how to deal with him again."

Nathaniel nodded, trying to convey by way of the twinkle in his eye that she didn't have to explain. No one spoke. The smell of sandalwood seemed to intensify, and for the moment everyone appeared to acquiesce to its calming effects. O, who had stopped working, was the first to come back to life, firing the tattoo gun and mumbling something akin to an apology. "All right. Maybe I was out of line. I just don't want you to get hurt, Winter. You know? You're like family to us here."

"You don't have to worry about me," Winter replied. "I can take care of myself."

*

North Davidson Street, aka NoDa, wore its bohemian heart on its sleeve: here a busker strummed an acoustic guitar while crooning a melancholic, British falsetto, begging not to be left "High and Dry"; there two women sporting multitudinous rings on a myriad of body parts held hands, sharing drags off a cigarette; everywhere the unconventional reigned, whether in the form of a crepe shop or a stirring graffiti mural of the Democratic nominee for president or a wine bar that catered to dog owners, NoDa was one area of Charlotte that refused to be polished into the city's shiny, banking exterior.

The moon above was a partial sand dollar, smudged by nothingness at the outer edges. The moon on Nathaniel's arm was a visual riddle, seemingly full beneath O's inky clouds but obscured enough that it begged multiple looks: both Nathaniel and Winter kept pulling up the sleeve of Nathaniel's shirt and pushing aside the protective plastic wrap, trying to determine if they were seeing what they thought they were seeing.

"Waxing gibbous," Winter decided, but as soon she'd made up her mind, she brought Nathaniel to yet another stop beneath a streetlight and took a closer look. They were a block past the busker, and from behind him Nathaniel could hear the tune reach its end, the melody surrendered. "Or is that the shadow of a cloud? The way O uses negative space really messes with your perception."

"I know," Nathaniel agreed, but he was distracted by Winter's closeness, her fingers grazing his flesh.

She rolled his sleeve back down. Then she studied him for a moment. He tried to hold her gaze, but the unabashed nature of it spooked him, so much so that he nearly looked away. She spoke before he could break the connection. "You're meeting me at a good moment in my life. I think you should know that. I've been a little...adrift...for a few years, but the last few months I've found my bearings. There was a time when I thought of myself as a hard-luck sort of girl, but lately, everything that happens to me seems to be infused with serendipity." A grin like a paring knife broke out on her face. "You're crushing on me pretty hard, aren't you?" She said it teasingly.

He searched for a clever retort, but the clock caught up with him. He sighed. Smiled. "Yes."

"Good to know," she said, and she skipped away from him a bit. She let her eyes trail behind her, leaving bread crumbs. "Come on, the pizza place is this way."

He followed Winter around the corner. The pizza joint, named Broosters, came into view. They walked inside together. While the hostess located a table, Nathaniel took a look around. To his left, a lively bar ran the length of the restaurant, every bar stool filled. To his right, small white tables that looked like decapitated mushrooms populated the room, the majority of them full. He thought he'd gotten the gist of the place when he noticed the glass double doors in the back leading to a courtyard. Through the doors, a fair number of people were drinking beer and/or playing lawn games. He saw a cornhole toss swallowed, followed by a muted "hurrah."

"This way," the hostess said.

Once they were seated, they ordered beers: a Sam Adams for him and a Blue Moon for her. Their conversation, so easy until now, sputtered for a few minutes, but by the time the drinks arrived they had drifted into backstory, that quintessential first date staple. She went first. She was from Charlotte via Greensboro. She was the eldest of two children, her parents' marriage still intact. Since graduating from college two years earlier, she had worked for a stint as a pharmacy technician, but had quit six months ago; more recently she had been substituting in local elementary schools. Nothing too revealing. There was more to her life story, Nathaniel knew, but she was waiting to reveal it to him in the fullness of time, or, perhaps, in the fullness of a couple more pints. He was enjoying listening to her, when, out of the corner of his eyes, he saw a trio of hale young fellows burst through the glass doors in the back, a college mop of auburn hair in the lead. Nathaniel recognized the undergrad swagger and the aquiline profile at once. Mike Tressel.

His ex's brother.

He tried turning his head but there was nowhere to hide: the mushroom tables were free-range, exposed for all the restaurant to see. "What's wrong?" Winter asked him.

"There's someone over there I'd rather not see me," he answered honestly. As he spoke, he cut his eyes at the bar and discovered that his wish was for naught: Mike had already spotted him and was headed his way, walking at what Nathaniel gauged to be a three-beer clip. Nathaniel had never known Mike to be a hothead, but, then again, he'd never seen him when he had a reason to be mad.

Mike was upon him in a flash. "Look at you," he snarled by way of hello. There was the slightest tremble in his voice. Boiling anger or the faintest fear, Nathaniel wasn't sure.

"Hi, Mike."

"Back on the scene, huh? How's the…what was it?…oh yeah, the writing. How's the writing going?" He spat the question like an insult.

Nathaniel's heart groaned. Divulging that he was trying to be a writer was a third- or fourth-date revelation, his own fullness-of-time disclosure. At least, that had been the plan. "It's going fine. Thanks for asking."

Behind Mike, his two friends had ambled up, posing as toughs. College kids with drinks in them. Not that they weren't capable of doing damage.

"It must be one hell of a novel if you needed to break off your engagement to my sister to finish it."

Nathaniel's groaning heart upshifted to moaning. "It was more complicated than that, Mike."

"Hi, Mike, is it?" said Winter, joining in without warning, a girlish lilt to her voice. "You may not have noticed, but we're in the middle of something here. So would you kindly fuck off?"

Mike studied Winter. Nathaniel saw the uneasiness spread across his face, the uncertainty of what this woman in the cheese-rind-red leather jacket might do. She was in possession of an undefinable quality that begged caution, and Mike & Co., though still feigning toughness, were caught off guard. Winter had raised the stakes, and Mike, angry as he might have been, wasn't ready to go all in.

"You're a real dick," Mike said to Nathaniel, pretending to ignore Winter. He turned as if to leave, but, at the last moment, reached out and fishhooked Nathaniel's pint glass with his index finger, toppling it onto the table. Nathaniel had to jerk away from the halved mushroom cap to keep from getting soaked. Mike and his buddies hurried out of the restaurant, bursting into laughter the moment they hit the door.

A waitress hurried over with a rag. "I'm sorry," Nathaniel said. He found himself reaching for the rag as if he meant to do the job himself.

"It's okay," the waitress said, ignoring his hand and busying through. A quick scan of the deathly quiet restaurant revealed pair after pair of human high beams shining down on him, drawn to the drama. He risked a glance at Winter. He was worried that she'd be upset, but, when he turned and saw that she did in fact look troubled, he was taken aback. In truth, he had thought she would make light of the matter in order to relieve the tension.

"You're a writer?" she asked.

Had he misheard her? Surely that wasn't the part of the exchange that had left her addled.

He shrugged. "When I'm not busy breaking off wedding engagements, yes."

The waitress finished. He sat down again, the seat thankfully dry. Winter paused until the waitress was gone before speaking.

"The professor? The one who's stalking me? He's a published author."

"Oh." So that was the concern. "No worries there," he deadpanned. He noticed that she was looking at him with eyes afresh, the way he had looked at her in the tattoo parlor after O elaborated on the stalker situation. Was it really the writing that bothered her? He kept waiting for the questions to start rolling in about his former fiancée, but they never did. Instead, she sipped on the Blue Moon, studying him with her emeralds. At last, he could take it no more. "You're not bothered by the fact that I broke off my engagement?"

She traced a reply into the condensation on the pint glass. Turned it toward him.

No.

*

The beers multiplied. The pizza—his a pimento with bacon, hers a mushroom with vegan cheese—transformed into math problems for the late-elementary school set, ever smaller fractions. The conversation rekindled. They wove in and out of each other's lives, the alcohol lubricating their discourse until the lines between them blurred; it soon felt as if they had known each other since birth and were rehashing a shared history. He let secrets slip. The story of his engagement to Angelica Tressel, for one. How Angelica had groomed him since college to become both an accountant and the husband of her dreams. How four months prior to their wedding he had rebelled, quitting the firm where he had slogged for three years and announcing that he intended to become a writer, damn the consequences. How he had told Angelica that she could leave him if she wanted. How she had taken him up on it, although in the leaving, the *who-left-who?* question quickly became muddled.

"What kind of writer?" Winter asked when he was finished, unbothered by the rest.

"Literary fiction," he answered. She exhaled as if the wrong response would have spelled doom.

He paid the bill. They stood at a crossroads in the center of the restaurant and turned right, out the double doors and into the courtyard. A fresh pint apiece. Soon they were using their free hands to wipe the respective smirks off a corn-holing duo who had been crowing about holding the boards for ten straight matches; Winter tallied the winning throws, winked the devil's own eyelid at her gobsmacked competitor, trotted over to Nathaniel, and planted him with a kiss. They held the boards for two more matches before retiring, undefeated.

The temperature had dropped. Beery warmth could no longer do the trick. They went back inside, ordered a sober-up water. Changed their minds and ordered shots. Whiskeys down the hatch. They weren't sloppy yet, but they were getting close. Nathaniel checked the time on the sly. Closing in on eleven o'clock. He remembered her car, parked twenty miles north. He wasn't about to bring it up.

"What do you want to do now?" he asked, leaning in and lingering at her neck.

"Me?" She damn near cackled. "I'm going home. I have a book to read."

She sprung off the bar stool. His flash-fried mind thought he was being jilted for a moment, but no, she pulled him along with her out into the street. The cold crept back in, and she crept under his arm. They walked a block in relative silence, enjoying this new intimacy.

They retraced the steps to his car, parked near the tattoo parlor. He checked his wooziness quotient. He was floating-in-a-swimming-pool dizzy, on the side of pleasurable that gave him pause for thought.

"Um…I don't think it's safe for me to drive you back to the mall."

She had separated from him and was foraging for a cigarette. "Then don't," she replied, winning a Camel from the pack. She lit up and blew bad-girl smoke in his direction, the "O" of her lips resolving into a three-sheets-to-the-wind grin. A moment of him staring stupidly at her and she cocked one hip to the side, her eyebrows rising in mock exasperation.

"The book?"

His thoughts were a slurry. "You want the book?"

"Yes, dear." She nodded behind her. "My place is a couple of blocks that way. Let's go back and *read* together."

Whatever *read* meant, he was game. Paperback in hand, they wound their way through deeply shadowed streets, the wind translating the last words of autumn leaves. Humble houses, many with their lights off, nestled into the neighborhood's substantial foliage like resting woodland creatures. The occasional lamp lit a window. It felt to Nathaniel like they were working their way toward the center of a maze.

Rounding a corner, Winter announced "Voila!" A simple one-story with white wood paneling stood before them, fronted by so many plants and shrubs that the house appeared a mother hen whose little ones were running loose and needed to be ushered back under her wings. Scattershot weeds plagued the drive, and, up on the porch, an abused set of patio furniture was scaly with peeling paint. It wasn't all disrepair. A well-tended ficus tree preened under the porch light, and the front porch railing appeared to sport a fresh coat of paint. The exterior of the house was both kempt and unkempt, a style suited to its occupant—at least in Nathaniel's view.

"It's a rental. I share it with a roommate, but she's out of town," Winter summarized. "Shall we?"

He followed the lovely twitch of her ass, her hand leading his. Once inside, she abandoned him at the door, walking into the dark kitchen and pouring two glasses of water from the tap. Her movements were languid and sensual, a mermaid lounging in the sea. Waters in hand, she drifted by him, humming, a siren's call toward the living room couch. He followed. She turned on a lamp. The black peeled open to reveal the dreamscape of the room, deep reds and browns bewitching the senses, a Moroccan rug on the floor. She handed him a water. Pointed at the book he had forgotten he was holding.

"Okay," she said, propping one elbow up on the couch cushion. "Read."

He thought she was joking, but no, her eyes were bright buttons, expectant. He took a quick sip of water before setting it down on a nearby coffee table. Then he opened *Shalimar the Clown* to page one, parted his lips, and read.

It was the story of a woman who couldn't sleep. The daughter of an ambassador. Rushdie's luscious prose wove its spell, and soon Nathaniel was engrossed in the narrative, every sentence an elaborate trap seeking to ensnare him in the world of the book. He likely would have been caught, but on page two Winter removed her shoes, on page three she removed her jacket, and then—wrenching Nathaniel's focus completely from the storyline—on page four she removed her T-shirt. A plagiarist no more. Nathaniel stopped reading and bent both eyes to Winter's brassiere, but with the signal of a finger she indicated that he was paying for the pleasure on an installment plan of words, so he continued. Another page and she unhooked her bra, but before removing it she requested his shirt. He obliged. By this point the story of the ambassador's daughter may as well have been a string of binary code, but the words still rolled off his tongue with convincing enough inflection, until, on page five, Winter began unbuttoning her jeans. At this he lowered the novel, a desperate look on his face. She laughed, a trilling cachinnation, and beckoned him over. He flung the book on the coffee table. Playfully bowled her over into the supine.

They were negotiating their bodies in the manner of the ages when, with startling force, someone pounded on the front door. Nathaniel, his thoughts hijacked by his senses, hesitated, processing the world anew, but Winter with a feral quickness scrambled out from underneath him and pulled her shirt on in a heartbeat, ready for the new reality. The pounding started again, a bone-jarring string of five. She made for the door. Nathaniel, catching on, grabbed her by the wrist. *No,* he mouthed. His heart was walloping on his breastbone like a strongman ringing the bell at a carnival. She nodded that she understood, but when he released her wrist, she rabbit-stepped toward the windows and peeked out the shades. Her reaction told him all that he needed to know: parking lot man had found his way here.

"I'll call the cops," he whispered, pulling out his cell.

She shook her head. She had an intense but faraway look in her eyes, like she was working out a complex math problem in her mind. The numbers, it seemed, didn't add up.

"Nova, open up, please…please!" the man outside screeched. His voice sounded not at all like Nathaniel had expected: it had a shrill, reedy quality, a cross between a startled songbird and an unpracticed Mike Tyson impersonator. And why had the man used the name Nova? Perhaps Nathaniel was wrong: perhaps it was a case of a mistaken address, and the man outside wasn't parking lot man after all.

"Go away, James," Winter responded, her voice imbued with a weary authority. The strange appellation had failed to trigger a reaction in her; Nathaniel decided that on the plane of existence where she knew the intruder, Nova must be her name.

"It will be different this time, I swear to you," James called out, sounding desperate. "You're the heroine, Nova, how could you even think that I would..." A desperate fist slam, the weak wooden door trembling. "Please! It's only a couple nights' disturbed sleep, and...you said it yourself, you never felt more alive than when you were inside my world. Please, I'm begging you." A pregnant pause. "If you don't, I'm finished as a writer."

James's voice trailed away and the world hushed, a hiatus in the dramatics. Nathaniel used the break to move to where Winter was standing near the window. She signaled for him to be quiet—the universal finger to the lips. He nodded, playing the cool character, but inside he was awash with adrenaline, his caveman self ready to fight or flee. He checked the gauge of his inner hero, determined it was leaning toward fisticuffs, should the need arise.

"James." Winter again. Hers was the voice at the other end of a suicide hotline, the angel answering a 911 call. "You're a talented writer. You don't need me. I know you think you need a muse in the flesh, but if you'd only give it a try, like we talked..."

"I have tried! For two years now I've bled out on the page, nothing begetting nothing. I don't have the type of talent that other writers have. I need you. Nova Norcross. Winter York. You."

A touch of steel in Winter's voice. "You know it's not fair to ask me, James, not after what…happened. You know that. We both agreed. I don't blame you for what happened, I've always believed you since you explained it to me, but I simply won't play a part in any more…stories…going forward. Maybe there's another girl, one with whom you could be honest up front…"

"No." James's voice had changed. The pleading tenor erased, a cold and soulless note instead. "There's no one else. Only you. It has to be you."

The ensuing silence was a prophecy of the chaos to come. Then: Boom! James lowered his shoulder and rammed into the door, making quick work of its weak frame and hinges. Nathaniel felt a hiccup of terror in his chest but he swallowed it down and stepped forward, stopping just shy of the blond-haired bull of a man who, with the third ram of his shoulder, had popped the faulty latch free of its strike plate and tumbled into the house. James was up in a jiffy—a boulder growing arms and legs—predator eyes searching, those same orbs taken aback when he saw the bare-chested man before him. He reassessed, the shifting light in his eyes suggesting a decision made. With slightly above average speed, he tried to sidestep Nathaniel, and lunged for Winter.

Nathaniel made a textbook tackle. Arms around the waist, wrapping up clean, he pulled the mid-forties man to the floor with aplomb all things considered, and did his best to pin him there. James fought back, but strictly Roman-Greco; Nathaniel immediately sensed that he didn't intend to throw a punch. It was surprising, considering his unhinged behavior up to that point, but their grappling made it clear that James wasn't eager for real violence, at least not against someone who might do damage to him in turn. They soon reached a stalemate: Nathaniel's youth and athleticism was an even match for James' extra bulk. It was all Nathaniel could do to keep James pinned to the floor.

"What the fuck, man?" Nathaniel muttered while they tussled. He might have made a more eloquent interrogation, but his exertions were such that he couldn't summon the necessary words. He loosened his grip once or twice, but each time he did, James tried to get at Winter, or what Nathaniel thought was Winter—she was hovering in his peripheral vision like a specter, or was she? She seemed to disappear and then reappear again, but it was tough to know for certain; his hands were too full for his eyes to be trusted.

"It's time for you to leave, James."

Winter. James stopped struggling with Nathaniel and lifted his head. Nathaniel followed suit. Winter was standing with a butcher knife in her hand, eight inches of angry stainless steel, the point of the knife following James's every movement. There was a look of deadly seriousness about her, and a bite to her voice that suggested the knife wasn't an idle threat. James, persuaded, rose from the floor in a nonthreatening manner, allowing Nathaniel to stand up as well. Nathaniel loosened his grip enough that James could stand, but he didn't let go entirely, and the moment they were upright, he stepped in front of James, blocking off Winter.

It was his first good look at the man. James was handsome in an ugly sort of way, like a pretty-boy boxer at the end of his career, the disfigurement of his face not so severe that it discounted its appeal. He was broad-shouldered too, and bulky in the flattering-not-fat fashion, the type of forty-year-old who would do well on the divorcee circuit. But there was also weakness: something about the way the lines in his face bunched together, wrinkles of doubt, self-loathing stripes. He was a man for whom it seemed life should have been easy, but it wasn't, and because of that he had decided there would be hell to pay, either for himself or everyone else.

"Ha!" James laughed, a little stabbing noise. He threw up his hands like he was in a room with unreasonable people. "I don't think you understand, Nova…"

"My name is not Nova," Winter interrupted, taking exception to the name for the first time.

"In my world, your name is whatever the hell I want it to be," James shot back.

Winter snarled. "Look around, psycho. This isn't your world."

The punch landed. James dropped his chin to his chest and started pacing an imaginary, yardstick-sized room, two steps this way and two steps that, considering and tossing away reply after reply. He had a caged-animal aspect to him, desperate to lash out at the keeper with the key. He worked his lips around a few mutterings. Nathaniel shuffle-stepped with him, worried that he would launch a new attack.

Then, suddenly, James stopped. Smiled. His face a horizon-swallowing sun. He lifted a hand, and, very slowly, very deliberately, placed it on Nathaniel's shoulder. "As you well know, my dear Nova," he announced, "my world is whatever I touch."

And with those words, he turned and walked out the door.

Nathaniel was both confused and relieved. He looked to Winter for clarification but she was undergoing a transformation of sorts, changing from the bad-A with the knife into a less self-assured creature, her face white with a dawning terror. She sputter-started after James, rocking not once but twice on her heels like a long-distance runner anticipating the starting gun, and then she took off after him, onto the front porch with Nathaniel following her, shouting into the night, "Don't do it, James! Don't do it!" But James was a dissolving shadow, dematerializing in the dark.

She turned to Nathaniel. Something fundamental had changed, a tear in the space-time fabric of their relationship, who they were now very different from who they had been only moments ago. He looked at her suddenly careworn face under the porch light and saw that she contained multitudes. She was trembling ever so slightly.

It frightened him.

*

"You can't fall asleep tonight," Winter commanded.

She was working both a cell phone and the coffee maker. He had been informed that the cup of joe was for him, whether he wanted it or not. He didn't drink coffee as a general rule, but the latent mystery of what had just occurred precluded the general rules of his life, or so he was beginning to believe. Winter was speaking in riddles that both quickened his pulse and made him want to laugh out loud. He would have dismissed her, but her tone was too matter-of-fact to disbelieve.

"Your life is in danger. I shouldn't have let him touch you, but I didn't think…" She trailed away. "He's changed, he's willing to put people's lives in play in order to get what he wants. So long as you're awake he can't hurt you, but if you fall asleep, especially tonight, he's going to lash out at me by going after you."

"What are you talking about… How?"

She looked at him as if he had asked a question that, while justifiable on its merits, she doubted her ability to provide an answer that he would believe. She returned to her cell phone and started up a conversation with it instead. "Text me back. Text me back," she murmured.

"*Who* do you want to text you back? *Him?*" he asked, incredulous.

The babbling coffee pot gave her another excuse to avoid replying. She put down her cell phone and poured two cups to the brim, the black ovals of liquid like a portal to another dimension. Handed one to him. They were standing in the dim light of the kitchen, miles and miles away from the couch. Nathaniel felt the first shifting of his drunk—a slight fatigue, a sudden tension behind the eyes—phase one in the bleary transition to a hangover.

"Yes," she replied at last. "I am texting him."

"But why?"

"Like I said, your life is in danger, and it will be until I speak to him. Actually, your life is in danger regardless, but he's after me, he's not after you, and if I give myself over to him..."

He couldn't believe what he was hearing. "Give yourself over to him? What are you talking about? Listen, I can look out for myself: awake, asleep, whatever. Don't worry about me. What you need to do is call the cops. Now. I'll vouch for you when they arrive. We'll have a restraining order against that nutcase in no time. I know I don't understand everything going on here, but calling the cops is the right thing to do. Trust me."

A tear hung from the corner of her eye like a crystal pear. He hadn't seen it form, but there it was, dangling like the physical manifestation of inexpressible sadness. A closer look at the melancholic cosmos of her face and he knew that everything he had said was wrong. He didn't have a clue.

He decided to shut up.

After a time, her eyes found his. She took a cavernous breath. Then, with obvious reluctance, she explained the mysteries of the evening the best she could. "Okay. I'm going to tell you what's happening here, but you have to listen to me all the way through."

He nodded that he would. She continued.

"When James touches someone, he is able to channel that person any time they fall asleep for the next seven days. Not only that, he can shape the course of their dreams. He uses this, um, talent, as inspiration for his writing life. I know because he once channeled me for a six-month stretch when I was his student in college. Every dream that I had ended up in a fantasy novel he wrote called *Savage Moon*."

He heard her, but he didn't believe her. How could he? She was saying things that couldn't possibly be true. He sipped on his coffee for cover. The caustic brew rampaged down his unaccustomed esophagus, a liquid Mongol horde. He swallowed the fire without blinking and took another sip, anything to keep from showing his disbelieving face.

Winter continued, "When you're in these dreams, he's in control. You have a sense of what's happening to you, but, like in a regular dream, it's nearly impossible to direct the action. What's worse, if he decides that something terrible should happen to you during the dream, you feel the effects of it in real life. For example, if you fight someone in your dream, you'll wake up feeling like you've been in a brawl. Your body will ache, you will suffer from adrenaline fatigue, etc., etc. No one can see the trauma on your skin, but you'll feel it on the inside. And that's only part of it. There are worse things that can happen."

She paused.

"Like what?" Nathaniel prompted. He thought he knew what was coming, but he still needed to hear her say it.

"Like, if he kills you in your dream, you die."

"How do you know?"

"It happened…to a friend of mine."

He sipped his coffee, uncertain what to say. It was all too implausible. This time, Winter sensed his skepticism. Frustrated, she angled her body away from him and took refuge in her own cup of caffeine.

They stood in silence for a few moments, until Nathaniel, pained by this new distance between them, reached over and tucked her hair behind her ear. The gesture was inordinately more intimate than he had intended, and Winter, taken aback, turned and stared at him the way a wild animal might stare at a beckoning human hand. He surveyed her across the spectrum of their time together, a mall chat and a tattoo outing and a pizza dinner and an evening of drinks and a couch makeout session suddenly transformed into something raw and real, something that required risk. It wasn't easy to take what she had said at face value, but he had known all evening that something about her was wildly different; plus, he wanted to believe her, so maybe that was enough. He could be proven wrong later. For now, however, he was going to see this through on her terms.

"I believe you," he said.

She peered at him with X-ray eyes. "No, you don't," she replied. "But that's okay. It's enough for now if you'll just do what I say."

*

They found their way back to the couch. He resumed reading, but this time there was no striptease, only the crashing tide of prose broken by intermittent coffee sips. The story of the ambassador's daughter blossomed into a tale of international intrigue, as character after character cast aside their humble purviews and tied their fates to worldlier arcs, until, over time, they became standard bearers for the clashing ideologies of the age. It was prime-rib reading, juicy and filling. Now and again Winter would glance at her phone, hopeful for a text reply. Nathaniel would pause until she was finished, and then he would resume reading, keeping his promise to stay active, and awake.

At one o'clock in the morning, Winter's cell phone buzzed to life. She read the incoming text with a strained, serious expression, her lips and eyebrows scrunching accordion-style. Finished, she announced, "He's agreed to meet me tomorrow at a public place."

"Where?"

She hesitated. "The public library."

"I'm going with you," he replied.

She looked at him but didn't respond. He decided to take her silence as a sign of tacit agreement. He thought of a different question. "Am I still in danger?" he asked, not altogether serious but curious nonetheless.

"He said he wouldn't hurt you, so long as I keep my promise tomorrow," she said. "But I still think we should play it safe tonight."

They needed a break from the book. Nathaniel suggested television. They tried watching one of the many 90s sitcoms that ruled the cable airwaves in syndication, but ten minutes in and Nathaniel's brain felt zapped, strung between exhaustion and caffeinated tensity. Winter felt the same, so they turned the TV off. On the borderlands of his body, Nathaniel could sense the impending hangover massing like an enemy army. His brain urged him toward sleep, or, since that wasn't an option, another beer. He could tell by looking at Winter that she was drifting into the same purgatory. He thought it wouldn't hurt to suggest a little hair-of-the-dog.

"Do you have any beer?"

She looked at him as if it wasn't the worst idea in the world. "We'll have one," she ruled. "But we need to make it last, and we should drink water too."

She produced a couple of Killians, two glasses of water, and a deck of cards. The instant the alcohol touched his lips, the army dispersed. Winter, while maintaining the troubled, no-nonsense air she had assumed since the incident with the writer, dealt out the entire deck with a noticeable increase in energy. "War," she declared when she was finished. It took him a moment to understand that she was talking about the card game. He hadn't played War since he was a kid, but the rules returned to him quickly enough, and soon they were slogging through battle after battle.

The game took ages to complete. Near-victories were dashed by improbable counterstrikes so frequently that to reach the verge of losing seemed the best strategy to win. At last, the game swung decidedly in her favor. Winter, whose demeanor had been guarded since the incident, allowed herself a moment of levity when she captured Nathaniel's final card. "You lose," she teased, a flirty smile possessing her lips. Then she remembered herself, and the smile disappeared. He sighed on the inside. As strange and discomfiting as the evening had been, he was still in the house of a woman that he liked. He wished that the universe would rearrange itself so that she would find her way into his arms again.

He needed to piss. "Where's the restroom?" he asked.

"It's through the master bedroom," she replied, pointing down the hall.

41

The room was unmistakably hers, the furnishings, colors, and smell all in concert with Winter's ineffable essence. In the corner of the room, wedged in beside the bed, a nightstand doubled as a small bookshelf. Beneath the soft lamplight, he could make out a handful of the titles. *The Monsters of Templeton. White Teeth. Cloud Atlas. The Left Hand of Darkness.*

Savage Moon.

Without thinking, he walked over and grabbed the book, and took it with him to the bathroom. Inside, he went about the business of urinating, but with his free hand he opened the book to a random page and steadied it on the bathroom sink. He speed-read over the waterworks.

"Where are they?"

Nova knew that Joessa meant the moonbringer zealots, but in the deep of the night she couldn't help but think that Joessa was referring to the horrors the new full moon was certain to unleash. She cast a glance at the satellite, wondering what in God's name the knotty mess of brown and greens portended. The memory of last month's full moon still traumatized her: a fur-tufted orb, and with it a host of howling, lupine creatures intent on devouring every human in sight, driven by some mad impulse to eradicate every human save those who worshipped the god of moons. She and Joessa had only just survived. But now that Nova and Joessa knew who the moonbringers were, and what they intended, they could put an end to it.

It would all be for naught, though, if they didn't reach the moonbringers before the nightmare began.

"This way, farther up the trail. Theo swore that they were conducting the ritual inside the park..."

CRAAAAAACK!

It was the sound of the earth severing itself, a cataclysmic ripping of roots from soil. Nova turned, unable to imagine the genesis of such a noise, and there saw, to her astonishment and terror, the midnight profile of a monstrous oak tree come to life. Its hundred limbs were frenetic with activity, swinging and slamming and reaching and grabbing, a promise of violence if ever they made contact; meanwhile, the tree's roots stirred in a slithering fashion, the many tendrils sliding in and out and over each other, propelling the oak forward.

The tree closed in on the two of them. Nova, taking no chances, took to the air, but Joessa, normally swift of foot, wasn't fast enough: one of the limbs swept her up and pulled her into the oak's leafy torso, the sounds of her screaming the only sign that she was alive.

"No!" Nova shouted. She dove for the oak, desperate to save...

"Nathaniel?"

Winter was on the other side of the bathroom door. "Almost done!" he said, which must have sounded ridiculous, because his stream had stopped some time ago. He zipped up and flushed. Washing his hands, he tried to decide what to do with the book, but by the time he had turned off the faucet, it was clear that no brilliant ideas were forthcoming. Out of options, he held the book to his chest and opened the bathroom door.

He emerged looking chagrined. "I had already noticed that it was missing," she said. She wore an expression like a knight's helmet, defensive and inscrutable.

He tried his best to sound contrite. "Curiosity got the better of me."

She nodded absentmindedly, absolving him of his sin. Her thoughts were distracted. "Did you read about my wings?"

"I think so," he answered, surprised by the question. "Not directly, but I did read a part where you flew. You were trying to save your friend."

She smirked. "That was a common theme."

A thought occurred to him. "Joessa," he tendered, "was she the one who—"

"May I have my book back, please?" she interrupted, sticking out her hand.

"Yeah. Sure." He handed it over. This was dangerous terrain, every question about the book a possible land mine. But *Winter* had broached the wings, hadn't she? He doubled back to the pinions. "In the book...in your dreams...you could fly?"

Her smile was a shimmering nickel in a wishing fountain, illusory and surreal. "I could. It was amazing, to be honest. Not worth the trade-off, of course, but there were times when I didn't want to wake up, because I didn't want to relinquish my wings." He could tell that she was talking to herself, not him. She was still keeping him at arm's length. For his protection or hers, he wasn't sure.

She smiled at him again in that same insubstantial way. It pricked his heart.

"I believe you," he said. It wasn't true, but he desperately wanted it to be.

"Not possible. You'd have to experience it to believe it."

"Then...let me fall asleep. Just for a moment. Maybe I'll get a glimpse, and you can wake me up before anything goes wrong."

"You say that because you're naïve. He could kill you"—she snapped her fingers—"just like that."

"How would he even know that I'm asleep?"

She shrugged her shoulders and rolled her eyes, annoyed. "What do you want me to say that would make you believe me? He would know, okay? But sure, if you want to take a little nap and risk your life, you go ahead. What do I care? I hardly know you."

Her words stung, but he didn't believe them. He sensed their brittleness even as she spoke them into existence, untruths daring to be shattered. "You do care," he challenged her. "Even if you hardly know me, you like me. And I like you. I've liked you since I first spotted you in the bookstore, and you've liked me since…since…since the moment I first wowed you with my cornhole skills. Or, I don't know, earlier, when I got the tattoo. For whatever reason that people decide to like each other, you decided to like me. And I know you're mad at me because you're mad at yourself that I'm involved now, but that's not my fault. So stop punishing me for it."

She looked taken aback. The hard gleam of her emerald eyes cracked, softening into aquamarine pools. Distant tears emerged on the tableau of her pupils like far-off thunderstorms. "What would you have me do? Pretend that your life isn't in danger, and sleep with you instead?"

"If that's what you need to do to work through this, who am I to stop you?"

She laughed, and though there was a catch of emotion in every exhalation, she seemed to have found her center. He laughed too. When she was finished laughing, she looked at him with a naked expression on her face. "I do like you," she said. She shrugged like she was dismissing the world. "What will be will be, I guess."

He wasn't sure how to interpret this, but he noticed that she took a half-step toward him. He in turn took a half-step toward her, and in a matter of moments they had bridged the entire distance.

*

The sun.

He was lying in bed when the star of the solar system made its daily entrance onto the American stage. Sensing the daytime shift, Nathaniel stood and walked to the window, opening the blinds to find the night crowning the new morning with a bruised-orange headdress. Nathaniel tried to remember the last time he had seen the sun rise, with no luck. His brain was all fuzzy, but it didn't bother him. He had reached the stage of exhaustion where he was impervious to self-criticism.

Winter was in the shower. Nathaniel listened to the soothing patter of the shower water, its lulling melody. For a moment he considered joining her, but decided against it; it was enough to listen and know that she was nearby. They had stolen a couple of magical hours together; he didn't want to push his luck.

As if in response to his thoughts, she called his name from the shower. Her voice was both feminine and slightly husky, a piano accompanied by the bass. He walked to the bathroom door. "Still awake," he answered. He stole a glimpse of Winter washing her hair through the clouded glass, the wonder of her curves below. He looked away, not wanting to seem pervy.

"You can take a shower too," she suggested while he hovered in the bathroom doorway.

"Okay," he said.

"And you don't have to wait outside," she said as the water died, a note of humor in her voice. He accepted the invitation and stepped inside, gazing openly at her as she stepped out of the shower. She raised you're-welcome eyebrows at him as she reached for a towel. He stripped down himself, the two of them taking turns taking in eyefuls, and soon they were crossing paths, a stolen kiss as he stepped into the shower and she stepped to the vanity. He twisted his neck for one last glimpse before committing his feet, curious to see the ivy tattoo in the light of day. It wound around the trellis of her spine, lush and verdant, spiraling to the nape of her neck.

He showered in silence, dreamily remembering the last few hours. When he was finished, he stepped out of the shower to find the bathroom empty. On the bathroom floor, yesterday's clothes. There being no other options, he donned the day-old apparel. Somewhere in the house, Winter was playing a concerto of dishware. He stuck his nose out the bathroom door and sniffed the air. *Eggs,* he guessed.

Walking into the kitchen, he saw that his nose had guessed correctly: eggs were on the menu. That and more coffee. Winter, scrubbed fresh, was wearing jeans and a brilliant white shirt bearing the inky silhouette of a city skyline. She served Nathaniel a plate of scrambled eggs and a cup of coffee with a brass tacks bearing. "After we've eaten breakfast, I need you to drive me back to my car," she said.

The car. He had forgotten about it. Again. "Okay. But then we're going to the library together, right? What time are you supposed to meet him?"

She turned her back on him and made herself a plate of eggs. "Ten o'clock. I'd rather you not go. If he sees you, it will cement your existence in his mind, which will put you at a greater risk."

"Are you suggesting that I'm supposed to be less worried about you than you are about me?"

She didn't reply. She filled up her plate and sat beside him on the small wooden table. Sipped her coffee. Nathaniel waited patiently, thinking it best to give her the space to reply. At last, she obliged. "There's nothing you can do. I'm the one who has to deal with this. And the last thing I want to happen is for you to end up hurt because you met me."

"But he'll touch you as soon as he has the chance, right? And then you'll be in as much danger as I am. I'm already in danger; me being there doesn't change that. But you've avoided him this long, there's no reason why…"

"Okay," she said, cutting him off. "You can come."

The abruptness of her about-face shocked him into silence. The speed with which she had changed her mind struck him as suspicious, but, having won the argument, he thought it best to keep his thoughts to himself.

The morning blurred. Shortly after breakfast they left the house and retraced their nighttime stroll, working their way out of the tightly coiled maze of human habitats, back toward Charlotte's industries of commerce.

They talked, but the conversation was stilted, hampered by the future; fortunately, the stress of their unease was mitigated by Winter's decision to take his hand in hers. Everything about holding hands felt right and true.

They reached Nathaniel's car. The interior smelled like a bread-baking oven. It was a warm and sunny morning for the season, much warmer than the day before, and for a brief moment after they entered the car, Nathaniel felt as if they were about to take a trip together, an impromptu summer jaunt. But a minute into the drive and the spell was broken by the autumn shadows on the road, tree glooms blotting the world with melancholy.

Winter suggested music. Nathaniel obliged, turning on the stereo. The CD in the player picked up where it had last left off, Caleb Followill crooning on the new Kings of Leon album. The track coming through the speakers was "Manhattan," a better song than the album's first single, in Nathaniel's opinion. Winter crinkled her nose after a minute or two, but when he started to change over to the radio, she stopped him. "No!" she said, pulling his hand back. He looked at her funny. She explained. "I want to listen to it. If I ever hear it again, it will remind me of you."

The way she imbued what she said with the suggestion of an uncertain future bothered him. He struggled for a means to hold on to her. "I don't have your phone number," he said. He pulled his cell phone from his pocket and handed it to her. "Will you add it to my contacts?"

"Uh-huh," she replied, looking caught off-guard. She slid open the phone and punched in the information with a dutiful precision. Finished, she handed the phone back to him with an unconvincing smile. He nearly asked if she had entered a fake number, but he didn't want to upset the already fragile equilibrium.

They reached the mall a little before nine a.m. Winter's car—a white Toyota frosted with dirt—sat stranded in the middle of the lot, looking like the last grimy snowbank at the end of the melt. Mall workers were trickling in from the parking lot's outer edges, crossing a galaxy of asphalt.

"It's not even nine o'clock yet," Nathaniel said as he pulled into the parking space beside the Toyota. He threw the car into park and turned to look at her. He caught the end credits of a downcast stare and a bitten lip.

"I want to get there early," she said, quickly meeting his gaze. "I don't want him to catch me off-guard."

"Makes sense."

A hush fell over the car. She held his gaze and he saw the truth in the whorled cosmos of her mica-flecked green eyes, the Shakespearean end in store. He wanted to protest, but he knew that it was pointless, and besides, the words hadn't been spoken, so they couldn't be argued. He felt a strong urge to do something irrational, like make a declaration of love, but her tongue beat his to the punch.

"Let me see your tattoo."

He rolled up his sleeve. She raised a finger and pressed the empty, epidermal moonscape, being careful to avoid the now-healing lines of ink. She let it rest there for a moment, making what felt to him like a permanent indention. Then, swift and silent, she leaned in and kissed him.

It was over in a timeless moment. When she broke away, she turned her head and opened the car door all in one motion, words trailing in her wake: "I'll see you at the library." And then she was unlocking the car, and then she was turning over the Toyota's engine, and then he was following her out of the mall parking lot, heading back toward Charlotte.

*

Following Winter was easy. She drove five miles per hour over the speed limit down the interstate, and she stayed in the middle lane, making her the simplest tail in the world. The other cars, speeding the customary ten, glided by as if on conveyor belts. Nathaniel, pleased that Winter wasn't trying to lose him, settled into the ride, coasting into Charlotte on a low-volume dose of Kings of Leon reverb.

It wasn't until Winter had committed to the Brookshire Freeway that Nathaniel realized he didn't know which library branch she was going to. He had assumed ImaginOn, the children's library, because it was an uptown landmark—the bright and colorful architecture grabbed one's attention—but now that he thought about it, he supposed that she could have meant any number of branches in the system. She appeared en route to ImaginOn, however, so he decided for the time being to believe that his assumption was correct. When Winter turned onto the Brevard Street exit, he was certain that he was right. Relaxing, he allowed a roughly vehicle-shaped gap to open up between their respective vehicles. The gap was quickly filled by a bullying Escalade looking to turn right at the traffic light. Up ahead, the light changed over to yellow. To Nathaniel's surprise, the Escalade drew flush with the light. Winter's Toyota slipped under the yellow, continuing up Eleventh.

Nathaniel glanced down North Brevard to his right, toward uptown, toward ImaginOn, the direction Winter's car should have been heading. Confusion reigned. He tried to spot Winter's car, but the Escalade was blocking his view like a Canton-bound lineman.

The oncoming rush of traffic prevented the Escalade from turning until the tail end of the light cycle. Nathaniel hoped to see Winter's dirt-freckled Toyota stalled at the next light, but the asphalt horizon was clear. The instant the light turned green, he gunned the engine. The traffic gods, however, were conspiring against him: the light at the next intersection ascended the ladder to red before Nathaniel could do the Honda's accumulated RPMs justice. He considered running the light, but the traffic floodgates had already opened.

Sitting at the red light, Nathaniel surveyed Winter's options. Ahead at the next intersection on the left an exit bled back onto the freeway, donating its miniscule offerings to the arterial mass of Charlotte traffic. He watched the great daily migration of automobiles on the freeway with dismay, knowing that if Winter had joined the flock, his hopes of finding her were zilch. His only option was to stay on Eleventh and hope that she was somewhere up ahead.

*

He traveled up Eleventh until it turned into North McDowell, searching for Winter's car. No luck. Frustrated, he parked his car on the street and pulled out his phone. Scrolling through the alphabet of his contacts, he felt a tremor of hope when he spotted both her name and a 704 number. He pushed the call button.

Four rings sounded without fruition. After the fifth, an answering machine picked up. Although it was immediately clear that the female on the machine wasn't Winter, the voice did sound familiar. *"You've reached Purity Tattoo. Our dance card is currently full, so if you're interested in getting inked, we recommend that you stop by the shop so we can get to know you in person. If, on the other hand, you enjoy talking to machines, feel free to leave a message after the beep. We check our messages at least twice a year."*

Nathaniel hung up. He felt the sting of Winter's lie, transparent as it had been at the time. And yet—she had left him the number of a friend, the digits a filament suggesting that she didn't want to cut off all ties between them. He searched his brain for the tattooist's name. Kelly Anne. He would have to go see her if…if…if he couldn't find Winter.

He checked his watch. 9:32. He smacked his dry lips together. The deep machinery of his mind jammed for a moment, and nothing made sense. The gears reengaged and a thought materialized: he hadn't slept in over twenty-four hours. He looked outside his car window. The world was bleeding at the edges, the brilliant fall colors running to the horizon. He fought against his exhaustion and its accompanying side effects by biting his lip. The taste of iron stirred him back to life.

ImaginOn. It was his only option. He threw the car back into gear and merged back onto North McDowell, searching for the turns that would lead him into the heart of the city.

*

The library teemed with a Saturday glut of children. Nathaniel walked the zany blue and orange interior feeling out of place, looking out of place. Children zigzagged around him like pinballs bouncing off air. It dawned on him that he had made a mistake: Winter would not have met James here. The instant he realized his error, he was approached by a member of the staff.

"Excuse me, sir, are you here with a child?"

"No, I…" He caught a mental glimpse of what he must have looked like, eyes bloodshot-red and a sloth-sluggish bearing. The staff member's face was one large, ringing alarm bell. "I thought I was supposed to meet a friend here. But obviously not."

"No, sir, I wouldn't think so." The woman looked certain of Nathaniel's latent criminality. "Perhaps you should leave."

He nodded. "A different branch, I think." He knew what he meant, but in retrospect it sounded like nonsensical jabber. He half-waved to the woman as he turned to go. "I'm leaving," he said. He walked outside as fast as he could without adding to the impression of his guilt.

*

He tried a different branch, but not before losing thirty minutes asking random Charlotteans for directions. The simplest solution would have been to return to ImaginOn and ask a staff member, but he couldn't bring himself to do it.

By the time he arrived at the Plaza Midwood branch, it was half past ten. Winter's mud-speckled Toyota was not in the parking lot. He went inside, hoping against hope to spot Winter's obsidian spill of hair. A quick inspection of the assorted manes in the library and he knew that she wasn't there. He looked for James Breach too, surveying the room for a haggard-looking lion, but the man he had tackled the night before was nowhere to be seen.

Deflated, he let his exhaustion fill him up like a balloon. Standing, he rested his floating head on a shelf. His sinking eyes latched onto the many eye-level book spines in an effort to stay afloat. The spines were tagged with three-letter words from a strange, abortive language: FIC and ABE; FIC and ADI; FIC and AGA; and so on. The FICs were stacked atop the other words, two words to a spine. Bubbles of comprehension popped in Nathaniel's brain. He evolved to upright once more. Started scanning the shelves for FIC atop BRE.

It didn't take Nathaniel long to find it. He plucked *Savage Moon* from the shelf and turned the book so that he could better look at the cover. On the top half of the cover an enormous, brown-green moon loomed on the horizon. Two shadows traversed its face: near the crest, the winged figure of a woman, and, on the horizontal plane, the jetting silhouette of a sprinting female. Below the moon, in a harsh, pseudo-gothic font, the book's title was spelled out in white. Below the title, in the same font but smaller, resided the author's name: James Breach.

Without another thought, Nathaniel took the book to the checkout counter. The staff member on duty remedied the problem of his lack of a library card with courtesy and speed. Book in hand, Nathaniel returned to his car feeling reenergized. A plan coalesced in his mind: he would return to Winter's place and wait. And while he waited, he would read.

*

Finding Winter's house turned out to be more difficult than he had anticipated. Her street was a snake entwined with tens of others, her house the egg lodged in its belly. He had nearly given up when a hedgerow of bushes on the corner of a street that he had passed at least twice snagged his attention. Out of the miasma of his mind's eye he saw the hedgerow from a different perspective, that of the late-night drunk. He turned onto the street, Larkhaven Lane, and found, seven houses down, the white wood-paneled bungalow where he had spent the previous night.

The driveway was empty. He parked on the street, facing the drive. Rolled down the window. The moment he turned off the ignition, his eyes became boulders trying to pin his skull to the headrest. Doing his best to keep his head upright, he pinched his arm. Slapped his face. Anything to stay awake. His attention shifted to the passenger seat. *Oh yeah,* he remembered. *The book.*

He opened *Savage Moon* and began reading. Groggy eyes. The words swam in and out of focus like darting minnows. *Fucking concentrate,* he chided himself. He summoned every ounce of energy he had left and slowly began to piece the sentences together. On the page, two college girls were at a party, but the mood was ominous, sour. Apocalyptic underpinnings. A background television suggested a world soon to be at war, an open laptop screamed news of an intercontinental virus, and a drunk partygoer made mention of a mentally unstable boyfriend on his way to the shindig. The girls fled into the night. Walking on the outskirts of campus, they came across a skin-and-bones man in a black suit, flipping a quarter that glinted in the moonlight in the air.

He was sitting on a bus stop bench, looking like a man with the universe under his thumb. He wore a smile fashioned from stolen joy and a suit the color of coal. The stitching on both was exquisite. Everything about his appearance screamed anachronism. He had a trilby for his bald head, but at the present moment the hat sat on the bench beside him. From a distance, he appeared to be flipping a quarter into the air. When the women approached, he pocketed the silver.

"Two wishes! One for the each of you! Tell me your heart's desire and it's yours!" the man called out as the women tried to hurry past him. Nova, made nervous by the man, kept her head down, but Joessa, full of vodka courage from drinking PJs at the party, shouted back.

"Did you say what I think you did, weirdo?"

The man stood up, put his trilby on, and advanced on Nova and Joessa, his smile growing ever wider. His many imperfect teeth were stacked in his mouth like tiny mountains in a crowded range. He had a debonair, king-of-thieves quality, and he gave the impression of one familiar with walks of life both low and high. Nova's breath caught when she saw him. Joessa laughed to hide her fright.

"I did indeed! As I've spent the night stacking the deck against the human race, I'd like to balance the scales a bit by granting the both of you a wish. Prove that I'm not altogether unsympathetic to the plight of your…kind. Granting wishes is in the contract, actually, but don't let my obligations to larger forces fool you. I'm happy to do it."

Nova pulled on Joessa's shirt, urging her to move on, but Joessa's feet were firmly planted. Joessa was laughing a blue streak. "Who are you to grant anyone a wish?"

"A fair enough question," the man replied. He pulled the quarter from his pocket and flipped it high into the air. "Heads I'll tell the truth, tails a convincing lie." He plucked the coin from the sky. Palming the silver, he gave it a quick glance. "Damned. The truth, then. My celestial name is Joshimer the Unholy, though lord knows I have others. In the old Mestoan tongue, I was referred to as Barubarra. The Ulaarts called me Shoni, or Sea Demon, which I found to be far afield. I've nothing against the Ulaarts per se, but, being a coastal people, they are a bit fixated on saltwater. When their moon went topsy-turvy, they looked for a sea demon to blame. Enter me. But I digress." He had cast his eyes to the sky, reminiscing, but now he refocused his gaze on Nova and Joessa. "The plainspoken call me god of moons."

"Let's go," Nova pressed Joessa.

But Joessa wouldn't budge. "Okay, god of moons, my wish is for eternal youth," she said, a challenge in her voice.

The god of moons tsk-tsked. "I do not traffic in the eternal. You need to wish for something that I can grant you here and now. But, before you do, let me offer you fair warning: the apocalypse is nigh, so take that into consideration as you make your wish. I would know because I've set it in motion."

Joessa scoffed. "Whatever, you old fraud." She turned on her heels to leave. Only Nova didn't turn with her. Instead, she spoke.

"Wings," she said. Her voice sounded like falling snow. "My wish is for wings. I want to fly."

The god of moons double-pumped his eyebrows, pleased. He put his fingers together as if he intended to snap them, but, once they were configured, he simply held the pose.

Knots of pressure formed on the inside of Nova's shoulder blades. Then, in a great explosion of pain, a pair of wings burst forth from her skin, the trailing caress of black *feathers exiting the holes until, with a mighty unfurling, the wings tore open the back of her shirt and tested the air. Nova shuddered in shock, clutching the remnants of her shirt to the front of her chest.*

"Holy shit!" Joessa exclaimed. She backed away from Nova in astonishment. "Can you...can you feel them?"

Nova could feel little else. She tried making the wings retract. They folded neatly into her back.

The god of moon's expression was devilish, his deportment ecstatic. "One satisfied customer! And now that I've made a convert," he intoned, grinning at Joessa, "let's hear your wish. Something tangible this time."

Joessa hesitated. Gears churning. The weight of a lifetime's desire on the tip of her tongue.

"I want to be rich," she said. "Mountains of money."

The god of moons smirked, but he made the same movement as before, the three fingers on his right hand assuming the snap position. The bus came round the bend at that very moment, the only vehicle to approach since Nova and Joessa had arrived. The bus stopped, and two men stepped out, black duffel bags in their hands. They approached and dropped the bags on the ground, their faces expressionless, vacant. Then they turned, reloaded the bus, and left.

"Go ahead. Open it up."

Joessa approached the bags. She leaned down and...

Rapping knuckles on the car window stirred Nathaniel from his reading reverie. Startled, he looked up to find a woman with hair the color of a burning lightbulb staring at him. She backed away, and motioned for him to roll down the window.

"Why are you parked here?" the woman asked once there was no longer a glass barrier between them. She looked about his age, or perhaps a little older. A serious, no-nonsense mien. She had a physique like a slim but sturdy money safe.

"Because I'm waiting on someone."

"Who?"

"My...friend. Winter. She lives here." He pointed at the house.

The woman looked suspicious. Her eyes were hard nuggets of authority. "She's coming to meet you?"

Nathaniel bristled against the line of questioning. "I'm sorry. How does this concern you?"

"I'm a cop," the woman replied. "I live three houses down. I'm off-duty today, but your little stakeout caught my attention."

Instantly Nathaniel saw himself from the female officer's perspective, with his day-old stubble and his sleep-deprived, Mariana Trench eyes. The inside of his head turned gummy. "I met Winter...the woman who lives here...yesterday. We were going to the library together this morning but we were separated. I thought I'd come back here and wait."

"Have you tried texting her?"

"Yes. I..." He could feel himself readying to botch the reply even as he searched for the right response. Unfortunately, his brain could summon naught but the truth. "She gave me...the wrong number. It was a mistake."

The woman gave Nathaniel a smile like a little sting. "Perhaps she did that on purpose."

Nathaniel fished for the right words. Complete, convincing sentences. "Look, this isn't what you think. Yesterday was our first date, and it went great. I wouldn't be here if it hadn't. Besides…I'm not doing anything illegal by parking on the street, am I?"

"No. You're not. But still…I feel like you should leave."

"Tough luck. I'm not going to leave."

A silence like a hung noose. Then: "Sure," the woman replied. She stared at him looking like the judge, jury, and executioner. "Did you know that your eyes are bloodshot? If I were forced to take a bet, I would guess that you are under the influence of either drugs or alcohol."

"I'm not. I'm just sleepy," he said. *And a little hungover,* he thought. Fortunately, he didn't say it.

"Hm," she replied. A dry smile graced her lips. "You know, I wouldn't be surprised if a cop car came rolling through the neighborhood soon. They do that from time to time. Who knows? An off-duty cop might call in a request. Maybe you should leave before that happens." She rapped the car door with the same knuckle song that her fist had sung when she approached. "In the meantime, since it's my day off, I'm going to go run your plates." She winked at him. "It'll give me something to do." Then she turned and left.

Nathaniel watched her go in the rearview mirror. He knew that he wasn't in the wrong, but sleep deprivation had drained his sense of self-assuredness. He felt guilty for just being alive. If there was one thing he was certain of, it was that he wasn't, at the present moment, in the right frame of mind to go toe-to-toe with the law.

"Who knows when Winter will come back," he murmured to himself. Saying the words felt like a betrayal of a sort, but, once they had been spoken, they were too perfect of an excuse not to take advantage of. He turned over the ignition, threw the car into drive, and drove away.

*

Nathaniel spent the remainder of the afternoon in a purposeless haze. He returned to his one-bedroom apartment in North Charlotte and watched college football. He hated the dull pageant, but it filled the time. It was the same two teams that were always playing on television; or, if it wasn't, it may as well have been.

At halftime, he took a shower. When he was fully sudsed, he realized that it was his second shower of the day. As penance, he scalded himself with hot water. Then, changing tact, he iced his bones with cold. Stepping out of the shower, he felt like a minor deity. One given dominion over trivial matters, like the water temperature of showers.

The thought crossed his mind that perhaps he was in love.

He wanted to take a nap, but he didn't. He was an ascetic now, and needed neither food nor sleep. By leaving Winter's house he felt that he had betrayed her in some fundamental way, but, so long as he stayed awake, he thought he might redeem himself. He tried to formulate a plan for finding her. Nothing came to him. He was distracted by something that he had forgotten. The forgotten thing's nebulous importance haunted him. He wandered the apartment, the plan and the forgotten thing just out of sight of his mind's eye. The football game ended in a swarm of home colors, the green field covered by orangey human insects. Outside, the autumn sun moped. The day was nearly done.

Hunger struck him like a hurled stone. He wasn't an ascetic, after all. Fresh jeans, a crimson-red polo. Back in the car, he saw the book. The forgotten thing. He nearly cried with relief. He drove to the Jason's Deli down the street, constructed a skyscraper salad. He sat in a booth by himself and watched yet another college football game on the restaurant's lone television. Boston College vs. Florida State. Unlike earlier, the teams were distinct entities, and the game enjoyable—a full stomach was making the world take shape again. He considered reading *Savage Moon* but decided it was beyond him at the present moment. The book sat in his car like an artifact, waiting to be pored over.

His phone tremored. He pulled it from his pocket expecting a miracle, but, before he remembered that Winter had never taken his number, he saw that it was his brother.

Are we still on for drinks?

Another item on the list of forgotten things. Nathaniel's brother, Zack, was four years younger than Nathaniel and a newly minted drinker, having turned twenty-one only six months prior. Zack enjoyed drinking; Zack enjoyed the late-night uptown life; Zack enjoyed coercing newly single Nathaniel into the role of big brother wingman. Nathaniel read the text over and over, unable to decide whether to brush his brother off or co-opt him into searching for Winter. He settled on: *Not sure. Something's come up. I'll text you back in a bit.*

Back outside, the blue-black of the gloaming was settling in to roost. Nathaniel felt another wind kick in. His wiring was glitchy but firing. The broken butterfly plan in his mind flitted around until he could see that there was only one option. He jumped in his car, and drove back into the heart of Charlotte.

*

She wasn't there. The house an empty cocoon. He nearly parked on the street fronting Winter's house but then he remembered the female cop. He parked on an adjoining street instead.

He returned to the house on foot. Still, no sign of Winter. He looped by the house again and again, hoping to see headlights turning into the drive; a muddy white Toyota parked outside; a raven-haired woman with a spiraling ivy neck tattoo unlocking the front door. Exhaustion chopped at his legs like an axe. If only he knew that Winter was safe, he could go home. Go to sleep. But until he saw her, there was no way of knowing. So he stayed.

He revisited his options, tromping through the mud and the muck of his thought processes. Besides knowing the location of the house, his only tether to Winter was the tattoo parlor. He tried the number she had given him once more. The same teasing message played. He considered driving to Purity Tattoo, but he couldn't imagine that Kelly Anne and O knew any more than he did. In all likelihood, they didn't even know that Winter was missing.

His phone buzzed. His brother Zack again. *You coming out or what?* He studied the text message the way one would a hieroglyphic. When at last he deciphered it, he pecked out a reply. *Still don't know. Give me a little more time.*

The instant he sent the text, a pair of headlights dressed him in yellow, the cylindrical beams moving from right to left as they searched for a driveway. Winter's driveway. The trailing fish of a car chased the worms of light, but Nathaniel, momentarily blinded, couldn't place the make or color. A second later, his color blindness resolved. The car wasn't mud-white; it was lipstick-red, a sporty little Mazda.

The car parked. A petite woman with short, feathery blonde hair exited the driver's side. With a workmanlike briskness, she made her way to the scaly-paint front porch, unlocked the front door, and went inside.

Without thinking, Nathaniel strode across the lawn. Reaching the front door, he rapped a no-nonsense question with his knuckles. The front porch light bloomed. Fingers played at shades. A moment later, the woman spoke from inside the house. "I don't know who you are, but I've already dialed 911 on my cell. If you don't leave, I'm going to hit the call button."

He decided to risk it. "Please don't do that. I'm looking for Winter York. I met her last night and today…she disappeared. I'm trying to find out if she's okay."

Silence. Then, "Are you Nathaniel?"

He was drowning; the question was a life preserver. "Yes." And again. "Yes."

The door opened. The woman, her feathery blonde hair shaping her head like a helmet of golden flame, eyed him with curiosity. "Winter's fine. She texted me two hours ago to tell me that she wouldn't be coming home tonight. She's staying at her parents'. She mentioned you in the text. She said there was a chance a guy named Nathaniel might stop by and ask if she was okay. I assumed she meant that you might stop by tomorrow morning, but I guess not. She said to tell you to go home, and, if you haven't slept, to go to sleep. She'll be here tomorrow around five o'clock if you want to take her out for a bite to eat."

He gulped in the news like desperately needed oxygen. "Really? She said that? Thank God. I was worried...she was meeting a man, a writer? James..."

"Breach. Yes, I know all about James Breach."

Nathaniel was caught off-guard. He looked at the woman. She was staring at him with cat's eyes. Sly, inscrutable orbs. She had a face like a female Terminator, the jawline attractive but steely. Coupled with the blonde hair, she looked like a Nazi propaganda poster in miniature.

"Are you...the roommate?"

"I am. Emily Winch," she said, extending a hand and a silver dollar smile. "Would you like to see Winter's text?"

He did, although he hadn't expected the offer. "Sure," he said.

Emily took out her phone, located the text message, and handed it over to Nathaniel. He read the contents of the cloud bubble. Emily had paraphrased the message quite neatly. The words were a tidy bundle of good news. In the text, Winter had also mentioned James's break-in the previous evening; she assured Emily that the danger had passed, and that it wouldn't happen again. At the top of the text, Winter's name and number. Nathaniel's mind transformed into a giant claw enclosed in Plexiglas, grasping at the stuffed-animal digits. *704-555-0180. 704-555-0180. 704-555-0180.*

"Thank you," he said, returning the phone.

"No problem," she replied. She stood facing him with a posture so open, it bordered on unsettling. It was difficult to believe that she was the same woman who was threatening to dial 911 a minute ago.

He repeated the numbers in his mind. *704-555-0180.* His brain was slick with sleep deprivation; it was hard to make the digits stick.

"This James Breach. You've met him?" he asked.

"Yes," Emily answered. "But only once, and briefly. Winter has told me all about him, of course. I know she doesn't like him, but he seems fascinating to me."

"What?" Nathaniel said, laughing uncomfortably. "You know the guy's insane, right? I was here last night when he broke in. He was going to…"

"Touch Winter?" It was Emily's turn to laugh. Her laugh made a sound like a tiny wood chipper. "And then what? Dream her to life in a book? Give her wings?" Her voice was lightly mocking. "I'm sorry," she said, although she didn't sound or look sorry at all, "it's not that I don't believe Winter. But you have to admit, the story is a little difficult to swallow. And, on the off chance that she is telling the truth, wow! It's hard to feel bad for someone who gets to live out being a superhero. You know?" She reached out and touched Nathaniel on the arm, and, as she did, she flashed the silver dollar smile again, a smile at once alluring and guileful. She withdrew her hand almost immediately, but slowly, so that he would know it wasn't a mistake.

"I d-d-don't know," he said, stuttering. It was all too much. Was Winter's roommate hitting on him? He reminded himself that he was exhausted: it was difficult to tell up from down, let alone an innocent touch from a flirtatious gesture. "I've been awake for nearly forty-eight hours now, so…"

Her face lit up. "He touched you, didn't he?! I thought as much after reading Winter's text, but, of course, I couldn't be certain. Lucky you! You'll know soon enough if Winter's telling the truth, then, won't you? Unless Winter has talked him out of it. That would be a disappointment, wouldn't it? If you fell asleep and nothing happened?"

She seemed a controlled person by nature, but, underneath the veneer of self-possession, Nathaniel detected a frenzy of excitement. Her excitement seemed both out of proportion and inappropriate. Why wasn't she concerned for him? More importantly, why wasn't she concerned for Winter?

And yet…a part of him agreed with her. The sleep deprivation and his worry for Winter had prevented him from processing his thoughts on the matter, but, now that he considered it, it *would* be a disappointment to fall asleep and not experience what Winter claimed to have experienced. Not at the expense of losing his life, of course, but what was the likelihood that he was in any real danger? James Breach might be nuts, but he didn't strike Nathaniel as a killer. At least not an intentional one.

"Maybe. Winter thought that staying awake was the safest option for the present. If what she claims is true, then I'd rather be safe than sorry."

"Sure." Emily's lips protruded and lingered as she spoke, teasing out the syllable. She kept her gaze fixed steadily fixed on him; her body language seemed to convey that she knew something that he did not. With a sudden bouncy smile, she continued, "Nathaniel, it was a pleasure to meet you. But I imagine that you're very tired, and would like to go home and get some sleep. I won't keep you any longer." She touched her fingers to her lips and blew him a kiss. "Sweet dreams."

She closed the door without ceremony, careful not to upstage the blown kiss. Nathaniel stood with his brow furrowed, confused. He staggered off the front porch in a somnambulant daze. What had just happened? The air was ripe with mystery, but the miasma in his mind was too thick for him to parse the competing fogs.

He was trying to process the strange encounter with Winter's roommate when his phone buzzed yet again. The text simply read: *Dude???* His reptilian brain rolled his eyes. He texted back: *Not coming out. Insane day. I'll explain later. Have fun.*

By the time he sent the reply text into the ether, his feet had navigated their way to the car. With nothing left to do, he started up the engine and headed home.

*

The drive home was an out-of-body experience. It wasn't until he was inside the apartment that he remembered Winter's number. He was pulling back the covers of his bed, prepping for the coming coma, when his mind spotted the wad of digits, sticking like used gum to a memory wall. *704-555-0180.* He laughed out loud. Retrieving his phone, he logged the number under Winter's name. Then he shot her a message.

Hey! Are you okay? I just spoke to your roommate. And I stole your number. She said you were safe, but I'm still worried about you. What happened today? About to go to sleep—thanks for the all-clear—but I'll stay up a few in the hopes of hearing from you.

He reread the message. He thought it sounded intense, even as a follow-up to a first date as insane as theirs. He needed to cut the message with a little flirting, but, now that he had let his guard down, sleep was gnawing at his mind like a dog at a bone. *Fuck it,* he thought, and he hit send. He lay down on the bed, watching the screen. He was hoping for a quick reply, but as soon as he hit the mattress, his eyelids came crashing down.

This time, there was no stopping them.

*

He was on a boat. The upper deck of a cruise ship. Salty ribbons of late-evening wind streamed through his hair, cleared his nasal passage. He had a glass of champagne in his hand. The champagne was the color of an ancient, exotic currency. An inoffensive pop song piped out of unseen sound speakers. It was the sort of parasitic song that loved to worm its way into people's brains and feast, but, at the present moment, it sounded innocuous enough. His elbows were propped on the railing. He was waiting on a woman—his lover—but there was no rush. They were on vacation, and they had all the time in the world.

He was meant to be enjoying himself. He was enjoying himself. It was hard to tell the difference.

Footsteps approached. He cast a glance over his shoulder and saw his lover approaching. She was wearing a breezy summer dress, blue seersucker, and long, golden earrings a shade darker than her feathery blonde hair. He noticed a gold necklace, too, one that he had never seen before. He couldn't discern the pendant. "My Zadie," he cooed as she drew near. The name was wrong, he knew—her real name was Emily, Emily Winch—but here, on the boat, she was Zadie. A part of his mind was at odds with itself, at odds with his present reality, but the reality was unbending, wedded to this dimension. The world's undertow urged him to let go, and so he did. He pushed away from the railing and reached out to embrace *his* Zadie.

But five feet away from him, she stopped. She stared at him wearing the devil's grin, a wicked, smiling scythe. "Nate," she said. "There's something I need to tell you." While he considered the slight change to his name, she reached up and rubbed the necklace at her collarbone with two fingers. The new angle made it possible for him to identify the pendant: a golden moon.

In an instant, the gloaming changed over to the night. It seemed that Zadie was summoning a vast and terrible evil. She chanted a name that he couldn't place. Her face was trembling, eyes and lips aquiver like Jell-O molds. Nathaniel looked at her with a growing horror, wondering if she was possessed.

Elsewhere on the ship, people were murmuring in fear. Fingers pointed at the sky. High above, the moon was changing color: the monochromatic gray was giving way to a deep, oceanic blue, the ovoid filling up like a cup. He glanced at the sky, but only for a moment. Zadie's countenance still held sway. At last, she finished her thought.

"I've fallen in love with someone else."

There was a thud on the bow of the ship like the hand of God, followed by a shrill screaming. Nathaniel struggled to stay upright as the bow dipped below horizontal. He dropped the champagne. Zadie laughed, a witch's cackle, but Nathaniel thought he saw fear in her eyes, fear held captive behind a character's mask. He broke eye contact with her, and looked to the front of the boat. By the light of the aquamarine moon, he saw the blue and orange tentacle of a massive cephalopod gripping at the deck.

He ran. Toward the action, and not away from it, some heroic, suicidal impulse winning out. While the masses struggled toward him, fighting gravity, Nathaniel sprinted downhill, toward those holding on for dear life to the deck railing nearest the tentacle. Stock photo people, but their screams were real enough. He honed in on a young couple. Concocted a plan, some impossible derring-do that involved leading the couple hand-over-hand up the port-side railing until they were safe. But then another of the leviathan's tentacles emerged from the sea and laid claim to the deck, and the world went vertiginous. His feet lost purchase with the deck. He tumbled and slid toward the sea beast.

He crashed into the railing at a terrifying velocity. His arms and legs reacted on instinct, wrapping tight around the metal cylinders that were his only safeguard from the monster below. All sound was apocalyptic: the screams of the ship's passengers, the moaning ache of the boat, the hellish sucking sound of the octopus. Nearby, the young couple that he had intended to save lost their fight with gravity. They fell like angels into the bestial void. Once Nathaniel's eyes were fixed on the monster, he couldn't look away. The octopus was a shapeshifting, amorphous thing: the ocean obscured and then revealed its blobby form to disturbing effect, like a dark wizard conjuring glimpses of a nightmarish dimension. The sight of it lanced Nathaniel's soul.

Yet another tentacle gained hold, causing the ship to surrender additional degrees to the vertical plane. Passengers everywhere plummeted to their deaths. Nathaniel wondered if Zadie would fall past him, but she never did.

His grip began to slip. His mind, which minutes ago had acquiesced to the reality of this world, fought savagely against the notion of his impending death. He didn't want to die. And yet he knew that if he fell, death would swallow him whole. *This is a dream,* he told himself, trying desperately to wake up. But no matter how hard he willed it, nothing changed.

The octopus—with the ship now fixed in its tentacles—began pulling the liner down into the briny depths. Nathaniel realized that his ever-weakening hold would soon be a moot point. He would die whether he held on or not. His will faltering, he considered letting go.

But then, overhead, a shadow crossed the aquamarine moon.

Salvation.

At first, he couldn't process what he was seeing. A blur of obsidian-black feathers. A long steel blade. Was it a bird? A person? The flying creature swooped down to the deck railing, and, raising the sword, revealed the face of a woman framed by raven-black hair. He recognized her. From where, he wasn't sure, but he knew that he knew her, from some other world, from some other life…

The answer came to him in a cold rush. The woman with the wings was Winter.

Winter struck the blow and severed the tentacle. The giant octopus recoiled in agony, causing the stern of the ship to drop. Nathaniel lost his hold on the railing, and his view of Winter. He tumbled back onto the ship. Looked to the sky.

Winter was circling the ship, sword brandished. Her flight had a raptor-like quality, graceful and terrifying. Nathaniel assumed that she would attack another of the monster's ship-gripping tentacles, but, instead, she went into a steep dive, down, down, down toward the octopus's head. Nathaniel hurried to his feet. Ran to the railing. Far below, he saw the gleaming of steel in the moonlight. Winter raised the sword and plunged the blade deep into the soft tissue between the cephalopod's oversized eyes.

The strike was true: the octopus didn't so much as spasm in death. Its tentacles slackened and slid away from the ship, and then the creature fell from its great watery height to its permanent resting place on the ocean floor. The ship slowly reestablished equilibrium. All was quiet. Nathaniel wondered if he was the top deck's lone survivor.

He wasn't.

Once more, he heard footsteps. He turned and saw Zadie. She was on the arm of a thin and bony bald-headed fellow wearing a suit and trilby who, for some reason, was flipping a quarter into the air. The man looked invigorated, like he'd just wrapped up a refreshing workout.

"You, sir," the man said, pocketing the quarter and addressing Nathaniel, "should be dead." He acted as if he were disappointed in Nathaniel. As if, by staying alive, Nathaniel had broken a prearranged agreement.

The man continued, "I suppose we need to remedy that. Don't we, Zadie?"

Zadie nodded like a marionette. Glassy eyes. Wooden stare.

The man laughed. Sensing a shift in the world around him, Nathaniel turned and saw the far eastern horizon blotted out by a craggy mountain of water. It was a tidal wave beyond comprehension, the stuff of children's drawings and Japanese woodblock prints. The cruise ship, massive though it was, ceded to the receding water like a bath toy. A capsizing was inevitable.

His heart sank. Death was coming. There was no avoiding it.

A dull *thunk* sounded beside him. He turned and his heart levitated. Winter. Only she wasn't Winter—she was Nova, her name an unexpectedly loving word on the bald man's lips.

"Nova, my beautiful creation. You work so hard to such little end," the bald man teased. She ignored him. She grabbed Nathaniel and pulled him into the air with all her might, trying desperately to rise above the oncoming wave. The two of them ascended like a Wright Brothers' prototype, clunky and slow but successful all the same. The skyscraper of water passed just beneath their feet.

Winter flew them away from the ship as fast as she could. Far below, Nathaniel thought he heard the bald man's laughter swallowed by the wave, but he couldn't see. The wave crashing, Nathaniel assumed that the cruise ship, Zadie, and the strange trilby-wearing, quarter-flipping man had been swallowed by the ocean.

They landed on a beach a short time later. Nova dropped Nathaniel into the sand feet before touchdown and then crash-landed into the dunes. Nathaniel sprang to his feet, uninjured, and hurried over to her. She was gimping on one leg. Fortunately, her magnificent wings appeared undamaged. She wore a coat of sand on her wings like a dusting of silver, the particles resplendent in the moonlight.

"Who are you?" he asked.

He hadn't chosen the question. In fact, it was the last question in the world that he needed answered; he knew exactly who she was. But it was as if his tongue was under the control of a remote entity. He felt like a puppet granted a modicum of free will, only to discover that it vanished the moment he consciously exercised it.

"I'm Nova Norcross," she answered, avoiding making eye contact. Still gimping, she eased herself down into the sand. He sat down beside her.

"Wow! I thought so. But then again, who else would you be?" He sounded star-struck, dopey. He desperately wished to gain control of his tongue, because he wanted to ask *Winter* questions, not Nova. But every effort at independent action was thwarted by the distant god of the dream.

His voice changed, lowered. "It's happening again, isn't it?" he asked.

He had no idea what he was talking about.

"Looks that way," Nova replied, glancing up at Earth's foremost satellite. "Based on its color and what we experienced, I'm guessing that this moon unleashes the powers of the deep."

"A Sea Moon."

Nova smirked. "Sea Moon, Ocean Moon, Poseidon Moon; the press can call it whatever they want. It's not the moon that needs to be stopped. It's the man and the cult behind it."

His dream self remembered something important. "My fiancée, she had on a necklace, a golden moon. She rubbed it between her fingers and then the world went dark, and that creature, the monster octopus…"

"What's your name?" she asked, interrupting him.

You know my name, he thought. But he answered, "Nate."

"Your fiancée's gone, Nate. Do you understand me?" She turned to him suddenly, a fire in her eyes, as if she had tapped into the serendipitous. Nova was talking, but, behind the mask, he thought he saw

Winter, trying to reach him. "She belongs to him now. Any attempt you make to try and rescue her will end either in your death or your enslavement. Do you understand?"

Nathaniel understood the subtext. Nate, on the other hand, was focused on the denotation. "But my fiancée's dead, isn't she? The cruise ship…"

"Doubtful," Nova spat, interrupting him again. "When he can, he usually protects his servants. And from the looks of it, she was his servant." A pause. "He's not dead. I can assure you of that."

Against his will, he put his head in his hands, ostensibly processing the loss of his fiancée. In truth, he didn't feel a thing.

After a minute or so, he regained his composure. "Who is he?"

"You wouldn't believe me if I told you."

"You do realize that I'm talking to a woman with wings, don't you?"

This won him a déjà vu smile. His confused heart rabbit-thumped at the sight of it.

"He's a god. Some minor deity given dominion over the earth after the previous god abandoned the post. He goes by a hundred different monikers, but I don't believe any of them are authentic. All I know is that he has to be defeated. And I'm the only one left who can do it."

He didn't know what to say to this. For a moment they sat in silence. The ocean breeze played at Nova's feathers, stirring a gentle song. Up above, the aquamarine moon feigned benevolence. Its placid hue suggested peace, not monsters of the deep and ship-swallowing tidal waves. Nathaniel felt himself letting his guard down. Some distant part of

78

his brain knew that he shouldn't, knew that in doing so he was playing into the worldmaker's designs, but it was impossible to sit on the beach and not find himself drifting into the storyline's undertow, one in which he fell deep and hard for the winged heroine.

"How can I help you? I mean, there has to be a way to defeat this…god, or whoever he is. Right? You can't do it alone."

She stood. "There's nothing you can do," she said in reply. There was a faraway look in her eyes, a bottomless, detached wisdom. She began to walk. At first, she limped away from him, but she grew faster with every step. When he realized what she intended, he stood and tried to stop her, but she was already aloft before he was fully on his feet. He watched in wonder as her black wings carved the soul out of the night sky.

Then he woke up.

*

It was past eleven a.m. He sat up and stared at the bedside clock in confusion, trying to make sense of the time. Outside, nature's soporific was at work: the steady patter of rain lulled Nathaniel to stay in bed. Feeling drowsy, he considered lying back down, but pinpricks of memory stirred him to life.

Winter.

Two days without sleep.

Emily Winch.

The dream.

He came to life.

Worried that he wouldn't remember the dream in its entirety, he rushed to recall the thread. To his surprise, he found that he remembered every facet of the dream in vivid detail: the sequence of events unfolded before him like he was watching a movie in his mind and could navigate with precision to whichever scene of the dream he wanted to study. Entranced by his own thoughts, he pored over the dream again and again, reliving every moment in explicit detail. He felt a giddiness overcome him: he should have died in the dream, but he hadn't.

Winter had saved him.

No, he thought. *Not Winter. Nova.*

Another thought. *If she hadn't saved me, would I have woken up?*

He brought a hand to his chin, faintly registered the lesser-Van-Winkle sandpaper stubble. *Shave,* he told himself. *Get on with the day.* He stood up.

With his first step, a knife-like pain stabbed him in his left ribcage. Recalling the dream sequence, he remembered the injury's origin: when he was tossed off the railing back onto the boat, seconds after Winter had severed the monster's tentacle. More evidence that everything Winter had told him was true. He continued toward the bathroom, grimacing with every step.

Halfway there, a thunderclap of memory.

The text message!

He rushed back into the room, eyes zooming to the bedside table, the cell phone's usual spot. It wasn't there. *Where is it? I was falling asleep*—he tornadoed through the sheets, catching up the electronic device in the spiral. Plucking the phone from the fabric, he brought it to life and looked to see if he had any messages. A tiny **1** sat atop the speech bubble icon. He mashed it with his thumb.

I'm fine. See you tomorrow.

He blinked his eyes. The five-word reply stayed the same.

I'm fine. See you tomorrow.

He looked at the time the text message had arrived. **11:03**. He glanced to see when he had written his original text message. **9:34**. A one-and-a-half-hours' difference. He tried to wrap his mind around the text. Had Winter written it under duress? Was the text a brush-off? Did she ignore his other questions on purpose? Was she pissed that he had obtained her real phone number? Was she even the person who had replied? Try as he might, he couldn't square the text message reply with the woman he had met; the five words rang false, both in style and content.

He sat the phone down on the bed. Closed his eyes. Took a couple deep breaths. Attempted to clear his mind. Sleep had restored him to his body (minus the ribcage injury), but, even after thirteen hours of shut-eye, he was still under the control of a helter-skelter mind. His thoughts felt as scattered as they had during his last days with Angelica, when every half-formed notion sprinted a torch through the wheat field of his consciousness, burning his ability to reason to a crisp.

The breathing helped. His mind quieted. Out of the stillness, a new thought occurred to him.

Walk away.

The simplicity of the solution floored him. Just walk away. This wasn't his battle. It was hers. And his involvement hadn't improved her lot one iota. If anything, he had exacerbated the danger and put her further at risk. Instead of focusing on protecting herself, she was going to great lengths to protect him as well.

Then again...

It was equally likely that he was the only person on her side, the one person she could trust. Now that he knew that she wasn't a liar, now that he had actually experienced everything she had claimed, he might be the only person who could help her end this nightmare.

Or...

He could continue trying to help her, and he could die.

Flustered, he put the collar of his T-shirt in his mouth and chewed. The masticating made him remember what Emily had told him on Winter's porch, before she transformed into his cult-kidnapped fiancée. *She'll be here around five o'clock tomorrow if you want to take her out to eat.* He nodded his head, trying to convince himself that this should be his working plan.

He looked at his phone. He considered texting Winter's number for a confirmation.

Instead, he texted his brother.

*

"Dude?"

Zack's mouth may have been stuffed with cow, but the incredulous *dude?* still worked its way out. He lowered the burger, signaling that his ravenous hangover could wait. Nathaniel was touched. Usually, the shoe was on the other foot, the burger in the other hand.

"It's true. Every bit of it."

Zack continued staring at Nathaniel, but the fingers in his free hand began foraging for a French fry. Priorities.

"You're telling me," Zack said, finding a fry and dipping it in ketchup, "that not only did you dream about this girl like she said you would, when you woke up your ribcage was sore from where you fell…in the dream?"

"That's what I'm telling you."

"Hm. That's weird, dude. Weird."

Nathaniel waited for further feedback, but after eating the fry in hand, Zack began scarfing down others, dropping the conversation flat.

"So?" Nathaniel prompted mid-gorging.

"So…what?" Zack's masticating mouth was a blizzard of potato mush.

"So…what should I do?"

Zack grabbed a napkin and wiped the grease off his fingers in a workmanlike fashion. He geared up for his reply by glancing to the side, signaling the coming affront.

"I don't know. Get your head checked?"

Nathaniel was braced for the sting, but it still hurt. "You don't believe me?"

"That you hurt yourself in a writer's dreamworld, or that you fell for a crazy chick?"

"You think I'm lying to you?"

"Look, man," Zack said, starting in on the fries again, "I think you had a great but really weird night out with a half-cocked girl, and now that she's slow-playing you, it's bumming you out. You've been out of the game a while, bro. There are some crazy chicks out there. You just gotta let this one go."

Nathaniel turned his palms up, cast his own side glance of mounting irritation. "I want you to be specific. Are you saying that you think I'm crazy? Or that you think Winter is crazy? Because everything I just told you is true."

Zack shrugged, a look on his face as if he'd been backed into a corner. "I mean, I'm hoping it's the girl, but…"

Nathaniel interrupted. "Do you know how many times I've been there for you when the shit hit the fan? Remember when what's-her-name kicked you out of her car on the interstate and I came and picked your drunk ass up off the exit ramp at three a.m. in the morning? Or that time you were arrested for brawling with the rugby team, and I bailed you out of jail so mom and dad would be none the wiser? And I didn't say one word in reproach, not a single…"

"All right, all right," Zack cut in, palms out, one a flash of meaty, pink skin and the other filled with burger. "Listen, I'm here for you. I mean, I'm literally right here, aren't I? But you've got to admit, the whole situation sounds pretty far-fetched. It's like the time you told me that you saw a ghost: I didn't *not* believe you, but I didn't believe you, either. And how could I? Ghosts aren't real! But what does it matter what I think? You're the one in the middle of it. But if you're asking for my advice, which is why you came to me in the first place, I think you should let this chick go. Anybody acting in your best interest would tell you the same.

Because whether this dream stuff is real or not, this girl is going down a rabbit hole, and you do not want to follow."

Nathaniel didn't know how to respond. He knew that his brother was right. But even as the logical part of his mind agreed with his sibling, the other part was reliving his every moment with Winter, winding around the spire of his cognitive processes like a shoot of ivy, growing and overtaking the whole.

They sat in silence. Zack, unaffected, started in again on the fries. Elsewhere in the Jack in the Box, fellow twenty-somethings were treating their Saturday-night hangovers with Sunday-brunch grease. Glancing around, Nathaniel suddenly felt out of his place. All he wanted to do was leave.

He glanced at his watch. Five o'clock was still half the day away.

*

He whiled away the afternoon in a trance. At half past four, he picked up his keys and got in his car. He drove to Winter's house on autopilot. He had no expectation other than to show up, to see. The image of her that he had in his mind was being erased, a quickly fading photograph. He knew in his bones that she wouldn't be there. He had ceded control of the story the moment he lost sight of her at that stoplight. Now he was simply hanging on to the plot in the hopes of reinserting himself into the drama. He imagined James Breach towering overhead, the puppet master with a pair of scissors at the ready.

But to his surprise, when he pulled up to the house, she was waiting for him. She was sitting in the Toyota in the drive, facing away from him, the soft cut of her celestial black hair smoothed against the driver's-side headrest. He looked around, thinking he might see Emily Winch or perhaps even James Breach, but no one was there except for Winter. He waited a moment for her to turn around and acknowledge his arrival. She never did. He got out of the car and walked toward the Toyota, uncertain what to expect.

When he reached the car, she rolled down the window. Then, without looking directly at him, she spoke.

"I'm moving. Leaving town. Don't ever contact me again."

He glanced to the passenger side and saw a suitcase, stuffed to the brim. In the backseat sat the miscellanea one might pack on the run, an assortment of clothes still clinging to hangers and haphazardly strewn pictures in picture frames and the rolled-up Moroccan rug and *Shalimar the Clown*, apparently the only book from Winter's collection that had made the cut.

"I want to help." The words came out somewhat half-hearted. He knew that he had only platitudes, not solutions. Still, he tried. "I'll do whatever it takes, I'll confront him myself, just tell me where..."

She interrupted him. "You truly don't get it, do you? Even after the dream. People died in that dream, Nathaniel. People that I loved. People that you knew!"

He didn't know how to respond. He didn't know what to think. (Who had died: Emily Winch?) Winter turned over the car engine with an aggressive swiftness. Then she locked her eyes on his.

"Don't. Ever. Fucking. Contact. Me. Again."

He knew that she had forced herself to say it for his sake, but that didn't mean it didn't hurt. She threw the car into reverse. Teardrop cocoons formed in her eyes, but before he could capitalize, the Toyota's tires spat gravel and he was forced to jump out of the way. He watched her go, but she didn't watch him, her neck craning backward as she whipped the car out into the street. Then she sped away.

He stood still for a moment after she had left, his heart dull with pain. It was over. Whatever the hell was going on, whatever danger she was in, there was nothing he could do about it. If anything, his continued involvement only exacerbated her danger. He took a moment to let the reality of the situation sink in. Moving on wouldn't be easy, but he could do it. After all, he had done it before.

He started to walk back to his car. But before he had taken two steps, a tall, peculiar-looking man rounded the corner of the street and came into view. The man was of a height that, while not freakish, certainly drew one's attention, and he had a build that, while not massive, was undeniably substantial. By itself the man's stature shouldn't have unnerved Nathaniel, but a slight static charge had come in on the air when the fellow came into view. Unnerved, Nathaniel risked a direct look at him. To his shock, the man's eyes were already locked on Nathaniel, a smile like a scythe on his face.

"Nathaniel Pilot! My man!"

The man was snappily dressed. He wore an unbuttoned blue blazer over a simple gray T-shirt, and chinos with crisp, brown wingtips. His skin was the color of white sand, and he had the countenance of a genial henchman, his good-natured visage undermined by a palpable, lurking violence. Nathaniel watched with a growing unease as the man drew closer. He knew that whatever was about to happen, it wouldn't be good.

"Who are you?" Nathaniel asked. "And how do you know my name?"

"Ha-ha! Right to the point! Okay, Nathaniel, I suppose it's only fair that since I know your name, you should know mine. My name's Kol Jones. And—no need to keep you in suspense—I am an associate of Mr. James Breach, whose acquaintance I believe you made two nights prior."

Kol drew within fifteen feet. Nathaniel took a step back, and went into a defensive crouch.

Kol laughed again, his "Ha!" like a cannon shot. "I heard you were a wrestler, Nathaniel," Kol said, mimicking Nathaniel's stance with one of his own. "You want to go a round? I'll warn you, though. I put up more of a fight than James."

Nathaniel kept quiet. He glanced this way and that, hoping to see a second soul, perhaps the female police officer or even Emily Winch (she couldn't really be dead, could she?) but there was no one. The neighborhood had a post-apocalyptic feel, like he had been left on earth to face the devil alone.

Kol, a wicked, self-assured smile on his face, dropped the wrestler's stance and came closer still. He stopped once he was inside the normal boundary for conducting human conversation, and there lodged himself, like he was taking up permanent residence in Nathaniel's personal space. Nathaniel became paralyzed, not with fear, but with indecision. He didn't know whether to fight or to run or to simply stand still and wait to see what occurred, which, by default, he was already doing.

"Mr. Pilot, Mr. Pilot," Kol intoned, the way a teacher might address a wayward student. "What are we going to do with you?"

Nathaniel adhered to his mouth-shut strategy. He guessed at Kol's age: late thirties to early forties. It struck Nathaniel that the sort of men who made ambiguous threats in middle age were often the ones who could back them up.

Kol leaned close. He smiled, his numerous teeth like polished tombstones. He opened his mouth, the smell minty fresh. "Do I scare you, Nathaniel?" he asked.

"Fuck you," Nathaniel said. He rocked a half-step back, wanting to hold his ground while trying to move out of knifing distance.

Kol rocked back as well, laughing. "You see, Nathaniel, that's what worries us about you! Your gumption! If Mr. Breach doesn't do something, if I don't do something, you might stew on matters for a day or two and then try to interfere again! So why not kill you now?"

A wave of adrenaline rushed through Nathaniel's body, enough to make him feel nauseous. Kol saw the dizzy, panic-stricken look in Nathaniel's eyes, because he laughed even harder.

"I don't mean *right* now, Nathaniel! I mean tonight! When you're asleep! If I'm giving you the heebie-jeebies now, just wait until you see me in a nightmare dreamscape brought to life by Mr. James Breach! I'm not going to lie to you. I'm a right nasty one. In that world, I go by the name of Burden Monks. There's this moon cult, see, and I'm a leader/enforcer type—Nathaniel, last night was my first time, and I'm still buzzing off it! I must have killed, what was it, five, six people? Now, most of them weren't flesh and bloods, but one was: James told me I'd be able to tell the difference, and boy could I!—when the light went out in that poor fucker's eyes, I knew that same poor schmuck had just died in his sleep, dreaming the same dream as me! Crazy! And to think that tonight—tonight that could be you! Dead!"

Nathaniel felt sick with fear. It was one thing to face down a mortal threat, quite another to know that the peril could hunt you down in your sleep. The remnants of his midday burger lunch worked their way up his esophagus. He vomited up chunks of meat and then retched helplessly while Kol leaned over and patted him on the back.

"That a boy!" Kol encouraged him. Nathaniel swiped his hand away. Kol laughed, making a sound like an overjoyed thunderstorm. "You are at last demonstrating the proper response!"

Nathaniel stepped away from Kol and attempted a lesser version of his defensive posture. "What do you want from me?"

"What do *I* want? I want to kill you! I mean…what a thrill that would be, right? Meeting you today, killing you tonight? But unfortunately, your girl Nova…I mean Winter…made it known that she would be a cooperative hostage if and only if you made it through the week alive. James has her behind the eight ball now that he's laid hands on her, but that doesn't mean he wants her resisting him going forward. She is the heroine, after all. So, I was sent to deliver the ultimatum. Go away. Stay away. Or die. Capisce?"

Kol waited for a reply, his toothy grin resplendent. Nathaniel felt his will giving way, his body a marionette to the absent puppet master. His mouth opened, and he said what he was meant to say.

"Yes. Okay. I got it."

Kol's grin grew to Cheshire Cat proportions. "Smart man! It is a disappointment for me, no doubt about it, but still…you have to respect it when a man makes the right call." The tall man bounced away a step. "Okay, Nathaniel. I have an afternoon to kill, before a night full of killing. For your sake, I hope you don't change your mind, but for mine"—he cocked his head at a forty-five-degree angle and locked eyes with Nathaniel—"I'd love to show you how much scarier I am at night."

Nathaniel didn't respond.

Like that, it was over. Kol spun on his wingtips and strode away, whistling a song.

A question flared in Nathaniel's conscience. He tried to snuff it out—*just let him go, let him go,* the voice inside his head said—but his want of knowledge was stronger than his fear. "Emily Winch?" he called out to Kol. "Is she dead?"

Kol stopped on a dime. He turned back around slowly, his grin leading the way. "Oh no. James Breach has big plans for her. But there were others who died, Nathaniel." He wagged a finger at Nathaniel. "Believe you me. There were others."

Kol continued wagging the finger for a couple of seconds after he stopped talking, like an automaton on the fritz. But then his smile shifted, lips collapsing around his teeth like sinister gates slamming shut. He turned around a little slower this time, but as soon as his back was to Nathaniel, he resumed his whistling and walked away.

*

Nighttime descended like a burdensome promise. Inside his apartment, Nathaniel watched television for hours without processing a second of it. The sandman whispered sweet nothings to him from time to time, but he knew it was only a tease. Going to sleep tonight wouldn't be easy.

At midnight, he crawled into bed. As expected, his mind spun into gear, the congress of his thoughts commencing a full-fledged debate over the events of the last few days. Whenever he relaxed, the possibility that falling asleep might cost him his life stirred him awake. Thirty minutes passed. An hour. He tried all the tricks: deep breathing, counting his breaths, detachment, standing up and lying down again, trying *not* to try to go to sleep. Nothing worked. By the end of the second hour, he was on the verge of getting up to read a book (a remedy he kept avoiding, mainly because the only book in his possession that he hadn't read was *Savage Moon*), but as he lay there considering it, he felt sleep's languorous pull, easy bait in shallow waters.

His exhausted brain closed around the hook.

*

He was the moon.

Or perhaps not. On a nearby celestial plane, a much larger moon the color of the deep blue sea lorded over the Earth with a dark majesty. He was but a mere satellite in comparison, a sketching, an outline, perhaps even a figment. It was difficult to get a true sense of himself.

He knew where he was. He might have been asleep, but the dream had the same strange hyperreal quality as his dream the night before, which meant he was a pawn in the hands of the writer-god James Breach. He assumed that at any moment the dream would lurch into the realm of nightmares, but, to his surprise, time rolled on, and nothing changed.

The dream lasted all night. From his tranquil perch in the firmament, he watched the Earth, surrounded by stillness. It was so peaceful and quiet that there were periods of time when he felt that he had fallen asleep inside his own dream. Toward the end, he saw a shadow pass over the Earth's surface below: the fully extended wingspan of a woman in flight. Looking closer, he realized that he had extraordinary vision, and could, if he wanted, see everything that occurred on the Earth below.

Shortly after, he woke up.

*

For five nights in a row, he had the same dream. The sixth night—a week to the day after he had met Winter—the dreams stopped.

It was only then that he fully felt the loss of her. The sensible decision he had reached after his confrontation with Kol Jones suddenly seemed cowardly; he felt the desperate need to make contact again. After a day of internal debating, he decided to try a text. When the text didn't go through, he risked a phone call, only to discover that the number was no longer in service.

Desperate, he tried the other number Winter had given him, the one for *Purity Tattoo*. The same message as before played on the other end of the line. It being a Sunday, he waited until the following day and tried again, to no avail. Frustrated, he made the decision to drive down to the tattoo parlor and see if Kelly Anne or O might know where Winter had gone. He knew that what he was doing was impulsive and stupid, but he didn't care. James Breach couldn't kill him now. The seven days were up.

When he reached the tattoo parlor, he immediately sensed that something was wrong. The parlor was open, and there were people inside, but the welcoming vibe from a week ago was gone. Walking through the door, a mournful energy overwhelmed him: it was as if the air itself were thick with sadness.

Inside, Kelly Anne was sitting on the pinstriped red-and-white couch beside a bespectacled woman in her late fifties. The two of them were flipping through a photo album. Behind them, an overweight kid who might have been in college wandered the shop with a nervous energy.

Kelly Anne looked up when he entered. "Hi," she said distractedly. But then, recognizing who he was, she did a double take and said, "Oh! Hi." Her eyes were cloudy with tears, and her voice was shaky, but she managed a smile and stood up to greet him. The woman with the glasses remained seated, looking uncomfortable, while behind them the boy stopped his pacing and glared.

"Hi," Nathaniel responded. "I'm sorry... I... um... is this a bad time?"

It was Kelly Anne's turn to look confused. "You don't know? You don't know. I thought maybe you were here on Winter's behalf to explain why she didn't come to the funeral."

"The funeral?"

"O's funeral."

O. Kris Kringle after spending a stint in a Siberian gulag, the big fellow who had inked the moon on Nathaniel's shoulder.

Dead.

The news disoriented him. Had O died of natural causes, or was this somehow connected to James Breach? Before he could connect the dots, Kelly Anne moved in, wrapping him in a full embrace and leading him by the hand to the couch. Suddenly he was sitting between the two women, and Kelly Anne was talking, taking control, a far-off voice that pierced his concentration and made it impossible for him to put two and two together.

"Nathaniel? It is Nathaniel, isn't it? Nathaniel, this is Maggie Graham, O's mom. And behind us is Sidney, O's younger brother. Maggie, Nathaniel here was one of the last people O worked on. He inked a moon—Nathaniel, would you mind rolling up your sleeve and showing her? We work on so many clients, but Nathaniel sticks out in my mind. He's a friend of a friend and, as I said, one of O's last tattoos. Beautiful, isn't it? Your son was so talented, Mrs. Graham. I don't know how... I'm sorry, I've cried so much the past week, but the tears just keep coming, I suppose that's natural. We had been business partners for so long..."

"How d-did it happen?" Nathaniel stammered.

Kelly Anne shared a brief look with Maggie before deciding that it was okay to continue. "He died in his sleep. Two nights after he gave you your tattoo. He simply went to bed and never woke up."

Nathaniel's stomach flipped. She was talking about the night of the dream, the night of the ship, the night of Winter with wings and Emily-aka-Zadie and the thin, bald-headed man flipping the quarter. But where was O in the dream? Where was O?

Kelly Anne continued. "I was showing Maggie the shop photo album when you walked in. I have an old Polaroid lying around that I love to use. When something strikes my interest at work, I don't think twice, I just stop and click. There are so many great ones of O—look, I love this one, he's smiling. He didn't smile a lot, but when he did, it was like the sun on a bright summer's day."

Nathaniel looked. O was smiling all right, beaming at some off-camera hilarity, but, magnificent as the grin was, it couldn't hold Nathaniel's attention. Instead, Nathaniel's eyes went to O's arm, and the bright orange and blue tattoo there. Immediately, everything fell into place: for a moment Nathaniel was in the dream again, dangling from the ship's railing while far below the orange-and-blue octopus waited with its maw open like an abyss. Remembering this, his thoughts fast-forwarded to when Nova Norcross plunged her sword deep into the soft tissue between the monster's oversized eyes.

He wondered if Winter had known at that moment that she was killing her friend.

"Are you okay?" Kelly Anne asked him.

He wasn't okay. Suddenly he didn't have the slightest clue what he was hoping to accomplish by being there. There was simply nothing to be done. Winter was gone. And he was in over his head. He knew that if he didn't get out now, if he didn't stay away from everything connected to Winter, it was only a matter of time before he ended up like O, dead in his sleep.

"Yes. I mean, no." He lurched off the couch, nearly knocking the photo album out of Kelly Anne's hands. "I... I'm sorry about O. I have to go."

Kelly Anne said something to him. So did O's mom. Maybe O's brother as well. But he refused to hear them. He rushed out the door and back into the autumnal chill, hurrying away from the tattoo parlor as fast as he could.

He never looked back.

Interlude

2018

An interview between James Breach, author of the Savage Moon *book series, and Mazzy Whittle, host of* The Hybrid Pen, *a podcast dedicated to interviewing authors of fantastical works of fiction.*

(Picking up at the 5:22 mark)

Mazzy Whittle: "—and with the ten-year anniversary of *Poseidon Moon*, the second book in the series, on the horizon, what better way to celebrate than with a television series! Tell us, James: When can we expect the pilot to air?"

James Breach: "It's a fluid situation, but, based on what I'm hearing from execs, either this fall or the following spring."

Mazzy Whittle: "How exciting! I've heard rumors that the network recently cast the Nova Norcross character. Is that true?"

James Breach: "They have."

Mazzy Whittle: "Don't be coy, James. Out with it."

James Breach: *(Laughs)* "You know I can't do that. The higher-ups over at *PHANTOM* would have my head. Or at least slap me on the wrist. I'll say this: you won't be disappointed."

Mazzy Whittle: "If the rumors are true, I'm sure I won't. James?"

James Breach: "…"

Mazzy Whittle: "James is smiling like a Cheshire cat. Delilah Blue it is, then."

James Breach: "You didn't hear it from me!"

Mazzy Whittle: *(Laughs)* "Moving on. Okay, James, I hate to do this, but I would be remiss if I didn't address the strange and surreal controversy that has surrounded the series for years now. I'm sure most of the listeners know what I'm referring to, but, for those who don't, do you mind if I provide a little background?"

James Breach: "I suppose."

Mazzy Whittle: "Please feel free to interject if you believe I've said anything that's incorrect or unfair. There are a small but vocal minority of…let's call them fans…who claim that they are the inspiration for a number of the characters in the series. Among that group, an even smaller subset has claimed—and I know how ludicrous this sounds—that you have the ability to tap into their dreams, and that, once inside their dreams, you write your books to life."

James Breach: *(chuckles)* "Something like that. Yes."

Mazzy Whittle: "We all know how preposterous this sounds, but, in a couple of cases—one of them disturbingly prescient—people who have claimed to be based on characters have turned up dead shortly after they met their demise in your books."

James Breach: "You're referring to the Kennedy Marks situation."

Mazzy Whittle: "Without a doubt it's the one that captured the public's attention. But there are others."

James Breach: "…"

Mazzy Whittle: "I want to hear your take on what happened with Kennedy Marks. But first, for those who are unfamiliar, Kennedy Marks left a trail of evidence in which he claimed to be the inspiration for the Carter Crowe character in the series, mostly in the form of videos that were posted on social media after he died. After Kennedy's untimely death, one of his relatives brought videos he had taken of himself to the attention of the police. In the videos, Kennedy claimed that his life was in danger because Carter Crowe's life was in danger in the books. We know this because the relative later posted the videos on various social media sites after the police cleared you of wrongdoing."

James Breach: "Yes."

Mazzy Whittle: "Kennedy's intimate knowledge of the book that you were working on at the time—"

James Breach: "Here's where I take issue—"

Mazzy Whittle: "Because of the discrepancy between what the published version of the book revealed and what Kennedy claimed?"

James Breach: "Yes. That. And—"

Mazzy Whittle: "The role that Officer Jorgen played."

James Breach: "Most definitely."

Mazzy Whittle: "Okay. I really want you to expound on this. But again, for anyone who's not up to speed, let's back up a little. You had a personal relationship with Kennedy Marks before his death, correct?"

James Breach: "Kennedy was a fan. I met him at a signing during the *Weeping Moon* book tour. I love my fans, but I was a little slow during the early years of my success in realizing that not everyone who was enthusiastic about my work was mentally stable. After I met Kennedy, we stayed in touch."

Mazzy Whittle: "Can you define what staying in touch means?"

James Breach: "Phone calls. Emails. The occasional lunch. Kennedy made the decision to move to Huntersville, North Carolina, which isn't far from Davidson, where I was living at the time."

Mazzy Whittle: "It didn't send off warning bells that Kennedy moved from…wasn't it Atlanta?…to be closer to you?"

James Breach: "In retrospect, it should have. But…what can I say… I tried early on to make genuine bonds with my biggest fans, and, if someone wants to move to a different city as an adult, who am I to stop them?"

Mazzy Whittle: "There have been others, right? Fans who moved or made drastic changes in their lives to be closer to you?"

James Breach: "Yes. It's fair to say that."

Mazzy Whittle: "Okay. Let me ask you this. Was Kennedy Marks the inspiration for the Carter Crowe character?"

James Breach: "I'm going to give a very writerly answer here, which might seem evasive, but it's the truth. The answer is yes and no. All my characters are amalgams of people I've met in my life. Carter Crowe was no different. Was he partially inspired by Kennedy Marks? Without a doubt. But to say that Carter Crowe was Kennedy Marks and Kennedy Marks was Carter Crowe would be false. That's not how fiction works."

Mazzy Whittle: "Fair enough. I know this is sensitive territory, but I'd like to ask you about the peculiarities surrounding Marks's death."

James Breach: "You can ask, but there's not much I'm going to say in response. Mostly out of respect for Kennedy's family."

Mazzy Whittle: "I understand, but the whole situation is just so…surreal. The autopsy said that Marks died of asphyxiation. But no one, not even the coroner, has been able to get their heads around why? The police report said that there was no sign of forced entry, and no physical marks on Marks's body consistent with strangulation. And then, when Marks's sister released the videos, Marks speculated that if he died, it would likely be because he was choked to death by Burden Monks, the biggest villain in the series!"

James Breach: "In the videos released on social media, Kennedy had a handful of theories as to how he might die. Being choked to death was one of them."

Mazzy Whittle: "He explicitly said that he thought being choked to death was the most likely way he would go. By Burden Monks."

James Breach: "As you'll recall, Kennedy… I mean, Carter Crowe…didn't die by strangulation in *Lightning Moon*. He was struck by lightning."

Mazzy Whittle: "Which leads us to the situation with Officer Jorgen."

James Breach: "I believe you mean former Officer Jorgen."

Mazzy Whittle: "Former Officer Jorgen. A year after the Charlotte-Mecklenburg Police Department cleared you of wrongdoing, Officer Jorgen—who by that point had left the force—claimed that Kennedy Marks's death was investigated as a homicide for a short period, and that you were the primary suspect. The main reason for this, he said, was because Kennedy's video predictions matched up exactly with the rough draft of *Lightning Moon* the police department found on your computer."

James Breach: "Okay, okay. *(Starts to laugh, stifles it)* I have quite a bit to say here, and I'm going to try to say it in a way that doesn't make light of the pain and suffering that the Marks family has gone through. Now, I know you said this at the top, but let me reiterate how ludicrous it is to think that what a writer writes on his or her computer has any bearing on what happens to a person in real life. So, above and beyond everything else…there's that. Second, I handed over my computer to the department of my own volition, because I had nothing to hide. Third, the only person who has ever said that I was a suspect in the case was Officer Jorgen, and that was after he retired. No one currently working for the CMPD has ever stated that. Fourth, as the police department has made clear multiple times, I have several alibis confirming that I was nowhere near Kennedy Marks at the time of his passing. Fifth, after I brought defamation charges against Officer Jorgen in civil court, we reached a settlement that precludes Officer Jorgen from speaking openly about the matter in public and or private. Beyond that, there's really nothing else to say."

Mazzy Whittle: "James, I understand why you're defensive. God knows I would be if I were in your shoes. But just to be clear: you're denying Officer Jorgen's claim that the scene describing Carter Crowe's death in the rough draft of *Lightning Moon* involved Carter Crowe being choked to death by Burden Monks."

James Breach: *(Laughs)* "I really…listen, Mazzy, there's nothing I would love more than to be specific about what you're asking me, but based on the advice of my lawyer and the terms of the settlement with Officer Jorgen, I can't."

Mazzy Whittle: "Okay. Sure. I understand. What about the others?"

James Breach: "What others? Surely you don't expect me to address all the nonsense that's on the internet?"

Mazzy Whittle: "Just a little of it. Was the Bridgette Ash character based on Ashley Bloom?"

James Breach: "That is a rabbit hole I'm reluctant to go down, for obvious reasons—"

Mazzy Whittle: "And Zadie Alaska—in real life, is she Emily Winch? Many of your fans made note that Zadie didn't die in the last book. Instead, she disappeared. Some have speculated that was a convenient way for the real-life Emily Winch to escape unscathed. Speaking of which, where is Emily? You had a relationship with her for a couple of years, and now...?"

James Breach: "Emily reached a point where she wanted more privacy in her life. Which I can understand. Wherever she is, I'm sure she's well."

Mazzy Whittle: "Now these are just the more, shall we say, credible accusations."

James Breach: "Referring to any of this nonsense as credible is a stretch."

Mazzy Whittle: "There are websites out there—I'm sure you've heard of *savagemoonmurders.com*—that make connections all the way back to the beginning of the series. I've even read speculation that the death of Joessa Fox way back in the first book is connected to the untimely passing of a student you taught when you were a professor—"

James Breach: "Okay. That's enough. I'm going to end this interview if there are any more questions in this vein."

(Four seconds of silence)

Mazzy Whittle: "James. You know that I'm a fan, and I don't want to make you unduly uncomfortable. It's only that the mysteries surrounding the series are so fascinating—"

James Breach: "I understand. But I have to draw the line somewhere. Please—no more."

(Two seconds of silence)

Mazzy Whittle: "Sure. Let's get back on track. You recently started writing the final book in the series, is that correct?"

James Breach: "Yes, now that the publicity for *Mischief Moon* is finished, I am writing the final book."

Mazzy Whittle: "Do you have a working title?"

James Breach: "I do."

Mazzy Whittle: "Care to reveal it?"

James Breach: "Um…no. Not just yet."

Mazzy Whittle: "Fair enough. Let's pivot to some of the plot points in the series that haven't been resolved. Like the Shadow Moon, for example. The Shadow Moon first appeared in *Poseidon Moon*, correct? The second book in the series?"

James Breach: "Yes. The Shadow Moon first appeared in Book Two."

Mazzy Whittle: "And it's been slowly working its way across the sky ever since. Most of your fan base seems to think that we're either headed for a collision or an eclipse. Care to weigh in?"

James Breach: "Ah, the Shadow Moon. Do you know that in all honesty I cannot remember what compelled me to put the Shadow Moon into the books in the first place? I've always been more of a gardener and less of an architect when it comes to writing, meaning that, when the Shadow Moon first appeared, I was operating on gut instinct. This will probably disappoint my readers who think that I'm a genius working four steps ahead, but I didn't have a master plan for the Shadow Moon when I first wrote about it. That being said, I'm determined that the Shadow Moon will have its say in the final book. Now I just need to know what that is!" (Laughs)

Mazzy Whittle: "Speaking of unresolved plot points, let's talk about Nova Norcross. With so many of the major characters in your books having died, it's telling that Nova is the only one who has survived from Book One. Which makes me super nervous for her now that you're writing the last novel. So, without telling us whether she lives or dies, can you let the readers know if there's going to be a definitive resolution for Nova in the final book?"

James Breach: "Oh, yes. One way or the other, Nova's story arc is going to reach its end. She will either escape the clutches of the god of moons, or she won't."

Mazzy Whittle: "I know millions of people will be picking up the book based on that information alone. Okay, James, I'm going to venture back onto thin ice for the final question. Is the Nova Norcross character inspired by someone in real life? Or is she an amalgamation of a few different people?"

James Breach: "We're going down this road again? All right. Fine. Let me ask you a question: don't you think it's funny that for all those who have come forward and claimed to be the inspiration for different characters in my book, almost no one has claimed to be Nova Norcross?"

Mazzy Whittle: "There have been one or two—"

James Breach: "No one who was taken seriously. And Nova Norcross is the primary protagonist of the entire series!"

Mazzy Whittle: "Are you insinuating that because no one credible has claimed to be Nova, those who claim to be the inspiration for the other characters are lying?"

James Breach: "To a degree. If I'm so reliant on using real-life muses as inspiration for my characters, how come no one has stepped forward to claim to be the most iconic character in the entire *Savage Moon* series?"

Mazzy Whittle: "That's a question I imagine only you can answer, James. And perhaps one other person."

James Breach: *(Laughs, sounding perhaps a little unhinged)* "Whoever it is had better come forward soon, then, hadn't they? There's only one book left, and I'm still on the fence as to how Nova Norcross's story ends."

Mazzy Whittle: *(Laughs as well, sounding unsettled and thrilled at the same time)*

(Dropping off at the 12:02 mark)

Part II
2016

Winter opened her eyes to find herself on the flipside of James Breach's mind.

She had survived yet another night. Yet another dream.

She was desperate to take a scalding hot shower, eager to scour the dreamworld from her bones, but she knew that she needed to check the phone first. Not her cell phone, but the burner that James made her use just for their interactions. She walked into the apartment kitchen where the phone rested on the counter. On the screen, a single text message awaited.

12:30. E.

E, she thought. *Dammit.*

E meant Orphanage Park. E meant James wanted to talk. Most weeks all she had to do was walk by James Breach in some public place close enough that he could reach out and touch her hand, but E meant that changes were in the offing, E meant a conversation, E meant that in all likelihood she would have to deal with Kol Jones before she dealt with James Breach. E meant that her whole day—and possibly more days to come—was fucked.

She took a deep breath. Tried to organize her thoughts. *Okay. First, call work.* She rung up the number to Poplar Road Animal Hospital, the veterinarian's office where she was currently employed as a tech. She prayed to God that anyone but Lisa would pick up, but after the second ring Lisa's condemnatory voice poured through the receiver. Even Lisa's "Hello, this is Poplar Road Animal Hospital. How can I help you?" sounded judgmental.

"Hey, Lisa. It's Winter."

"Uh-huh."

This isn't going to go well. "Listen, I can't come in at ten o'clock today. Will you let Dr. Walchip know? I'm dealing with a family issue."

"The same one as usual?" Lisa's inflection was deadpan.

"Yes. Please tell Dr. Walchip that I'll be in as soon as possible. And I'll be more than happy to work an extra shift to make up for time missed."

"Sure. I'll tell him."

Good, Winter thought. *She's giving me the cold shoulder treatment. I can hang up and deal with the fallout later.*

"Thanks. I'll try my best to be in by two o'clock."

Winter was reaching for the red *end call* button when Lisa's trailing voice called her back to the line.

"You really shouldn't bother. The doctors were discussing your…um, *situation*…the last time this happened. Which was what, last week? Anyway, I heard them say that the next time was the last straw. No matter how many extra shifts you offer to work, what they really need is a technician who shows up when she's scheduled."

Winter knew that there was no point in engaging. "Okay. Thanks, Lisa. I'll speak with Dr. Walchip about it when I get in."

Lisa chuckled on the other end, a caustic little laugh. "You know, I'm actually looking forward to seeing you today. It's not every day you get to see your least favorite person in the office lose their job."

And with that, Lisa hung up. Winter took a deep breath. Deep in the grinding machinery of her mind, she remembered the offer James Breach had made to her eight years ago, at the start of their "second beginning," as James liked to call it. *If there's anyone who makes your life a personal hell, tell me. I'll meet them. Touch them. Then I'll arrange it so that they're dealt with in the books.* Her response had been quickfire. *Someone who makes my life a personal hell? Besides you?* James had let it drop—at the end of the day he was a non-confrontational wuss, all things considered—but even years later, Winter had moments when James's offer tunneled to the surface of her thoughts. She had never once seriously entertained the notion; the thought of dragging someone into her nightmare, let alone killing them, made her want to retch. Even so, she felt guilty at how persistent the memory was. Worse than anything, it made Winter feel like she was somehow complicit in James's evil.

Besides, odds are, after today I'll never see Lisa again. The thought was bittersweet. Like every job she had taken since the "second beginning," Winter knew that her time at Poplar Road Animal Hospital would be short-lived. There was a time when James was forced to make allowances for her work, but that was before the *Savage Moon* series became a phenomenon. Now he didn't give two fucks for her personal schedule.

Kol Jones had laid out James's new philosophy to her shortly after the money started to stack up. "Mr. Breach will give you sufficient money to live comfortably. And he insists that you take it. You can continue to work. Or not. Mr. Breach doesn't care. His only requirements are that when he calls, you come. Other than that, feel free to live your life the way you want." And so her every employ came to an end the moment James Breach's demands on her schedule exasperated her bosses.

Still, she kept bouncing from job to job. Not because she needed the money. But because she needed consistent people in her life. Even if it was only for a short time. Even if it was people like Lisa.

She looked at the time. Still early. Now that she wasn't going in to work, she had an entire morning to kill.

Only one thing to do, she thought. *Keep brainstorming ways to escape.*

*

In the beginning—the very beginning of the second beginning, that is—she was confident that she would find a way out.

That was what she told herself as she slipped her car into the rushing stream of I-277 traffic, leaving behind the boy in the blue Civic with the new moon tattoo. *One week,* she thought. *Make sure Nathaniel is in the clear. Then stay awake a couple of days in a row and disappear.* She held out all manner of wild hopes in that moment, daydreaming even as she pulled away from Nathaniel that in good time she would find him again and they would resume falling in love.

But the instant she saw James, all confidence left her. He had an eerie calmness about him that she had never seen before, a calmness so at odds with the manic energy of the previous night that it was like he was an entirely different person.

They met in a large furniture showroom in the University area near the under-construction IKEA. When she reached the parking lot, she let the engine idle, waiting to ensure that Nathaniel hadn't somehow kept her in sight and followed her back north. After five minutes with no sign of him, she went inside.

James was waiting for her near a gray chamois leather sectional in the front of the store, hands clasped together like a contemplative priest. He flashed a surgical smile. Then he motioned that she should follow him.

They wound their way into a maze of bourgeois chairs and sofas. At last James came to a stop in front of a trio of wingbacks, a pair of muted burgundies flanking a floral print. But James didn't sit. Instead, he extended his right hand.

Winter channeled all the power that she could muster. "If I do this," she said, "you promise that no harm will come to the man you touched last night. Right?"

"That's right," James replied, his voice high and dry. "But only if you do this. Otherwise…"

She knew that there was no point in prolonging the inevitable. She offered him her right hand. He took it in his own, gave it a disagreeable squeeze.

The deed done, James took a seat on the floral print, visibly exhaling as he settled into the chair. He motioned that Winter should sit on one of the burgundies. She considered remaining standing as a show of defiance, but all at once she felt extremely tired, the sleepless night and the reality of what she had done catching up to her like a plague of weary demons. *It's happening again,* she thought. *After all this time.*

"I didn't want it to be this way," James said. "I wanted you to understand. To be my willing muse. But now...oh Nova, you've put me in such a difficult position."

She didn't respond. What was there to say? Before, she had hoped that she could reason with him. But now that she had given in, all that was left to do was pray that he kept his part of the agreement. Any commentary on her part could only imperil that.

"I made a choice three years ago," he continued. "A difficult choice. If you had known how close I came to saving Joessa, and not you—"

"Her name was Jessalyn. She was my college roommate."

Winter had meant to keep her mouth shut, but James calling Jessalyn by her character name was too much. In response, James simply sighed, another cheerless breath. He refused to look in Winter's direction.

His avoidance unnerved her. Something very bad was about to happen. She could sense it.

"Yes," he said after a long delay. "Her name was Jessalyn. But I didn't choose Jessalyn. I chose you. Winter York. Nova Norcross. And because I made that choice, you're alive today. And now I've made another choice. I refuse to live in guilt any longer because of my...abilities. I refuse to deny my talent. My destiny. And no one, not even you, is going to stop me from becoming what I'm meant to be."

And then, still without looking at her, James Breach stood up and walked away.

For a moment she was confused. Was it over? She expected at any moment for James to turn around, but instead he kept walking, winding through the furniture maze, advancing steadily toward the exit. Her heart lightened with each step he took, hoping against hope that the worst of it was over.

It was then that the man appeared. She was so focused on James that she didn't initially register the newcomer's presence. But once she saw him, she had difficulty looking away. He was uncommonly tall, with a wave of short brown hair and skin the color of curdled milk. His dress was impeccable. He struck Winter as formidable, but in a peculiar way; from across the room, he called to mind a stately minotaur roaming a furniture labyrinth.

Instinctively, Winter knew that she didn't want to meet him. To her horror, the man walked up to James, and the two began talking. Watching this, she hoped against hope that he was just a salesman making his pitch. But at that very moment the man looked up, located Winter, and gave her a chilling smile.

When he was finished talking to James, the man continued walking her way.

She considered jetting, but the man's long, effortless strides devoured the distance between them in seconds. Not knowing what else to do, she stood up to meet him. Even standing, she had to crane her neck to look him in the eye.

"Ah," he said when he was upon her, "the opposition."

She didn't respond. The man had a bloodcurdling quality that was latent in James; Winter had the impression that he was the manifestation of James's worst desires.

"Who are you?" she asked in spite of herself.

"Who am I?" The man's smile ballooned to monstrous proportions. "Why, I'm Kol Jones. I have a different name as well, but that one is a mystery. Don't worry—you'll learn it soon enough."

Winter felt the hair on the back of her neck stand up. She looked around the showroom for another living soul, but there was no one, not a salesperson or a customer in sight.

"Nova Norcross," the man continued. "In the flesh. My oh my. This will be fun."

She felt a surge of anger. Before she could fully process what she was doing, she poked the man hard in the chest. "Listen, you weirdo. Whatever it is you're here to do, get on with it. Or fuck off."

Kol showed stop-sign hands. "Easy! Let's not get off to a bad start. Not in real life. We need to have a working relationship in the here and now, because James gave me the impression that our dusk-to-dawn connection might be a bit tense." He laughed as he spoke, a dark undercurrent of a chuckle. "But as you wish. Brass tacks it is. The reason I'm here is because James wanted me to pass along his expectations of you as we embark on this new endeavor, as well as the risks you'll be incurring if you do anything…foolhardy or rash."

Winter's skin crawled. "James's expectations? What are you talking about?"

Kol shook his head, *tsk-tsking* in mock disappointment. "Now, Winter. I know it's been a whirlwind twenty-four hours, but surely you've taken a little time to imagine the many ways Mr. Breach might keep you captive this time around? No?"

She didn't respond.

"I understand. After all, James has been a bit soft up to now, hasn't he? Though I do believe that's changing. At first, he was reticent to put the plan into action. Even last night, before he went to your house, he still believed you could be convinced to willingly play your part. But after the wrestling match with your beau, he knew that it was time to cross the Rubicon. Now there's no going back."

Winter's heart thundered in her chest. She tried to keep the fear out of her face, without success.

Kol assaulted her with yet another lunatic grin. "Here I am, blabbering on, when what you're concerned with is details! Allow me to give you a rough outline. James has located the names and addresses of nearly forty people you have close connections with. Family members, friends, odd acquaintances. I'm not going to name them all—James believes a little suspense will work to his advantage over the long run—but, so you know that he's not bluffing, here are five."

Kol produced a crisply folded piece of paper from his pants pocket. In short order he rambled off the names and addresses of Winter's maternal aunt, Winter's best friend from her former high school, a former coworker at CVS pharmacy, Winter's boyfriend her sophomore year in college, and, unbelievably, one of the twins in Winter's neighborhood that she used to babysit when she was in high school.

Winter remembered the previous night. How difficult it had been to convince Nathaniel of the truth. The thought of convincing five more people, let alone forty…they would have her committed to a psych ward before she convinced even a fraction.

"Like I said, that's only a sample. James has options galore. So if you do something stupid, like, say, refuse to fall asleep! Or…go missing near the weekly deadline! Then James is going to go on a little scavenger hunt of your friends and relatives. You might be able to save a few, but make no mistake—in the end, people that you know and love will die."

Time slowed to a standstill. The present moment scored itself in Winter's mind. A part of her would always be chained to this instant, like Prometheus at his rock. This was her punishment for fleeing a lesser punishment: an eternity of worry for the ones that she loved.

"Good," Kol said. "I can see that my words are hitting home. Let's carry on, then. For tonight, and tonight only, you will be staying in a hotel. James has made reservations for you to stay in the Holiday Inn in Huntersville, not far from his home. Tonight, our dear writer's pen is going to be quite active, and he wants to ensure that you don't try anything reckless. We're going to go there directly from here. I'll be staying at the hotel as well. Keeping an eye on things, so to speak."

Winter choked down her fright. "If you think—"

"The things I think could fill a book!" Kol interrupted, laughing. "But not to worry, Winter, my agreement with James is predicated on my good

117

behavior in this realm. No doubt you've picked up on a fair amount of masochistic energy radiating off my person, but I'm storing that up for my forays into the *Savage Moon* universe. James has assured me that there will be ample opportunity for me to indulge my baser instincts there. But I digress! After tonight, James insists that you leave your rental home and move a little closer to his neck of the woods. He's open to your input, so long as you don't return to the rental house. Your *novio nuevo* will move along quicker if he can't find you. Which is important, as he's one of the two people we know you've shared our little secret with."

Winter's head spun. *One of two people?* There were *only* two people, Nathaniel and her roommate. But she didn't dare mention Emily's name. Not without proof that they knew.

"I can't leave my home," she protested. "I have a rental agreement, neighbors, a…"—her tongue stuck on the word, fearful that by speaking it, she was dragging the very person into the conversation that she wanted to keep out—"a roommate. I can't just—"

"Emily Winch!" Kol interrupted, interjecting Winter's roommate's name into the conversation with triumphant panache. "Nothing to worry about on that end. James met with Emily yesterday. Emily is making arrangements to find a new roommate as we speak. And if you're worried about not seeing her again, don't. Your daytime interactions might be coming to an end, but, as you know, it's possible to get to know someone in a completely different light at night."

Oh, no. Winter was surprised, but not shocked. She remembered Emily's many probing questions when she explained the situation with

James to her; the glints of fascinated envy in Emily's eyes; the puckish quality of the text Emily had sent to let Winter know that she wouldn't be returning home on Friday. It all added up to the terrible truth: James Breach had found Emily, and he had seduced her with promises of extraordinary adventure in the *Savage Moon* universe.

Winter remained speechless. What was there to say? A great war had begun, a war she hadn't prepared for properly. For the time being, there was nothing to do but play defense. Lashing out would only double their resolve to subjugate her, and, as they already had the upper hand on this account, she was reticent to give them cause to unleash the full store of their ammunition.

There would be a time for rebellion. Only not today.

Kol looked sated. "You appear to have retreated into a state of acquiescence. Yes?"

Winter nodded.

"Good. James was convinced that you would continue to fight, but I felt confident that you would listen to reason. Nova Norcross isn't a stupid woman, so why would Winter York be?" Kol grinned like an eel. "But Nova *is* a problem solver. And that will be when it gets fun. When you start plotting a way out. I have to admit that a small part of me was hoping you'd put me on my toes today...but all in good time." He motioned toward the door. "To the hotel, then?"

Another nod.

Together they walked out of the showroom.

*

The twists and turns of the ensuing forty-eight hours damaged Winter's soul. Trapped, she capitulated to her captors' every demand, hoping to minimize the damage, but instead the horrors compounded on one another, until the very thing she had been desperate to avoid took place.

First, she sent the fake text to Emily as ordered by Kol, for the purposes of keeping Nathaniel at bay until the following day. When Nathaniel discovered her number and texted her anyway, she replied with a short, emotionless response. Then she went to sleep and reentered the *Savage Moon* universe, where, with fear clanging in her heart, she encountered Nathaniel, and, to her surprise and almost unbearable relief, she whisked him to safety instead of watching him die. No longer afraid for Nathaniel's life, she couldn't help but indulge in the pleasure of being back inside of James Breach's world. She experienced the thrill of flight again, a surge of power at being Nova Norcross, and a godlike sense of proportion after killing a monstrous octopus. But then, in the span of a sleeping heartbeat, Nova Norcross was injured in a fight with a member of the moonbringer cult and nearly knocked unconscious. Lying there, she knew in the core of her flickering consciousness that James Breach was determined to show her that her life was his to do with as he pleased.

Then, the black miasma of the morning. Kol, swaggering around her at the Holiday Inn with his madman's grin, the many murders from the previous night glistening in his teeth. And she, his captive, waiting...for what? A text, as it turned out. A little after ten o'clock in the morning, Kelly Anne's number buzzed through, and with it the darkest of messages. O was dead. The news orbited Winter's fractured mind like a collapsing planet, a terrible thing to behold but at too far of a remove to connect to the circumstances of her own dying world. Or it was until Kol saw the change in her, and moved in for the kill.

"Bad news?" he asked.

"Yes," she replied, aware of the malice in his voice but not thinking it sufficiently excessive to warrant additional concern. She decided to tell him because there was no one else to tell. "My friend O. He died last night."

"You mean your friend with the octopus tattoo?"

Stupidly, she thought, *How does he know O?* But almost immediately the truth began to circle, like a shark sensing blood. A split second later, her brain was overrun by a horde of half-formed hypotheses, monstrous theories that, no matter how grotesque they appeared in her mind, could in no way match the horror of what Kol was about to say.

"James stopped by *Purity Tattoo* yesterday. I'm surprised your friends at the parlor didn't mention it to you." A sunburst of white enamel as he saw the look on her face. "Or perhaps they did! It's all coming together now, isn't it? James kept his promise. Nathaniel is still alive. And he'll stay that way, so long as you cooperate. But James also wanted you to know how serious he is. Try anything foolish, and you'll end up killing more of your friends. The same way that you killed O last night."

For a brief moment she was back in the dream, descending from the heavens like an avenging angel, steel gleaming in her hand, driven by James Breach's pen and the power coursing through her body and the *Savage Moon* sense that this was what she had been born to do, all without realizing that she was about to end the life of a friend embodied in the form of a monster.

A monster much like herself.

From that moment on, the day was a black-hearted blur. All she wanted to do was escape. But she couldn't escape, could she? Not from James Breach and Kol Jones, anyway. All she could do was keep those that she loved from being hurt, including the boy that she had fallen for the night before. Nathaniel Pilot.

That afternoon, when Nathaniel approached her in her driveway, she focused all of the day's anger and fear and directed it toward him, hoping to drive him away. She fled before her emotions betrayed her, tires peeling, eyes wet with tears, trying to suppress the last vision she saw in her rearview mirror: Kol Jones turning the corner at her driveway, walking toward Nathaniel.

I'm never going to see him again, she thought.

And for years and years, she was right.

*

The drive to the park was glorious. Open road under beautiful blue skies smattered with a handful of puffy marshmallow clouds. It was the type of drive that begged for convertible tops and open windows, for wind-rummaging hands, for thoughts of Kerouac and the possibilities at the end of the map.

But not for Winter. What concerned her were the sounds coming from the speaker system of her hermetically sealed transport, namely the audio version of *Bloodsucker Moon*. She was listening, as she always did, for clues. Something to help her better understand how James Breach's world worked. Something to help her pinpoint the flaw in the design.

"Where do we go?"

Diadolo lay dead at their feet, already blackening to ash at the edges. The massive stake that Carter had driven through the vampire's heart protruded into the air like a gruesome signpost, warning people away.

"I don't know, but we have to get out of the open. Standing here, we're..."

A noise started up in the nearby trees, an animalistic, high-pitched keening that refused to harmonize, instead keeping its discordant character even as the sound grew to ear-splitting proportions. It was the sound of infestation, the sound of echolocation.

The sound of bats.

"Quickly," Nova said. "Before they—"

But it was too late. A massive colony of bats shot out of the trees and into the open. The cloud was so black and so thick that for a moment it blotted out the blood-red moon high above.

"Go!" Carter shouted. "Fly!"

Nova gave her friend one last look and took to the air. She raced ahead, searching for cover, knowing that if she didn't find shelter, the bats would catch up to Carter and make a bloodless husk out of him. She considered the field house, but it was too far away, and she knew Carter would be dead before they could break into the Garden Home. But surely there was somewhere to hide in the sprawling arboretum—

It was then that she saw it. A brick-lined walkway overflowing with ivy, nearly stoppered on both sides by a surfeit of vine.

She threw her wings wide and circled back. "This way!" she screamed at Carter, before one-eightying once more, directing her friend toward the walkway. Behind her, the screeching black cloud closed in, thousands of tongues singing the same bloodthirsty song.

She landed in front of the walkway, with Carter twenty yards behind her. "Hurry!" she shouted. Already she could feel the power growing in her fingertips, signifying her strange connection to the plant. Behind her, the shoots took heed, growing at her behest, the many leafy tendrils closing off the open spaces with a workmanlike efficiency. But she couldn't close the front until Carter was safe inside.

By the time Carter made it, a handful of the winged bloodsuckers had caught up to him, with thousands more on his heels. Nova screamed telepathically at the ivy, which shot over the entrance with a fury, but that didn't stop the bats from bleeding through. Forty, maybe fifty made it inside, flying, biting, attacking. Those that didn't make it struggled in the vines, mad with the fury of the moon.

For longer than she could process, Nova warred against the winged beasts, snapping their necks and bashing their heads on the brick as they bit at her body. A few feasted on her wings. She lashed out at these the hardest, grabbing them by their heads and squeezing their skulls until they burst.

Finally, they killed the last of the attacking Desmodontinae. But the screeching continued: hundreds of the bats were trapped in the vines, singing their hideous songs, while outside the cloud reformed again and again, swooping and searching for a way to get inside.

"Are you okay?" Nova shouted over the din. It was almost pitch-black inside the ivy shell.

"I think so," Carter replied woozily. "I've lost a lot of blood."

Winter paused the audio book. She had listened to this section of *Bloodsucker Moon* hundreds of times, trying to recall what the experience had been like for her inside the dream. Because in the dream the experience had been different. Whereas in the book there was a clear delineation between Nova and the shoots of ivy covering the brick-lined walkway, in the dream it hadn't been so clear cut. There she was *both* Nova and the ivy. *But how?* she wondered. Even stranger, when she had been embodied in the plant, she hadn't felt entirely under James Breach's control. Instead, she had felt a sense of autonomy, a sense that James Breach's pen wasn't acting on her so much as she was acting on James Breach's pen.

It has something to do with my tattoo, she thought for the thousandth time. She knew for a fact that James was aware of her tattoo; he had commented on it more than once. She hated his fascination with the tattoo, mainly because she had gotten the tattoo during that precious period of time when she was free of his control. A twisting, turning shoot of ivy, climbing from the bottom of her spine to the nape of her neck, courtesy of her old friend Kelly Anne. It wasn't the only ink on her body, but it was the only tattoo that had made its way into the books—likely because it was the only tattoo James could see. When James first started writing about Nova's connection to ivy in the *Savage Moon* universe, it felt as if James had stolen her tattoo from her, and claimed it for his own.

But if he knows about the tattoo, why did it feel different when I was embodied in the ivy? Why did it feel like James wasn't entirely in control?

She pulled into the park. The park was set back off the road, giving it a wonderfully secluded feel while simultaneously making it the last park where you'd want to meet the people you most feared. But the choice wasn't hers. She parked in the upper parking lot, hoping to cross paths with as many people as possible before making her way to the preordained meeting place: a gazebo adjoined to the pond at the park's lowest point. If history was any indicator, Kol Jones would intercept her on the wooden walkway leading to the gazebo. He'd do the dirty work of threatening her, allowing James to preserve the illusion that theirs was a purely transactional affair, and not the deeply fucked-up power dynamic that kept Winter at his every beck and call.

That was what Kol Jones did for James Breach, she understood. He shouldered all the ugly responsibilities borne out by James's decisions, leaving the writer free to pretend that he was simply a writer, and not an evil puppet master.

As predicted, they were waiting for her when she crested the hill. James was sitting in the gazebo, affecting a writerly air, while Kol stood like Cerberus at the wooden walkway gates, sporting multiple personalities instead of heads.

The second she saw Kol, he looked her way. A wolfish grin spread across his face.

She took a deep breath. *Okay,* she thought. *Here we go.*

*

It was the standard drill. James was heading out on a book tour and needed Winter to meet him in Boston the following week, and then

Denver the week after that. He let Kol describe all manner of horrors that might befall Winter's friends and family if she didn't show, before stepping in and cordially extending an invitation to multi-night stays in five-star resort hotels, along with offers of tickets to any plays/concerts that piqued Winter's interest, and a per diem that would have made a professional athlete envious. She rejected each and every perk, opting instead for a same-day return flight from Boston and an early-morning flight back from Denver. She had long ago decided to use as little of his money as possible. Doing so gave her a little power back. *I might be your prisoner,* she thought, *but I'll be damned if I give you the pleasure of seeing me enjoy my captivity.*

The meeting over, Winter remained in the gazebo, allowing James and Kol to leave. Kol had waited for James, of course, and now they walked back up the hill together, James a few feet ahead. They didn't talk; they rarely talked in Winter's presence. James's doing, she imagined: he liked to foster the illusion that Kol's role in his operation was largely incidental. Twice Kol turned around and gave Winter a look that made her shudder. His looks were even more unsettling now that she had seen what Kol—or rather Burden Monks—was capable of in the books.

At last, they disappeared. Winter checked the time. *1:14.* She knew that she should leave and go to work, but now that she was alone, the day's beauty made itself manifest, making her want to stay. It was the rare summer day that wasn't oppressive; a butterfly knife of a breeze cut at the heat and humidity with a playful cunning. Winter sat in the gazebo for an additional five minutes, alternately opening and shutting her eyes, allowing the breeze and the sun and the quiet to cleanse her mind of her enemies.

When she stood up to leave, she didn't see a soul. Earlier, there had been a mother and two children on the playground equipment, but no longer. It was a sprawling park with ill-defined, tree-pocket borders, beautiful in all respects but perhaps not the first park a person would choose to find themselves alone in. Still, Winter was unbothered. She thought it reasonable to assume that she had already experienced her quota of danger for the day.

She was making her way back to the upper parking lot when a man appeared, stepping out from behind a large oak tree near the playground equipment. He materialized in a way that made it clear he'd been hiding. Winter was flummoxed by his appearance, and then unnerved when he started walking parallel to her in the direction of the parking lot, closing the distance between them by ever-shrinking degrees.

She sped up, hoping to beat him to the parking lot, but with every nervous glance to her right she saw that he was keeping pace. With one last look, Winter dropped all pretense, and took off for her car at a dead sprint. On the borderlands of her peripheral vision, the stalker did the same.

Fortunately, Winter was fast. She had always been fast, even as a kid, but in the years since James Breach had reentered her life, she had grown even faster. Daily pilgrimages to the gym had become the norm. There she sprinted like a madwoman on the treadmill, outpacing monsters both imaginary and real. In the process, she had become Nova Norcross in the flesh, only with wings on her feet instead of her back.

Pulling the keyless remote from her pocket, Winter unlocked the car door. Her pursuer had faded from her periphery. Reaching the car door, she opened it and jumped inside to the sound of her pursuer's footsteps closing in.

"Nova, it's me, C—" she heard as she slammed the car door shut. She thought she recognized the voice from an oddly familiar dimension, but she didn't look up. She locked the car doors, jammed the keys in the ignition, turned the ignition over, and threw the car into drive. The shadow of her pursuer hovered above her, knock-knocking on the glass, shouting words that she processed on a delay. Tires squealing, she sped away. But as she drove away, the man's words became clear in her mind. She looked in the rearview mirror, and she realized that she knew who he was.

They had, after all, spent much time together in dreams.

Winter hit the brakes. In the rearview mirror stood the man she had teamed up with in *Bloodsucker Moon,* the man who had helped her fight against the multitude of vampiric creatures sent by the moon god. A friend, an ally, one of the few people living who knew what it was like to try and survive the dreamworld that sprang forth from James Breach's mind.

Carter Crowe.

*

"Holy hot damn. Girl, it is you. You nearly killed me! But I suppose that's what happens when a person goes chasing after Nova Norcross. Not that Nova's your real name." Carter Crowe's eyebrows took the lift to a floor further up his forehead. "What is your real name?"

Winter had had her guard up too long to surrender personal info that easily. "Um…"

Carter rolled his eyes. "Fine. I'll go first. My real name is Kennedy Marks. I'm originally from Buford, GA, just outside Atlanta. About a year and a half ago I met my favorite author at a book signing, where he wowed me with an experience that I'm still paying the price for. What followed was a descent into a sort of ecstatic hell that I have become convinced will end in my death. I decided that before I died, I would try and make common cause with the one person on the planet who knows exactly what I'm going through. That is, if I could find the cold-hard, ass-kicking bitch." He smiled and made a theatrical presentation of Winter's person with an upturned right palm. "Voila."

Winter smiled, in spite of herself. Kennedy Marks had quite a bit in common with Carter Crowe. Both were lean and barrel-chested, both were in possession of a verbosity that might have seemed excessive were it not so razor-sharp, and both, it appeared, were gay. She supposed the only characteristics Carter Crowe possessed that Kennedy Marks did not were precognitive abilities and a touch of superhuman strength.

"I'm Winter," Winter said. "Winter York." Personal confession not being Winter's forte, she elected to skip that portion of the introduction. "So how did you find me?" she asked. "Did you follow James or Kol?"

"Who do you think?" Kennedy replied. "Those are two evil sons of bitches, but at least James doesn't wear his malevolence on his sleeve like a badge of honor. It's difficult enough dealing with Burden Monks at night. Why would I want to increase my odds of running into him during the day?"

Winter nodded. She knew the *Bloodsucker Moon* storyline well enough to know that Carter Crowe's path had intersected with Burden Monks's multiple times, a fate she wouldn't have wished on anyone—not even Lisa from the vet's office. James Breach was setting the two characters on a collision course, and, as even the dimmest-witted of book critics could have deduced, only one would survive.

"So you're saying that you followed James to find me. Because you think James is going to kill you…that is, kill Carter Crowe? And you want my help?"

Kennedy made a pass at his midnight-black coiffure without actually touching it. "Yes, but only because you need my help too. James might be a New Testament preacher when he's talking plotlines over lunch dates, but in case you haven't noticed, he's fire and brimstone in the pages. Everyone's number comes up sooner or later. Joessa, Theo, Bridgette. Probably me next. You might be Nova Norcross, but the series has to come to an end eventually. And when it does…"

It wasn't as if Winter hadn't considered the possibility that James would kill her in the end. The *Savage Moon* series had long taken a perverse pleasure in killing off its characters. Who was to say that Nova Norcross's death wasn't in the cards as well? James feigned care and compassion

131

when in conversation, but Winter had lived through enough nightmares to know that the writer's empathetic concerns ended when he put pen to paper. She had seen it firsthand. There wasn't a day that passed that she didn't relive the horror of seeing the moonwolf Grismark wring Joessa Fox's porcelain-white neck before feasting on it, only to wake up and find her roommate Jessalyn Bright lying dead on their dorm room floor from a neatly severed spine. The police report had settled on an inebriated fall, but Winter knew better.

She had been there.

"Okay," Winter said. "You don't need to convince me. I'll help you."

Kennedy's lips curled in a manner consistent with a smile. "Swell," he said. "Let's get started."

*

Kennedy had parked in a neighborhood a mile clear of the park, before roughing it through the woods to find a spying vantage point. Winter returned him to his vehicle—surprisingly, a magma red Ford F-150 pickup truck—and made a promise to drive directly to an out-of-the-way coffee house in Midland called The Daily Grind. "The odds of us running into James are Cash 5 low, but in Midland we're talking Powerball probabilities," Kennedy reasoned. "And, don't take offense, honey, because I saw your earlier commune with nature, but I've had enough of the great outdoors today."

They drove through the ever-mutating expanse that marked the edges of suburbia, developments giving way to shops giving way to gas stations giving way to greenery that had yet to be subsumed. Crossing a bridge over Highway 49, trees and grass gained the upper hand, and the drive became a country idyll. Winter watched as the clock on the console changed over to 1:41. Now, she supposed, it didn't matter whether or not Lisa was telling the truth about her firing. Failing to show up sealed the deal. Her days as a vet tech at Poplar Road Animal Hospital were over.

The Daily Grind was stationed at the corner of a strip mall. To its credit, the coffee shop had done its best not to let cookie-cutter capitalism dull its aesthetic. Signage on the front exclaimed *Wine, Coffee, Books, & More!* Inside, all was as promised: three stacks of bookshelves displayed their wares beneath paintings by local artists, two abstracts and a blue and yellow portrait of what appeared to be an amiable demon. No-frills wooden tables and chairs nodded to convention, but there was also a creamy blue couch that screamed *offbeat!*, and a Moroccan-style rug on the wall.

For Midland, it constituted an impressive effort.

Kennedy waltzed into the shop with the self-assured ease of an established regular. "Hey darlin'," he schmoozed to the girl behind the counter, "what's brewing?" Cheesy or not, the girl grinned. Five minutes later, Kennedy and Winter retired to the creamy blue couch with a café latte and cappuccino in hand, respectively.

"Do you come here often?" Winter asked.

"First time," Kennedy replied, settling into the couch like he owned it. "But when I was planning our little rendezvous, I thought it would be best to switch up the routine, just in case. I've actually made a spreadsheet of places within fifty miles of my lovely rental home in Huntersville where

I might safely escape the prying eyes of…let's call them our captors. I doubt James is keeping an eye on me personally, but I know his henchman keeps tabs."

Smart. Winter had long known that James Breach made it his business to know her daily routine. It hadn't happened often, but once or twice she had spotted Kol Jones in the shadows, watching her go about her daily life.

Caffeine soldiers marched their way to the sluggish quarters of Winter's brain, rousing Winter to life. She was excited to be in Kennedy's presence. For years she had been sleepwalking through the waking hours, trying to reserve energy for the night. But now she was in the presence of someone who knew exactly what she was going through. Someone who was interested in flipping the script. Someone who could help her shift the battle to the hours when the sun was up.

"I'm going to assume that if you went to the trouble of tracking me down, you have a plan for dealing with James Breach."

Kennedy winced, but with a thespian flair. "A plan? Maybe." He gave Winter a sharp once-over, as if looking at her for the first time. "We're about to tread into dark territory here, and I need to know…" He trailed off. "How do you think the series ends? For you?"

"I think I survive the *Savage Moon* universe," Winter replied. "Everything about the arc of the series suggests as much. But I don't think James means for me to outlive his books. Out history is too complicated. The last thing he wants is Winter York walking around without being captive to his dreamworld. So yeah…I think he kills me." She paused. "But it's better than the alternative."

"Which is?"

She lowered her voice. "James kills my friends and family. He has a list of names and addresses. I've seen it. Or at least a part of it. Kol made it clear in no uncertain terms that if I step out of line…" She trailed off as she experienced a pang of panic that James or Kol knew that she was here talking with Kennedy. If they did—

The memory of O's death still haunted her daily. For years she had been comforted by the thought that Jessalyn's death, as horrific as it had been, was an accident, the result of James Breach exercising powers he didn't yet understand that he possessed. But O's death was no mistake. James Breach had killed the tattoo artist on purpose. And if James was willing to kill O, Winter had no doubt that he would strike down more of her friends and family with his mortal pen. Especially if he discovered that she was conspiring with Kennedy. Her thoughts spiraled as she considered the possibility that James might wait to reveal his knowledge of her malfeasance until she was deep inside a dream, where, with paralytic hopelessness, she would discover a loved one on death's doorstep—perhaps in the clutches of Burden Monks, or as the prey of some as-yet-unimagined moon monster—while high above the page, the moon god hovered, ready to exact retribution for her mistake.

Kennedy reached over and took hold of her hand. "That's a heavy burden to carry," he said.

Winter felt hot tears welling up in the corners of her eyes. When was the last time someone had commiserated with her over the predicament that was her daily existence? Not since Nathaniel, she supposed. Eight long years without sharing her fears. Eight long years bottled up inside. Eight long years pretending to be okay during the days, saving her strength for the perils of the night.

"You know what it's like," she said, blinking away tears. "James is holding you hostage too."

Kennedy tilted his head to the side and gave Winter a funny grin. "James and I are playing a different game," he said.

"What do you mean?"

Kennedy shrugged. "We play pretend. I pretend that I'm no wiser to what's going on than I was when I first met James. James pretends that he isn't going to off me in the books. It's more civil that way, and it keeps Kol Jones at bay, which I prefer. But the illusion is crumbling. James knows it, and so do I. Now I need to make my move before James makes his."

Winter stared at Kennedy disbelievingly. He brought his café latte to his lips, then pulled it away to reveal a faint foam milk moustache.

"You're still friends with James?"

"We certainly pretend to be."

She bobbed her head at him rooster-style. "Then why don't you disappear? Fail to show up the next time he wants to meet with you and then rough it without sleep for a few days?"

Kennedy scrunched his nose once for effect. "Like I said, it's all pretend. James knows how to hurt me the same way he knows how to hurt you. He's made threats. He may have disguised them as jokes, but they were threats all the same."

Winter sensed that this was sensitive territory, but she decided to tread anyway. "What threats has he made?"

Kennedy sighed. His face looked momentarily awash with pain. "Threats about a boy, if you must know. Let's call the boy…Charles. I still rue the lunch date when I mentioned his name. I'm a talker, if you couldn't tell: give me an hour of your time and I'll give you half my life's story. I'm more bottled up than I used to be, but I digress. Anyway, a couple of months after I divulged Charles's existence, James revisited the topic over a fig and pistachio salad. He started joking about including Charles in one of his books. By that time, Charles and I hadn't been in a relationship for months, but I still loved him. James knew that. I laughed along nervously, hoping James would drop the subject, but instead James looked me dead in the eye and said that he was serious. He said that he wanted to include Charles in the books, and that he had gone so far as to look up Charles's address in Georgia. Then he recited Charles's address to me. I just sat there, stunned stupid, fearing that Charles's life was in danger. James held that moment between us, and then he started laughing. He said that he was only joking. He swore to me that he had gone to the trouble of learning where Charles lived just to see the look on my face when he told me the address. Of course, it wasn't a joke at all. It was intentional. He wanted me to know what he could do to the people that I loved without saying it outright. He wanted me to know that he was prepared to hurt me if I reneged on our deal."

"Your deal?"

Kennedy smiled a melancholic little smile. Sighed another plaintive sigh.

"I wasn't in the best place when I met James. That first night, after the book signing, I did what more than a few others have done before me. I made a Faustian bargain with James. For the price of entering the *Savage Moon* universe as a central character with powers, I promised James that I would allow him to channel me until my time in the series was over."

"Did you know what that entailed?"

"Not exactly. James glossed over the rougher bits. But I didn't press him for details, either. Like I said, my life was a bit of a mess at the time, and frankly, nothing seemed more appealing than escaping into the universe of a book series that I absolutely loved. Also, I might have convinced myself that I believed the rumors about James's powers, but, like anyone, I didn't *believe* believe until I experienced it firsthand. How could I? As an uber-fan, I thought I knew the *Savage Moon* universe up and down, but, as you know, reading the books is a far different experience from *being* in the books."

Winter nodded. She understood in practice, even if her reality had been different from Kennedy's. For her, the books had *always* been a secondhand experience. She had read them, of course, but the details, no matter how well-wrought, had always fell flat in her mind. Reading the *Savage Moon* books was like reading a bootleg version of her life. Funnily, the experience had had the opposite effect on books she read by other authors. Now she couldn't help but imagine that every character she encountered in a book was in fact a real person suffering the same way that she did inside the pages of *Savage Moon*. Some days all she could think about was the possibility that every person in the world lived a double life as a character in a novel, subject to the whims and impulses of a capricious author-god.

"When did you know for certain that James could kill you?"

"I had an inkling pretty early on in *Bloodsucker Moon*. You were there, in fact. It was the night that we killed the vampire and were chased by the bats."

Winter laughed behind her cappuccino. "You won't believe this, but I was listening to that scene in my car earlier today."

"You listen to the audiobooks?" Kennedy asked.

"I do." She hesitated, before finishing her thought. "I'm searching for clues."

Kennedy cocked his head to the side and gave a wondering smile. "Clues, huh? Let's get back to that. But to answer your question, I first had a good idea that James could kill me when I woke up after the dream and could still feel the bat bites on the inside of my skin. It was...wild. I kept checking the mirror, wondering why I couldn't see the damage. It made no sense. My skin was burning, I could *feel* the pain, but when I looked in the mirror—nothing."

Winter knew exactly what Kennedy was talking about. Her memory logged back to those disturbing mornings in college when she would wake up battered and bruised from the supernatural adventures of the previous night, but with no visible signs of her suffering. If Jessalyn hadn't been going through the exact same thing, she might have lost her mind. "This might be cold comfort, but at least you knew enough to connect the dots. When it first happened to me, I didn't have a clue what was going on. Me or my roommate. The dreams were exhilarating, sure, but after I started experiencing morning aches and pains, I was frightened to death. Then my roommate died. If Professor Breach hadn't come clean, I never would have figured it out."

Kennedy's eyes grew saucer-wide. "You didn't know that the dreams were because of James?"

"Not at the outset, no. He was just the creative writing professor who kept brushing up against me and my roommate in class. But after Jessalyn—er, my roommate—died, he came and found me. He looked half sick. It wasn't until he started talking that I realized he was eaten up with guilt. He thought that he had played a role in Jessalyn's death, but he didn't know for sure. Then he asked me if I had been having any strange dreams recently. I thought he was playing a sick prank at first, but his tears and his contrition were too genuine to discount. As a test, I asked him questions about the dreams that he couldn't possibly know the answers to unless he was telling the truth. By the time I was finished, I not only believed him—I had forgiven him. He truly hadn't known that he had the power to kill. When he left, he swore that he would never use his *powers* again, and he swore that he would tear up the manuscript that he had written."

Kennedy rolled his eyes around the universe. "That clearly didn't happen."

"No, it didn't. But before the first book came out, he sent me a long email promising that the book's publication was the extent of him going back on his word. He said he was determined to make it as a writer without relying on his powers. He wished me a long and happy life, and he swore that would be the last I would ever hear from him."

Together, they held a moment of silence for James Breach's broken promises.

The sound of the espresso machine stirred them back to life.

Kennedy puppy-dogged his head to the side. Apparently, it was a go-to mannerism. "You mentioned that you were listening for clues in the audiobook. What type of clues?"

Winter opened her mouth to reply, then stopped. Before she gave up any more of her secrets, she wanted to hear Kennedy's endgame. "I'll tell you, but first I need to know where we're heading with this. You said you had a plan. Or at least you insinuated that you did. So tell me—how do we get out of this?"

Kennedy leaned forward. His expression tied the lines on his forehead into knots. "You want me to say it? Okay, honey, I'll say it. But you better not act shocked." He leaned in even closer, channeled a subterranean whisper. "If either one of us wants to survive, we have to kill James Breach."

*

They said their good-byes a half-hour later. After years without real human intimacy, Winter had experienced a new level out of the blue.

Plotting-to-kill closeness.

The question, of course, was how. Kennedy's suggestions were too real, too visceral, too godawful like murder. The only palatable idea he came up with was hiring a hitman, and that, Winter knew, was because it removed the two of them from the act by degrees. Winter had looped Kennedy in on her tattoo theories, but, try as they might, the jump from *point A: the ivy tattoo appears to work on James Breach's subconscious* to *point B: let's use that information to kill James Breach* was a long one. By the time the meeting was over, they hadn't settled on a strategy. They only knew that they needed to settle on one soon. From their most recent dreams, it was obvious that James had started a new book, the one Kennedy believed he was destined to die in. But it was early in the writing. They needed to get to work, but they assumed they had time.

They agreed to meet again in three weeks, after the book tour was over. As a general rule, James didn't write on book tours, so they were in a safe zone. Kennedy didn't have Winter's qualms about accepting the perks of their position—"why wouldn't I?" was his logical defense—so he planned to stay in a number of the cities James was touring, indulging in the finer things. Kennedy's laissez-faire attitude toward James's manipulative munificence tempted Winter to reconsider her own position, but ultimately, she held firm. Unlike Kennedy, she wasn't playing a game with James. It was clear where she stood.

She spent the next two weeks preparing for the coming coup. She purchased burner phones. She typed in word searches on the internet that left her convinced that the cops would burst open her door at any moment. She made the round trip to Boston and back in the amount of time that passes between an early breakfast and a late lunch, trying to maximize on every available minute that James Breach and Kol Jones were out of town. She read revenge novels, hoping to psyche herself into the mind-set that she thought was necessary to kill someone.

She thought she was ready.

Then, the unexpected.

It was the day before she was set to fly to Denver. A Wednesday. She had spent the day reading *The Art of War*, prepping, like a twenty-first-century male of the species, for the combat to come. Around five p.m., she realized that she hadn't planned for dinner. Setting the book aside, she decided that she wanted a vegan pizza from Trader Joe's. She was no longer a vegan per se, but she still enjoyed the occasional vegan meal, so every now and then she made the trip to the University area for her favorite frozen meal.

She was standing at the back of the checkout line, yellow cardboard box in hand, when she saw him. He walked in through the sliding glass doors wearing a sleeveless Nike top and black mesh workout shorts, toting a little goldilocks girl on his arm. She *knew* that it was him, but she might not have believed it was him were it not for the tattoo. But there it was. Resting high on his right deltoid, a moon derived largely from the negative space of his skin, partially obscured by an ink-saturated night sky.

Too late, she looked away. His gaze, however, had already been drawn to hers, guided by the magnetic pull of their past.

She was overcome by a maelstrom of emotions. She both wanted and didn't want to speak to him. She considered pretending that she didn't recognize him if he approached, but the idea turned into a pillar of salt in her mind. She checked her peripheral vision.

He was walking toward her.

She turned to face him. Summoned a smile from unfathomable depths.

He looked like an archaeologist struggling to process the enormity of his find.

"Winter?" he tendered. The little girl on his arm peeked out from beneath the palanquin of his clavicle.

"Nathaniel," she replied. She understood that pretending that she didn't recognize him had never been a realistic option.

"Hey. Oh wow. It's really you. I, um—" he struggled to find the thread. The little girl, satisfied that she'd seen all there was to see, rooted back into his chest. Nathaniel glanced down at the child. "Winter, this is Isabelle. My little girl."

And there it was.

"Hi, Isabelle," Winter said, though her eyes never left Nathaniel's. The girl didn't look up. Winter dropped the pretense that she was interested in the kid. "Are you married?" she asked. The question was too forward, but she needed to know for sure. She tried to ask the question evenly. She hoped that her voice sounded steady.

Nathaniel's face colored ever so slightly. "Yes. I got back together with Angelica. My old girlfriend. After."

A little demon whispered in her ear, *Say: After what?* But she didn't give in. She knew that the anger she felt toward Nathaniel wasn't his fault. "Congratulations," she said. Her words sounded perfunctory because they were. She was trying her best not to be angry at him, but that didn't mean she had to be happy for him.

He gave her a look that traversed the borderlands of concern. "How are *you*?" he asked.

She gave him a blank look. Responding didn't seem possible. Waves of emotion crashed just beneath the surface. *How am I?* The seconds ticked by. She wondered if she had loved this man. She wondered if it was possible to feel an emotion as deep as love for someone after only one night. She knew that even if it hadn't been love, it was still the closest she had come to loving someone in her adult life. But then James had murdered their near-love. Or, no: James had forced her to murder their near-love, their becoming-love, their embryonic-love. And she had murdered it, to save Nathaniel's life. She had locked eyes with him in her driveway and told him to Never. Fucking. Contact. Me. Again. And then she had sped away, praying to whatever deity would listen that he *would* listen to her. Praying that the blow she had struck against their near-becoming-embryonic love would be a fatal one. Praying that he would disappear from her life forever.

And it had worked.

She had never been more grateful for or resentful of anything in her entire life.

"Please go away," she said. Were there tears in her eyes? Was the wave cresting?

His soul looked strung between two telephone poles. "Of course you're not okay. I've seen the controversy about the book series. I've read the books. Not because I enjoy reading them, but because..." He drifted off, his *because* lingering in purgatory, unable to ascend to a subordinating conjunction.

"Because why?" she asked. Something firmed up inside her. A tear dangled from the precipice of an eyelid, but she knew there would no others.

"Because..." Another pause. He looked like a swimmer out of his depth.

"There's nothing you can do, Nathaniel." She liked the feel of his name on her lips. Suddenly she understood what this moment was for. It was a chance to say good-bye again. To get it right. To say what she had wanted to say last time, omitting the *Never. Fucking. Contact. Me. Again.* part. "Nothing at all. There never was. This is going to end however it ends. If you had tried to save me, it would have only added another casualty to the tally." She felt a wonderful lie coming on. Perhaps the most beautiful and perfect lie to have ever crossed her lips. "And now look at you! You're a dad! A husband! I can't tell you how happy that makes me. It's what I wanted more than anything. For you to escape unscathed and live your life."

She could see the wheels churning, his mind scrambling. "I don't know, Winter. Sometimes I think…sometimes I still think—"

The child began squirming in his arms. Isabelle seemed to intuit that her father was treading into dangerous territory and wanted to warn him away.

His train of thought broken, Nathaniel glanced down at his daughter. As good fathers do.

Winter capitalized. "It was so good to see you, Nathaniel. But your daughter needs you. And I need to buy this pizza." She forced herself to laugh and turned away. The line had moved, and she used the opportunity to walk toward the cash register. She busied herself with the distraction of items in the checkout line, pretending to be interested in the many varieties of xylitol and natural sugar gums before her.

A half-minute later she peeked behind her.

Nathaniel and his daughter were nowhere to be seen.

*

Kol greeted her at the airport. He looked slightly less menacing than usual, like a jaguar who had ingested too much catnip. He explained the reason why once they were safely ensconced in the rental car, speeding away in a silvery splash of a Mercedes.

"Edibles," he said. "Sour gummies. Indica. An all-body high." He nodded at the glove compartment. "Help yourself."

She popped open the latch. Inside was a bag filled with fairy-dusted rectangles—reds, yellows, and oranges.

"No thanks," she said, closing the box to keep from being tempted.

Kol bared his teeth. It might have been a grin. "I know. A girl has her principles. How about this? The offer stands on the drive back. That way, if you're so inclined, you can pop one in your mouth the second you're free."

Before she could reply, he looked out the car window and started cackling. She followed his gaze. A statue of a monstrous blue stallion reared over the landscape. "The locals call him Blucifer," Kol explained. "Part of the statue fell on the artist and crushed his leg during construction. The artist died from the complications. It's beautiful and terrible at the same time, isn't it?"

It was. The statue had an apocalyptic grandness to it. She followed it with her eyes as they drove past, entranced. She couldn't help but think it an omen, a sign.

"I'm considering pitching the statue to James as inspiration for his next book," Kol continued. "Only I can't come up with the correct title. *Horse Moon? Equine Moon? Stallion Moon* sounds the best, but even that leaves a little to be desired, doesn't it?"

Fuck you, Winter thought, but she didn't reply. She'd be damned if Blucifer ended up in her dreams, him and thousands of his clones thundering below while she soared above some godforsaken prairie. Blucifer wasn't inspiration for James.

Blucifer was inspiration for her.

"Where is James meeting me?" she asked.

Kol's eyes burned red, same as the horse's. "Coors Field. He's going to a baseball game. Never cared for the sport myself, but James is a fan.

There's a statue in front of the stadium. That's where you're meeting him. After that, you're free to go."

*

Winter preferred meeting James in public. They had a system for exchanging skin-to-skin contact that was inconspicuous, hand grazing hand, and then Winter would be on her way. In private, James always let the touch linger—not in a sexual way per se, but in a way that demonstrated power, both in his dominion over her day-to-day life and in his ability to siphon her essence for his own purposes. But not in public. In public James Breach was usually distracted, either by his environment or by his plans for the day, and their interaction was often reduced to the moment itself, the simple act of hand brushing against hand. Meetings on book tour amplified the distracted effect. Winter had long ago made it clear that she didn't like traveling to meet James, and James, busy with his itinerary, went about their skin-to-skin check-ins with the disposition of a man preoccupied by more important matters.

All of which suited Winter just fine.

James was waiting for her beneath the statue. He always looked a bit off-footed whenever they rendezvoused out of town, the polish of his ongoing performance art—mysterious and urbane author on tour—scuffed up by the necessity of waiting for Winter to arrive. She relished the lost-boy look of him as she approached, the anxious way he shuffled his feet. He had never really looked like her estimation of an author, and now, pushing fifty, the pretty-boy pugilist look he had cultivated was waning as well.

See, he won't be that difficult to kill, she thought.

Winter lengthened her stride. To the west, the sun dissolved into the horizon, leaving behind a smear of Neapolitan colors.

She imagined approaching James with a knife in her hand. In James's dreamworld, she was forever wielding one weapon or another, but in real life she had never once held an instrument for the purpose of physically harming someone. Or wait—had she? Suddenly the memory returned to her. Standing in the living room of her rental house in NoDa long ago, butcher knife held tight, ready to gut James Breach if he didn't release Nathaniel.

And now, Nathaniel was free. He was married, and he had a little girl. All these years later, the only person still suffering was her.

I should have gutted James for myself, she thought.

At that moment James spotted her. His eyes immediately flitted away, lighting on the distant horizon. High above him, the statue of the baseball player mirrored James's pose: the player's arm rested on a shoulder-slung baseball bat while James's arm rested on the statue's base. Together their respective gazes worked on the approaching skyline.

Winter closed in.

James's hand slid down the statue's base, extending ever so slightly. A waiting gift of another week of enslavement.

Winter imagined walking by without touching his hand, disappearing into the mountains. Consuming edibles until the worry of what might happen to friends and family was lost in the fog of an all-encompassing high. Marrying a mountain man with enough guns to arm a small militia.

Having a daughter of her own, indulging in the everyday pleasure of toting the little girl around on her arm. Reclaiming what had been taken from her. Giving herself the same gift that she had given Nathaniel.

She arrived at the statue.

She reached out her right hand and let the tips of her fingers brush against James Breach's.

*

"You're staying for the game?"

Kol twisted his eyebrows into devilish knots. His expression was coated in stoner-glaze, but Winter wasn't fooled. The machinery of an evil mind ground beneath.

"I am. It's nice out, and I'm not in the mood to sit in my hotel room."

"It's unlike you. For you, sitting in your hotel room and doing nothing is a point of pride."

Truer words had never been spoken. Still, Winter plowed ahead. "I'll Uber to the hotel later. And I'll Uber back to the airport tomorrow morning. You should take the night off. Tomorrow morning too."

"I don't like surprises. Neither does James. That's why we want to know your itinerary beforehand."

"Surely he doesn't keep minute-to-minute tabs on all of his special friends? I can't be the only one."

Kol's eyebrows engaged in a series of strange calisthenics. "No, but you are the most important." He feigned contemplation, grinned a wicked grin. "Fine. Get an Uber tonight, but in the a.m., I'm chauffeuring. Eight fifteen for a ten o'clock flight. Be ready."

Winter sat out in left field, a Coors Light in one hand and a plastic baseball cap full of elote-topped tater tots in the other. She had a slight headache from the change in altitude, but she downed the beer nevertheless, relishing the slipping space.

She watched everything but the baseball game.

Four rows below Winter, a young teenage couple spent the evening making out. Occasionally they took breaks from kissing to laugh and eat popcorn. When they thought no one was watching, they would paw at each other's bodies, then titter about it. A sort of timeless joy came off their skin in waves.

To Winter's right, sitting on the opposite side of the left field foul pole, a husband-and-wife duo orchestrated an evening with their two small children, a boy and a girl. It was exhausting to watch, but not without its charms. Along the way ice cream was spilled, a succession of bathroom trips spanned two innings, the little boy had a crying fit, and the little girl fell into a Van-Winkle-deep sleep. But when at last the family folded up shop in the seventh inning, the boy hugged his father tight around the leg and the little girl delivered a peal of laughter into her mother's ears. Even from where Winter was sitting, it was obvious that the outing had been a success.

At the far end of Winter's row, an old man wearing a Rockies cap sat alone. He watched the game like a forgotten god from on high, content in his solitude.

A murder of drunk men near the outfield wall heckled the Pirates' left fielder. They appeared engaged in a spiraling competition to see who could make the biggest ass of themselves.

Throughout, Winter downed one beer after the next. She was an experienced drinker, and knew her limits, but tonight she loosened the reins, allowing her altitude high to piggyback on top of cup after plastic cup until her head was swimming.

During the 8th inning, she made the decision to take a walk around the stadium. When she stood, she laughed a little at how unbalanced the world had become. Quickly righting the ship, she worked her way toward the concourse.

Once on the cement walkway, she allowed her eyes to roam. Winter knew what she was doing, though it seemed entirely unimportant whether or not she admitted it. *Besides,* she thought, *I'm not even doing it well.* From time to time, she would linger at the top of the stairs leading to a section of seats and look out at the crowd. But try as she might, she couldn't spot James, nor any guest he might have in tow.

She walked past a beer vendor closing up shop. She found a twenty in her pocket, then proceeded to flirt in a manner that made her feel like she was having an out-of-body experience.

She made a conscious decision not to judge.

Prohibitively purchased beer in hand, she continued on her quest.

She noticed that the concourse was filling up with more and more people. She heard comments about a lopsided score. She sighed. *Likely they've left,* she thought.

Winter's bladder tapped her on the shoulder. She peeled her eyes. Searched for the universal lady with the triangle skirt.

She was honing in on the restroom, weaving a course a little less direct than A to B, when her eyes did spy a friend. *I thought you might be here,* she thought to herself, smiling on the inside. She fell in step behind him when he turned, forgoing the triangle-skirt side and opting instead for the sign with a circle head and straight legs.

"Hi," she said once they were inside the restroom.

Kennedy Marks turned. The flabbergasted look on his face was worth the price of admission.

"Honey! Honey?" He gave her a closer look. "Oh, honey, you're drunk."

She supposed it was true. She stole a glimpse of her surroundings. She laughed a little at the porcelain lineup, then a little more at the men craning their heads toward her voice.

"I wanted to see you. Here with him. I wanted to see how you pretend. I wanted to see...whether or *not* it's pretend."

Kennedy's expression went cold. "You decided to risk both our skins by following me into a public restroom at a baseball game? I understand if you don't trust me. We hardly know each other. But this is stupid, and you know it. He's right outside, for heaven's sake! He may have seen you follow me in here, for all we know."

Kennedy was right, of course. But she chose to ignore him.

"You really think you can do it?" she whispered. "Kill this man you've spent so much time with?"

Kennedy bored into her with cold, blue eyes. A drunk Rockies fan walked past, leering, but they paid him no mind. "Yes. Without a doubt."

"Let's do it tonight," she said, to gauge his reaction. "Lure him back to your hotel room, and we'll finish the deed together."

"You're worried if you can trust me," he said. "But look at it from my perspective. What about any of this makes you think that I can trust you?"

She was overcome by a wave of sadness. Instead of replying, she leaned in and kissed him full on the lips, tears welling in her eyes.

Kennedy gently pulled away from her. "Honey," he said.

She smiled a lonely, six-brew smile. "Who else is there to kiss?" she asked him.

Kennedy was gracious with his non-reply. He mirrored Winter's sad smile with one of his own.

Winter dried her tears. "Leave," she said. "I'll stay behind for a few minutes. I doubt the peeing men will mind." She paused, giving him a look that was both sincere and contrite. "If you can't trust me, then I can't be trusted by anyone."

Kennedy nodded. He kissed his fingertips and brought them just shy of Winter's lips. "I sought you out, remember? The cold-hard, ass-kicking bitch? We're in this together." He smiled. "I'll call you when I get back home."

And with those words, he turned and was gone.

*

Blucifer bathed in the dawn's morning light, undiminished.

Winter waited until Kol had pulled the Mercedes curbside at Denver International, then asked for an edible. She popped the fairy-dusted orange rectangle into her mouth as Kol popped the trunk for her luggage.

"Look at you!" Kol began, ever patronizing. "Nova Norcross coming out in the light of day! Enjoy your fl—"

She slammed the car door on him mid-sentence.

*

Five days later, she rendezvoused with Kennedy in the agreed-upon Charlotte University parking lot, quick and quiet. Burner numbers were exchanged.

"I bought a gun," she told him. "A handgun. And a shotgun."

"Honey, I've had a gun," Kennedy admitted. "It might be the only way." When she looked at Kennedy, she usually saw Carter Crowe, but not when he was biting his lip. "I'm learning James's routines, but...there's the matter of Kol. That son of a bitch follows us, you know."

Winter did know. It hadn't happened often, but on a handful of occasions she had spotted Kol's soulless self tracking her during the day. Unlike their face-to-face encounters, when Kol eagerly played the part of the belligerent bully, it was clear at those moments that he was trying to remain hidden, out of sight. It was terrifying to imagine how many times he had tailed her without her knowledge.

"Now that we're working together, we can use that to our advantage." In-between sentences Kennedy kept up the mastication, treating his lower lip like overtaxed gum. Winter hadn't known Kennedy for long, but, all the same, it was a very un-Kennedy like mannerism.

"What's wrong?"

"I'm worried that I may have triggered James's suspicions."

Winter's heart stutter-stepped. "Why?"

"I've been trying to nail down his routine. I'm looking for a soft spot...for an opening. Yesterday I got up early and parked at a gas station directly across from a dog park that James likes to frequent."

Winter wasn't exactly sure why, but the thought of James owning a dog made her angry. She had pared her life down to only the most necessary interactions, and her torturer was out cavorting with a canine? "He owns a dog?"

Kennedy tilted his head to an *I'm-not-sure* angle. "He's never mentioned it to me. Maybe it's his, maybe it belongs to someone he knows. Regardless, he escorts a golden retriever out to a dog park near Concord Mills two or three times a week. While he's there he...makes friends. Touches shoulders. Shakes hands."

"Oh." Winter understood. The dog was a device for getting close enough to people to bring them into the *Savage Moon* world. Sacrificial lambs. Fodder for the depraved violence of Kol Jones/Burden Monks and the moonbringer cult.

"I thought while I was waiting that I would go inside and buy a lottery ticket. I had my Powerball in hand when James walked in. He spotted me straight away. A short interrogation ensued, but I was able to parlay my genuine surprise at seeing him into enough time to manufacture a plausible lie."

"Which was?"

He raised his eyebrows. "We all visit the mall from time to time."

For a pinch, it was a good ruse. "And he bought it?"

"He certainly appeared to. I'm not as confident that he'll remain convinced after a little time passes." An incisor chawed on pink. "Later that same day, I spotted Kol staking out my house."

Winter nervously cast her eyes hither and yon. "How do you know he didn't follow you here?"

"If he did, he's a damn detective. I'm well versed in the googology of evasion; I used every trick in the book to drop a tail. And I went to all that trouble even though I'm ninety-nine percent certain that he wasn't following me in the first place." He gave Winter a consoling look. "At the end of the day, as creepy as James and Kol are, they don't keep tabs on us at all times."

The manifold possibilities of what Kol's tracking Kennedy might mean swirled in Winter's mind. But she knew it was time to push her fears to the side and take ownership of the present. Kennedy had been doing too much of the heavy lifting; if Winter was really going to be a part of this, it was time she did her share. "What now?" she asked. "What else do you need to know about James's schedule before we make our move?"

"I've thought..." Kennedy trailed off, searching for the words, uncertain. Winter felt a pang of sadness watching him. Seeing Carter Crowe looking tentative and unsure, Winter could only imagine how

Nova Norcross looked to him. Here in the real world they were reduced by the frailties of their flesh, the miasma of their minds. The danger of making the wrong move was just as real in the books, but, because the decisions in James's dreamworld weren't really their own, it was easy to submit to their characters' bold sense of purpose. In the books, James would either kill them or he wouldn't; their decisions mattered not at all. But here in the real, the decisions, and the repercussions of those decisions, were their own.

At last, Kennedy found the thread. "...there's a walking trail that leads deep into the woods behind the dog park. It dead-ends. The path is part of the Carolina Thread Trail, but it's still unconnected. Very few people walk it. I've been there myself and sat for an hour without seeing a soul." He paused. "Occasionally, when James is finished at the park, he will walk the dog down the trail." Another pause. "There's a way to access the trail through the woods without parking at the dog park. If we were there first...if the moment was right..."

Winter nodded. It took her a second to register that *she* was biting her lip. "When do you think he'll visit the dog park again?"

"In two days' time. Friday morning. He usually arrives a little after nine. But there's no point in taking the risk of tracking him. If he spots one of us, he'll know it's not a coincidence. If we decide to go the route of the dog park, we need to be all systems go."

"Let's do it, then," Winter said. She made her voice as hard as iron. "Let's be all systems go."

Kennedy grimaced, gently sucking his teeth. "It's quicker than I had planned. Hell's bells, girl, when we do this, we've got one chance to get it right. I'm still working out the kinks—"

"Tell me," Winter interrupted. "Tell me exactly what you had planned. Every day that we put this off, we risk not waking up from our dreams. You especially. Now that James has started writing again, there are no guarantees."

Kennedy nodded. James's work on the follow-up to *Bloodsucker Moon* had begun the night after he returned from the book tour. The new dreamscape was filled with storm clouds and lightning bolts, and the moon, roiling in the heavens, was the face of barometric turbulence. "Okay. I'll tell you what I had in mind. Then, together, we'll decide if it's time to act."

*

Winter received a text from James the following morning. **B**, a bump and run at a Harris Teeter. She waited in the produce section. Hands collided near the green onions, then James was on his way. No words exchanged.

She desperately wanted to go to the firing range. Her pistol purchase permit had arrived the day she returned from Colorado, after which she promptly went out and purchased a 9mm SIG. She had already purchased a .12 gauge shotgun—gun laws around long firearms were less restrictive—which loomed in the corner of her closet like a restless shadow. She had tested the shotgun at an outdoor firing range early on during James's book tour, a taxing ordeal that left her with both a bruised shoulder and bruised ego; her newbie-ness was evident for everyone at the range to see. But she was determined, and by the end her YouTube prep work and the helpful coaching of a range worker left her confident that she could, at the least, load the shotgun and fire it at a target. She wanted to do the same with the SIG, but with James and Kol back in town, she was wary of being discovered. So instead, she became an internet expert, learning everything there was to learn about the handgun while watching video after video of enthusiasts loading and firing the weapon. In the dark of the apartment, she practiced holding and aiming the gun, imagining, based on YouTube, what firing a SIG would feel like. It was not the same as going to a range, but it was better than nothing.

In between her dark visualizations, she texted Kennedy on the burner phone. She relished the warmth of his presence. She had been alone for so long that not even the psychic weight of planning a murder could dispel the joy she felt from connecting with another person.

She was texting Kennedy the second night, the Thursday, when she caught a glimpse of herself in the hallway mirror. She had the SIG in one hand, the phone in the other. Kennedy was bitching about his dinner: **cold chipotle, prelude to a stress shit**. She laughed and looked up, and there she was. The ghost of Winter York. Her once pearlescent skin had turned pale. Her hair, formerly a dark razorblade, now framed her face like a murky, melancholy shadow. Even the ivy tattoo that twisted up her long and daring neck looked faded. She was still striking in her way, like a swan that captures the eye from afar, but, up close, one sees that the creature is damaged.

I might have been a person, she thought.

Though she continued staring at the mirror, her thoughts strayed. She remembered how hale Nathaniel had looked when she saw him at Trader Joe's. She remembered the little girl, Isabelle, sheltering in his arms. The perfect package of her. Winter closed her eyes. She searched for the woman that she had once been. And then, in the mirror of her mind's-eye, she made a perfect memory: she was standing beside Nathaniel in Trader Joe, only now she was the Winter of old, and the little girl, whose features had changed to resemble her own, was reaching for her with eager arms and calling her by the universal name.

Mommy.

The image faded. She opened her eyes. The mirror regained the frame. She stared at the murderer in the making. She laughed a little, a manic sort of titter.

Then she cried.

When she was finished crying, she felt wrung out, but in a good way. She had not shed a tear in years. Doing so made her feel human again.

She knew that the sensation was only temporary. After tomorrow, a good crying fit would no longer feel the same. After tomorrow, the perfect memory that she had made might become irretrievable. Murderers were different people than murderers in the making, after all. Her sincerest hope was that James's death would help her regain her life. But she also knew that the cost of killing him might mean forever saying good-bye to the person she had been all those years ago when she stood on the precipice of falling in love.

She looked down at the phone. She felt emboldened knowing that Kennedy was on the other end. Unlike the scores of people in her life that she lived apart from to protect, Kennedy was an equal, someone in the same position as her. She was responsible *to* him, but she wasn't responsible *for* him.

She loved him for that.

She walked back into the living room and put the 9mm down on the coffee table. Then she texted Kennedy back. **Thx for the info. Still trying to scrub the mental image.** A thought occurred. She typed it to life. **Should we skip sleeping tonight?** It dawned on her why that wouldn't work even as Kennedy spelled it out.

No, no, no. It would be the same as sending a big red flag. Just remember...tonight's the last night. Tomorrow we dream our own dreams.

She nodded at the burner. *My own dreams,* she thought. She had those occasionally; they often devilishly took the form of a James writing session, fooling her unconscious mind into believing that she was in the writer's world before plunging her into the depths of her deepest fears. She often died in her own dreams, and, believing that she was in James's dreamworld, she would awake in a terrible panic, certain that she was, in fact, actually dead.

Better to dream a thousand dreams where I believe that I'm dead than to dream one where James actually kills me.

A chasmic yawn separated before and after. Living in the mind of a murderer in the making was exhausting. She needed shut-eye before the morrow's offerings. Going to sleep, she knew, would not be an issue; her body had long ago adapted itself to the thrills and terrors that awaited her in the land of nod.

She pecked at the phone.

You're right. On that note, I'm going to bed. I need the rest. See you in the morning. She paused a second before adding: **Here's hoping JB is too knackered to write tonight.**

Seconds later the phone buzzed a reply. **Rest up, honey. If he does write and I see you in the moonlight, let's kick a little ass together one last time.**

*

Bellicose cloudbanks stormed across the sky, waging war against the land. They spat rain and hail while gnashing electric knives in their dark-bloom teeth. Behind the shape-shifting clouds, the moon held sway. This particular savage moon was less visible than its predecessors, but, perhaps because its appearances were only intermittent, it was all the more striking for it: all at once the moon would emerge from behind the black veil of storm clouds, illuminated, agitated, roiling with a pent-up fury. Previous moons had often deceived, hiding their calamitous intentions behind a façade of beauty. Not the Lightning Moon. It promised death and destruction, and it intended to deliver.

She—Winter York, Nova Norcross—stood hunkered together with him—Kennedy Marks, Carter Crowe—beneath a picnic shelter. The raging storm appeared intent on ripping the world from its hinges. While they strategized, the viscera of a nearby creek spilled over into the park.

"We need to get moving. The god of moons isn't here. Neither are his followers."

Carter was right. She was disappointed but unsurprised. No matter how good their intelligence, the god of moons and the members of the moonbringer cult rarely materialized where they expected them to. The moonbringers were persons who, like themselves, had been imbued with powers invested in them by the moon god. Unlike Nova and her allies, who had quickly realized the error of their ways shortly after receiving their powers from the moon god and had worked ever since to bring his reign of terror to an end, the moonbringers used their powers to sustain the myriad incarnations of the savage moon. The moons persisted until Nova and Co. found a way to disperse the cult. Victories were always short-lived, but Nova and her allies fought on, determined that one day they would not only bring an end to the moonbringers, but also stop the god of moons himself.

She looked at Carter/Kennedy. The wind was driving sideways, pelting them with horizontal rain. Her wings ached for the sky, but flying tonight wouldn't be easy. "You're right. It's time to go."

He read her thoughts. "Can you fly?"

She shrugged. "Maybe. The wind is more problematic than the rain." She scanned the park one last time for Burden Monks and the other cult members. "It's as if the storm has dispersed the cult's energy. I know that they're close, but..."

Carter nodded, flummoxed. "Same here. It has something to do with the storm. The nexus of their power is fluid, shifting." He wiped rainwater away from his eyes. From out of nowhere, the blank stare of intuition fell upon him. It was one of the two powers given to him by the moon god—the ability to predict, to foresee. At least to a degree. "West," he said. "We need to go west. We'll find them there."

The water from the overflowing creek suddenly galloped toward the picnic shelter. Nova and Carter exchanged *time-to-go* glances. He sprinted toward higher ground. She gave the skies a tentative try. Strong flier that she was, the wind tonight was unmerciful; twice she was nearly tossed to the ground. Using a burst of concentrated effort, she caught up to Carter as he crested a nearby knoll, her feet skipping down on terra firma.

"I... I'm..." She felt unexpectedly vulnerable. There was a part of her mind—she thought of it as *the Winter Echo*—that strove to remind her that the invincibility she felt as Nova Norcross was not real. But once she was in James Breach's dreamworld, it was easy to forget. To be reminded was unsettling. "...struggling to fly. The storm..." Her words trailed away.

The chivalrous Carter Crowe took her by the hand. "No worries, we'll stick together." They bounded toward Carter's SUV in the parking lot, a black Escalade that looked like the chariot of an avenging god. Once inside the cocoon of dry, Nova tucked away her wings. Carter turned the ignition and off they sped, battering through the winds and strafing rain. Nature conceded the vehicle's advantage. They forded a flooded bridge with relative ease. Scattershot hail bounced off the Escalade's formidable exoskeleton. The wind howled but couldn't shake them from their self-appointed course.

All at once, the sky turned from black to light gray. Parted clouds revealed the Lightning Moon. Its roiling, riotous face quieted, becoming the pale color of bone. A moonbeam tracked from the sky to the road in front of them. A figure appeared on the asphalt, long legs straddling the forever yellow lines. He wore a coal-colored suit and an ash-gray trilby. He flipped a piece of silver into the air, again and again. As the Escalade approached, the god of moons snatched the quarter from the air and pocketed it. Then, revealing a scimitar smile, he turned a palm toward the SUV and, using forces unknown, brought the vehicle to a stop.

"What do we do?" Carter asked.

Somewhere inside of her mind, the *Winter Echo* experienced a terrible foreboding. But, as always, it was Nova Norcross who answered. "We confront the evil son of a bitch," she said.

They stepped out of the Escalade. The sky above had turned a dark royal blue, filled with pinprick stars. Nova glanced skyward. Directly overhead, the Lightning Moon. To the receding west she could see the Shadow Moon, continuing its slow voyage across the sky. *To what end?* she wondered, but it was a futile endeavor, as pointless as wishing on one of the pinpricks. Nova/Winter had long understood that the *Savage Moon* universe operated under a few basic principles: chief among these being that the god of moons held power when the moonbringer cult was able to conduct the rituals that kept the present incarnation of the savage moon alive. The Shadow Moon, however, was a mystery. And, as far as Nova could tell, it appeared destined to exist as such until James Breach revealed its purpose.

She returned her attention to the horror at hand: the god of moons stood alone in the middle of the road, patiently awaiting their undivided attentions.

"My lovelies," he began. Was that sentimental earnestness in his voice? As always, it was difficult to tell. "You work so hard. You believe...I suppose you have to believe, don't you?...that one day your actions will bring about my end. Because the truth would be unbearable. But a difficult truth is no less a truth. And the truth is this: It is my pleasure that you oppose me. And my pleasure, as always, is fulfilled."

He was taunting them. The *Winter Echo* knew that he was right. There was nothing they could do to him. The god of moons was immortal. Invincible. Nevertheless, Nova continued circling to his left, while Carter circled to his right, looking for an angle of attack. They were actors in a production, destined to play their parts.

The god of moons grinned, unconcerned. He rediscovered the quarter in his pocket. "Which of the two of you shall I entertain this evening?" he asked. He showed one side of the quarter to Nova. "Heads," he said. The other side he showed to Carter. "Tails." Nova and Carter caught eyes from across the expanse of their ever-widening breach, the look being in effect an unspoken promise to attack the instant the quarter was in the air. The god of moons swiveled his head, laughing, exhibiting the patient, predatory knowledge of a cat lounging in a flower bed while two birds hover nearby, shrilling empty threats. "Do you know," he asked, "that there are times when my powers extend to knowing the outcome of a quarter flip before the coin is even in the air?"

And then the quarter was aloft. Nova and Carter instantly attacked: she swooped in on vengeful wings, brandishing a bloodthirsty blade, while he advanced from the opposite direction, fists at the ready. But before they could close the gap, the god of moons disappeared. "Where did he go?" she asked. She looked to Carter for an answer, only to find that he had surrendered to one of his precognitive fits. She moved toward him in concern, sheathing the sword. Carter's spell lasted barely a second, but it was as powerful as the Lightning Moon above, a concentrated burst of rapidly flitting eyelids exposing peeks of white marble beneath. When Carter's pupils returned, he bore bad news. "Heads for you, Burden Monks for me," he said. He wore a plaintive, lost-soul expression, and she knew that there was more to the vision than he could say.

The *Winter Echo* screamed: *Kennedy!* She offered him all of her love in one sorrow-filled look. But it was a dream inside a dream, a book inside a book, and, as such, it lived and died inside of a fleeting moment in time.

She was sucked backwards into the air, as if being jerked into the heavens by a celestial rope. An invisible hand brought her to a halt. Her wings took over by instinct, and there she hovered, awash in the blue-black dark. She could feel the Lightning Moon behind her, bone-pale and quiet, waiting. Far below she could see Carter Crowe, reduced. She tried working her pinions toward the land, but they would not cooperate.

The god of moon's voice washed over her like a cold and unforgiving sea. "Carter Crowe is on his own now, my dearest Nova. Your time together has come to an end." She turned her neck and there the bald-headed god stood, feet firmly planted on a pedestal of air. Trilby in hand, he tossed the hat toward the horizon, where, instead of succumbing to gravity, it continued on an infinite line, leading Nova's eyes on a collision course with the most terrifying bank of thunderclouds she had ever seen. The trilby was swallowed up by the clouds like a small fish disappearing into the great emptiness of a killer whale's mouth, there and then gone, so small as to perish unnoticed.

The god of moons laughed. Nova studied him while channeling the *Winter Echo*, searching for signs of her real-world torturer inside of this omnipotent beast. There were glimpses, subtleties, similarities even, but in the end, it wasn't him, or, if it was him, it was only one possible version, no more real than a million others he might have dreamed up. *Bring his name to your lips,* the *Winter Echo* insisted. Nova resisted, knowing the outcome, but the *Winter Echo* won out. She brought her tongue to the roof of her mouth, only to have the syllable stick. He would not allow it. Which meant, of course, that the god of moons was in fact James Breach.

His laughter intensified. She thought she heard him say, telepathically, *Permission denied!*

The laughter gave way to words. "Don't focus all of your anger on me, my lovely. You're missing the show!"

She followed his pointing finger, which drew a vertical line from the advancing bank of brutish thunderclouds to the highway, where, to her horror, an army of moonbringers was advancing on Carter Crowe. Leading the charge was the moonbringers' chief masochist, the sadistically joyful Burden Monks. He had the look, Nova thought, of a nattily dressed centaur: his chest was puffed out, and the twin engines of his body sloped into a torso made up of the other moonbringers, on whose power he advanced like a one-man cavalry of the supernatural.

"Let's have a closer look, shall we?"

The god of moons flew them closer to the fray, jerking Nova by the invisible rope. Helpless with fright, she watched Burden Monks and the moonbringers advance on Carter Crowe, the storm of the ages nipping at the cult's heels. "Carter!" she screamed, but he could not hear her. All of his attention was attuned to the impending onslaught.

The blur of combat commenced. Carter Crowe barreled into the moonbringers, wrapping up Burden by the waist and tackling him to the ground. The moonbringers were stunned. Burden Monks, he of the supernatural strength and fiendish designs, was pinned on the asphalt, warding off blows thrown by a relentless Carter Crowe. A surge of hope flooded through Nova's chest. But then, but then...Carter gasped, pulling back, as if stung by fire. *Oh no,* Nova thought. Burden flung Carter from his person and she could see that the villain's fingers were aflame. Burden possessed a nefarious multitude of powers, but the ability to scorch others by the simple act of touching them was the one that Nova and her allies feared most. Laughter rang out of Burden's mouth, the crazed, deranged cachinnation of a murderous mind. The villain rose to his feet. Cracked his knuckles. Charged.

The instant the two men crashed into one another, the storm erupted. Scores of lightning bolts hot-trotted from cloud to ground, urged on by a satanic symphony of thunder. Everywhere madness. The moonbringers reveled in it: howling like wolves, they surrounded Carter and Burden, dancing orgiastically in the frantic rain. Nova, aloft, could see everything clearly; the storm sheet had stopped short of her perch in the sky, leaving a crystal-clear view. She watched in horror as Burden gained the upper hand. Scorch marks bloomed on Carter's body like scar flowers, blazing orange before cooling into a damaged black. Carter, weakened, was pushed time and again into the fury of the circle, where the moonbringers inflicted additional punishment before returning him to Burden's greedy, violent arms.

The rain stopped with a theatric abruptness. Burden Monks stood behind a depleted and defeated Carter Crowe. Pillars of lightning framed the scene. A curling bicep worked at a windpipe. It was Burden's preferred method of execution: first, he weakened his victims by burning them, and then, he strangled them to death.

Carter's face blossomed into blue.

Nova screamed for mercy. This time, Burden and the moonbringers heard her. They looked up. Hissed. Screamed obscenities. Laughed. They fanned out in a straight line, with Burden standing at the center, laboring with his death work. They stared at Nova with death-hungry eyes. Burden's were the hungriest of all. The feast at hand had left him unsated.

Nova didn't see them. She only had eyes for her dying friend. Carter Crowe. *Kennedy Marks.* Her heart breaking, she watched with unbearable sadness as he slipped into the next life.

She hovered in the sky for what seemed like an eternity, lost in sorrow. It wasn't until she heard the god of moons speaking that she came back into herself.

"My dearest Nova. How many friends have you seen die before your very eyes? Too many, no? And still you persist in resisting me." He chuckled. "Truth be told, I admire you for it. I do! I've gifted so many humans with powers, and yet you, the very first of your kind, refuse to maximize your potential by becoming a moonbringer. It's inspiring. Truly. If it were not for you and those poor sad-sack allies of yours, my dominion over this planet would be a fait accompli. But on you troop, suffering the agonizing loss of one friend after the other, believing that somehow, in the end, you will find a way to win."

"I will find a way to win," Nova responded. The *Winter Echo* listened on, uninvolved. "You can kill me now, if you like. If you don't, I will spend every waking moment trying to find a way to bring an end to your reign."

"Kill you?! I don't kill, my dear girl. I create. It's the creation of chaos, yes, but it's creation all the same." His eyes burned tiger bright. "But what I really want is for you to join me. Become a member of the moonbringer cult. You are my most prized creation, Nova Norcross. I won't rest until, of your own free will, you give yourself over to me."

For once, Nova's words were aligned with the *Winter Echo*. "I won't give you my soul. You know damn well that's not a price I'm willing to pay."

He turned his palms up, confessional style. The moonbringer pendant—a golden moon, the gift the god of moons gave to all those who chose to become his servant—rested in his right palm. The ever-present quarter was in his left. "So you say. But know this, Nova

Norcross. You may be my first. And you may be my favorite. But the day draws nigh when the moonbringers will have dominion over the entire planet. It's why I'm here, after all! And when that day comes, if you yourself have not joined their ranks, the death that has been visited on so many of your friends will at last arrive at your doorstep."

A clap of thunder shook the foundations of the earth, coupled with lightning so close that Nova could taste its metallic flavor. When it struck, the spell lifted: Nova's wings were her own once more. Without a moment's hesitation, she flew at the god of moons. To her shock, he didn't move. She grabbed hold of the deity with a single-minded determination to end his existence. *The sword,* she thought, *gut him with the sword.* But they were grappling with one another, and she couldn't free a hand to grab the weapon. Together they tumbled through the air, fighting for control. *How?* she wondered. *Why?* But no answers were forthcoming. *He's allowing this, it's the book, he's writing this, it's only the book,* the *Winter Echo* advised, but, as she had never touched the god of moons before, Nova Norcross couldn't help but wonder if a new epoch had begun.

If I can lay my hands on him, anything is possible.

To the west, a bank of ivy pored over the graded side of the highway. She tried to guide them in that direction. The storm, expanding rapidly, swept them up in its hungry maw, a black-bellied tract churning with wind and rain. The god of moons laughed, or sobbed, or smiled, or frowned: she was too close to him to tell. *Fly west,* she thought. *Throw him in the ivy.* To her disbelief, it worked. Spending all her strength at the last second,

Nova Norcross freed herself from the god of moons and flung him into the greenery.

Nova's mind, already inside the greenery, went straight to work, swallowing up the god of moons with ravenous speed. *Choke him,* she thought. The leafy tendrils heeded her command, grabbing at the villainous deity's throat with abandon. The god of moons, cognizant of what was occurring, tore at the vines with his hands, but for every plant fiber that he ripped away, two more took its place. *It's working,* she realized with amazement. She channeled every inch of her being into the ivy. The shoots began working at his wrists, making it so that he could not protect his throat. The moon god's corporeal form, frantic with panic, began to still. She thought that she could detect the beginnings of his skin turning blue.

That's for Carter, you fuck, she thought. The *Winter Echo* suggested a revision. Her inner voice complied, a tear appearing in her mind's-eye. *No. That's for Kennedy Marks.*

The god of moons was dying, dying, dying.

And then...

The world exploded.

White light bright light hot heat nothing nothing nothing.

Nova lurched into a semiconscious state. She was lying on her back, staring up the storm-black sky. Somewhere in the catacumbal depths, a cloud break revealed a vengeful sphere.

The Lightning Moon.

She lay still. Waiting. Idly, she wondered if her wings were still attached to her body.

The god of moons appeared. He looked down on her in bewilderment. In wonder. In fear.

She closed her eyes and fell back asleep.

Waited to wake up.

*

Consciousness. The mornings after a night in the Savage Moon dreamscape were always a bruised and tender affair, but this was worse: Winter's body and mind screamed in agony the second she awoke. *Kennedy's dead, Kennedy's dead, Kennedy's dead* ran the steam train of her brain, while her body grasped at the extent of the trauma, feeling, fruitlessly, for the charred remnants of her wings.

Get up. Get moving. You need to leave. Now.

She rolled over and pried a finger through the window blinds. The hollowed-out emptiness of a pre-dawn black stared back. *James will send Kol Jones after you the second they are awake.* Her hand searched for the bedside alarm clock. An illuminated **4:57** answered the touch.

Get up! Get up! Get up!

She sat up. Her insides were ash-covered coals. Whatever the damage done, she knew it would not last; dream pain was like a hyperreal impression that carried over into the waking world, but, so long as you survived the night, the effects were only temporary. It was only if you died…the vision returned to her of Kennedy breathing his last, his neck locked in Burden Monks's bicep. Tears tried to make their way to the surface, but she stanched them at the source. There simply wasn't time.

She grabbed both burner phones from the bedside table. One for Kennedy, one for James. No text messages. She forced herself to send one to Kennedy. **Did you survive?** The words stared back, accusing her of a cold bluntness. She considered sending another message, warming the words, showing her distress, her suffering, but in her heart of hearts she knew that at the other end there was only a corpse who would never read it. If by some miracle Kennedy texted back, then she would write a reply deserving of her emotions.

Slapdash, she packed a timeworn Adidas gym bag full of clothes and toiletries. Enough to see it through.

She opened the closet. Retrieved the restless shadow in the corner. Wrapped it up in two large towels.

The SIG was waiting for her on the living room coffee table. She stuffed it in the gym bag.

In the parking lot of her apartment building, she popped open the trunk to her Hyundai Elantra and threw the towel-wrapped shadow inside. The gym bag and the 9mm she placed on the passenger seat. Before driving away, she took a long look at the night sky. The moon was a peaceful crescent white, and there wasn't a cloud—storm or otherwise—in the sky.

*

The plan was to follow through with the plan.

By herself.

For the moment, there was time to kill. She wasted it driving the tributary backroads that existed in the no-man's land of Cabarrus County. The Hyundai headlights guided the way like a caffeinated lightning bug, too jacked up to blink. When she wandered too far into unfamiliar territory, Google Maps guided her back.

Lorde's *Pure Heroine* played on the car's stereo system. She had finally stopped buying CDs a year back, only to find that she enjoyed listening to CDs more than she did utilizing a streaming service. It was difficult losing herself in the music this morning, but, to some effect, the songs worked their spell, creating a barrier between Winter and reality. "A World Alone," the closing track, rose in time to the sunrise.

She began making her way toward the dog park.

I should fill the car up with gas, she thought. The tank was a quarter full, and, on the outside chance that all went according to plan, she wanted to distance herself from the scene of the crime as quickly as possible. She tried not to think of everything that could go wrong. The plan had been for Kennedy to pull the trigger, and for her to be ready with the getaway car. But that plan had died with Kennedy, and now she was left to ponder the million possible missteps that might take place along the way. *It's all happening too fast,* she thought. *We aren't prepared, we haven't considered every possibility, we haven't—*

Her train of thought was struck dumb by the obvious. This was not happening too fast. If anything, it was too late. The *We* of her thoughts no longer existed. Kennedy was dead. And now that she had nearly destroyed

James Breach inside of his own dream, any future foray into the Savage Moon universe might end in her death as well.

She filled the car up with gas at a QT. The pulse of the workweek morn was quickening, traffic pumping through the asphalt arteries. The sun, clear of the horizon, blasted mid-summer heat. While standing at the tank, her thoughts went to the burner phone she used to contact Kennedy. *Once the police find it, they'll trace it to me.* The complications that might derive from that possibility chilled Winter to her bones. She opened up the car door and, unzipping the duffel bag, retrieved the flip phone. She almost looked back at the last text message that Kennedy had sent her, but stopped herself out of fear of the emotions it might engender. Before she could change her mind, she snapped the phone in half and tossed it in the trash receptacle.

With the gas tank topped off, she made her way to where they had planned to drop off Kennedy, near the back of the woods leading to the dog park. Only now she needed to find a place to park. She and Kennedy had arranged to communicate a pickup using the burner phones, but now the person driving the car also had to make their way through the woods alone. She had her choice between parking at a brick-and-mortar business strip and the streets of a nearby neighborhood. She pulled into a parking space in the business strip, but then, catching sight of a surveillance camera, she changed her mind and opted for the neighborhood.

She parked the Hyundai on the inconspicuous corner of a shaded street, worry gnawing at her bones. She realized, in a panic, that she didn't know how to conceal the 9mm. She made the decision to dump half the contents of the gym bag onto the passenger seat floorboard. Then she repacked the gun.

Taking the gym bag with her, she got out of the car and started the long walk toward the woods.

While she walked, she scanned the area for witnesses. Two young children dashed in and out of front-yard sprinklers, while a mom sitting on a porch chair played on her cell phone. An elderly man walked the streets. A delivery truck zoomed from door to door. The lot of them seemed oblivious to her presence.

Reaching the woods, she slipped into the tree line like a baptismal candidate disappearing into the river.

The woods were fecund with summer growth. Poison ivy ran rampant over the forest floor, leaves repeating ad infinitum in threes. Winter couldn't help but think of the Woodland Moon from the first novel, one of three savage moons that she experienced with Jessalyn in James Breach's debut. The woods in the book were both infinitely more terrifying and yet somehow more sanitized than this one. And unlike the ivy in *Savage Moon*, the ivy in the real world paid her no heed.

A slithering underfoot. Winter screamed, a staccato burst. The shiny black scales of a snake glided to safety.

This is insane! she thought, her heart pounding. She stood still for a moment, waiting to see if anyone had heard her scream. Nothing. Only the sounds of the woods. She gathered herself. *Keep going. This might be your only chance.*

She walked, ever onward. Kennedy had said it was a quarter mile or so from the tree line to the trail. She knew that she was in the right place, but the enigmatic quality of the woods made her wonder if she had somehow ventured into a different world altogether. *If only,* she thought, but even that joy was dampened by the subsequent consideration that perhaps she was dreaming, stumbling about in a nightmare of James Breach's design. Just then she heard the joyous barking of dogs some distance away. A few steps later, she came upon the trail.

She looked around. She was standing at the bottom of a small hill. Further up the incline, obscured by hundreds and hundreds of trees, she could make out the far reaches of the dog park fence. The dogs and people, however, were inside the fence's interior, out of sight. She studied the path. It was broad and flat, having wound down the hill south of the fencing. As long as she stayed out of sight, it would be easy to surprise anyone who walked down to the flat part of the path.

Not surprise them, she corrected herself. *Kill them. Kill him. Kill James Breach.*

She took a deep breath. Forced her murderer-in-the-making mind to pick a hiding spot. An oak tree the width of a Mini Cooper spoke to her. Winter walked over to it, nodded internally, and sat her butt on the forest floor.

Once settled, she opened the gym bag and retrieved the pistol.

*

Twenty minutes later, Winter heard footsteps. And whistling.

Her heart responded like a tom-tom drum, threatening to explode out of the top of her skull. Thoughts struggled to form in the maelstrom. Still, a few managed. *Wait till he's closer. Till there's no chance for escape. Be sure it's him before you show the gun. Does James whistle?*

Whistling seemed a very un-James-like thing to do.

She whipped her head around the side of the tree trunk. A man of South Asian descent was approaching at a brisk pace, arms swinging freely at his side. Spotting Winter, the man startled with surprise. Not knowing what to do, Winter ducked back behind the tree trunk. She quickly returned the gun to the gym bag, her face turning secretly crimson.

"Miss? Ma'am? Are…are you okay?"

Winter didn't know if she should answer. Or if she should show her face again. *Who knew that trying to murder someone could be so embarrassing?*

"Yes!" she called back with too much gusto, a slight tremble in her voice. She stayed hidden on the opposite side of the tree trunk. "Just enjoying the woods!"

The man responded with silence. Winter pricked her ears, but heard nothing. The silence unnerved her to the point that she prepared to reach into the gym bag in case she needed the gun for an altogether different reason. At last, she heard footsteps. Her heart resumed its thunderous beating, making it impossible to tell if the man was coming or going. Flustered, she looked around the side of the tree.

To her relief, the man was walking away.

What a disaster. She wondered if the man would feel compelled to report the strange story of the woman in the woods to the authorities.

She calmed herself. Steeled her nerves. *Stay. Don't leave. This might be your only...*

Her thoughts were interrupted by the buzz of the other burner phone. The one she hadn't thrown away.

A text appeared on the screen.

12:30. E.

Her heart jumped in her throat. It was James. And he wanted to meet. But where was he messaging her from? Was he in the park at this very moment, walking his dog? *Get it together,* she told herself. Her fingers started moving on the flip phone, typing out a response. **I'm going to kill you, you murdering psychopath. I'm going to avenge my friend.** She stared at the words, relishing the harsh substance of the message. The act seemed to calm her; the words were a bridge between being a murderer in the making and a murderer in the moment, a bridge she intended to cross any minute now. Feeling more in control of herself, she erased the message, and typed a new one. **Today is your last day on Earth.** Then she sat back and, staring at the phone, imagined pressing send.

She continued creating and erasing messages until a new sound, another *whistling,* drove her fingers from the phone. She tried to put the flip phone back into her shorts pocket, but, when it didn't slide smoothly in, she stuffed it into the gym bag and pulled out the gun. The whistling drew nearer. *Surely, it's not the same guy,* she thought. The tune certainly wasn't the same. Whereas the first tune had been jolly and freeform, this one sounded strange and minor key, but cut with wild discordant notes, like an ironic funeral dirge. She tried to imagine the type of person who would whistle such a tune.

To her horror, an image of a very specific person formed in her mind's-eye.

Winter's heartbeat rattled her breastbone. She slowly pulled the 9mm from the Adidas gym bag. Then, as swiftly and smoothly as she could manage, she peeked around the side of the tree.

The nattily dressed nightmare known as Kol Jones was walking down the asphalt path, leading a golden retriever on a leash.

Winter moved without thought. Like a dream. Like Nova Norcross. She stepped out from behind the tree and onto the path and strode toward Kol Jones. The 9mm at her side.

The dog, sensing danger, stopped short and barked. Kol, ever jaunty and arrogant, urged the dog forward. He strained his neck toward Winter, trying to figure out who she was. Aviator sunglasses and the forest shade hampered his vision.

Then, all at once, Kol Jones saw. Kol Jones understood.

Winter raised the gun.

Kol dropped the dog's leash and turned on his heels.

Winter pulled the trigger twice.

Pop-pop.

Part III

2019

Nathaniel kept his eyes peeled for ghosts. Specters aged a decade plus one. He seemed to recall a street lamp under which Winter had rolled up his sleeve and admired his new tattoo. *But which one?* Under every lamppost he expected to see a younger version of himself smiling down at a bewitching cut of a woman wearing a cheese-rind-red jacket. But to his disappointment, the couple never appeared.

"Hurry up. We're already late." Angelica didn't like to be late. Not to work. Not to play. And not to dinner with Nathaniel's brother Zack and Zack's new fiancée. She pounded the NoDa pavement in black Tieks, urging Nathaniel forward like a dog sled in reverse, *mush, mush.* Nathaniel sped up enough to keep pace. His mind's-eye kept trying to envision a slightly different NoDa, but he stayed sufficiently in the here and now to follow Angelica's go-go Tieks.

High above the Tieks, Angelica's bouncing blonde hair tumbled down a green tent dress.

They turned a corner and arrived at the restaurant. Angelica turned to Nathaniel. "How do I look?"

Nathaniel gave Angelica a languorous smile. Then he made her wait for the reply. She half-grinned, half-glared at him. It was a game they played. The great balancing game. They had once been terrible at it, but over the years they had refined their respective styles so that now they appreciated, even enjoyed, the moves and countermoves. Her move had been the brisk walk. His, the drawn-out response.

Balance.

"Like Denna," he replied, referencing a female character from one of his favorite fantasy books. She cut her eyes at him. "Like the indefinable beauty of an indescribable sunset." She smiled. She turned around and grabbed the door handle. He looked at her ass. "Like candy!" he whispered loud enough for her to hear. Angelica continued walking inside, but, while holding the door handle, she turned and winked at him.

Zack and Ariel were already seated on the far side of the restaurant. It was a tapas joint, predictably named *Less Is More*. The middle of the restaurant was crammed with wooden high-top tables while the walls were lined with black leather booths. Nathaniel and Angelica curlicued their way through the tables to the booth in the back where Zack and Ariel were seated. Halfway there, Nathaniel noticed the glass double doors in the back leading to a courtyard. He did a double take, his head swiveling from left to right.

It's the same place where I went on my date with Winter. Only renovated.

Zack stood up to meet them with a big, beefy grin. Ariel scooched to stand as well, but Zack didn't clear enough space, so she ended up saying hello by way of a little wave, still seated. Angelica took charge, hugging Zack and then maneuvering him out of the way so that she could hug Ariel. Nathaniel and Zack bro-hugged, hand clasps and back slaps. Then everyone took their seats, with the couples facing each other.

Zack opened the conversation. "Have you eaten here before?"

Zack's question caught Nathaniel by surprise. *Yes,* he thought, *eleven years ago. Back when it was a pizza joint.* But he gave a charier response. "I haven't eaten in NoDa in a long time."

"You're in for a treat. It's one of our favorite places," Zack said, looking at Ariel. They nodded together the way new lovers do. Nathaniel grinned on the inside. Angelica, he knew, was doing the same. The sardonic slacker-Zack of old had recently been replaced by the earnest, open-minded man before them. It was still taking some getting used to.

"We've been looking forward to it," Angelica replied. "It's tough getting out with the kids, and, when we do, we never seem to venture into the NoDa area. I think we've talked about eating here? But it hasn't happened. This is a treat."

Nathaniel nodded dumbly along, although, in truth, he knew exactly why they never ended up in NoDa. For years and years, he had subtly given potential NoDa trips the slip: usually it was as simple as persuading Angelica to choose a different restaurant, but occasionally the excuses were more involved, and, once, he had even feigned a sickness. Tonight had been a surrender of sorts. Ariel had arranged the outing, and, rather than sabotage a meal that Nathaniel knew meant a lot to his brother, he had decided that it was time to confront his NoDa ghosts.

The small talk continued. Zack, long the irreverent bachelor, went out of his way to keep the conversation civil. What was funny was that Ariel didn't strike Nathaniel as the type who cared one way or the other. She was a slight young woman with strawberry-blonde hair and a smile that looked like it had been nicked from the easygoing store. In short:

Angelica's foil. But, from the looks of it, the two women were getting along splendidly.

Watching Angelica and Ariel hit it off, Nathaniel couldn't help but wonder what Angelica would have thought of Winter. Would they have gotten along? He had his doubts. They were different from each other in a different sort of way. *Or maybe,* he thought, *the similarities dovetailed inside of their differences would have set them apart.* He knew that they were both strong women. Courageous women. Independent-minded women.

Nathaniel checked himself. *Angelica is a strong, courageous, independent-minded woman. Winter, you hardly knew.*

The sharp point of Angelica's elbow returned Nathaniel to the here and now. "Ariel asked you a question," she said.

He turned and faced his brother's fiancée, apologetic. "I'm sorry. Do you mind repeating it?"

Ariel graced him with a forgiving, rosy-cheeked grin. "Not at all. I was asking how you and Angelica ended up together. Now that I'm going to be in the family, I would love to hear the tale." She clicked her fingernails on a martini glass. "The unvarnished version, of course."

The unvarnished version? He hesitated. An eleven-year-old memory raced across his consciousness like a comet against the sky: Angelica's brother Mike, sloshed and standing above him in this very restaurant, berating him for breaking off the engagement. The same Mike that he had enjoyed a Cage the Elephant concert with last month. All of that was in the past, of course, but being here was not only a reminder of Winter, but also of the bumps in the road along the way to a successful marriage.

"Er…it took us a while to work it out."

"To say the least," Angelica piped in.

Ariel brought her elbows to the table and puppy-dogged her head forward. "Ooh…interesting. Tell me more."

Nathaniel reluctantly continued. "We met in college. Angelica was…um…"

"I was dating Nathaniel's roommate at the time," Angelica admitted, letting Nathaniel off the hook. "But when I laid eyes on Nathaniel, I thought he made the better fit. So, I orchestrated the switch."

Zack guffawed. "And Natty-boy was an innocent bystander in all of this?"

Nathaniel and Angelica looked at each other. Both gave little shrugs. "I mean…yeah," he said at last. Everyone laughed. "I was a passive bystander to my own life's story back then. When Angelica came in and started calling the shots, I thought it best to let her take charge."

"Until you didn't," Angelica reminded him.

"Until I didn't," he concurred.

"So…there was a breakup?" Ariel's green eyes came alive with impish delight.

"Yes. There was a breakup."

Angelica laughed. "Nathaniel let me know in no uncertain terms that *he* was the master of his own destiny. Not me. A more confident woman would have found his declaration of independence sexy, but I didn't like the idea of a man that I couldn't control, so….difficulties arose. The last straw was when he decided that he no longer wanted to be an accountant.

We were engaged by then. I made it clear that I expected to marry an accountant." She took a sip of her lager. "Soon after, he dumped me."

"I wanted to be a writer."

Ariel's eyes flashed with delight. "Zack lent me your book! It was *so* good. I love fantasy."

My self-published book, Nathaniel thought. But he said, "Thank you. I'm proud of it."

"He's super talented," Angelica chimed in. Underneath the table, she gave his knee a squeeze.

Nathaniel managed a queasy smile. He knew that Angelica's praise was both sincere and well-intentioned, but the scanty reality of his writing accomplishments always made him feel like a primary school child being praised for an especially good coloring. "I try. Even if I'm not in danger of achieving mainstream success. Or of quitting my day job."

"I thought it was amazing," Ariel said. "It reminded me of one of my favorite fantasy authors. The *Savage Moon* guy? But I digress: How did you end up back together?"

Nathaniel's brain buckled at the mention of James Breach. Sensing that something was awry, Angelica took over. "I can't speak for Nathaniel, because he's always been fairly mum about the months when we were apart, but, as for me, I had a *come-to-Jesus* moment when I went on a date with this guy named Brad. It made me realize that I was missing out on the love of my life for the stupid reason that I wanted the love of my life to be someone he wasn't." She circled the top of her pint glass with a finger. "Also, that I didn't want to date anyone named *Brad.*"

Laughs all around. Angelica lowered her gaze, the playful predator. "Once Brad was dealt with, I went looking for Nathaniel."

Nathaniel, now recovered, picked up the thread. "By then I was substitute teaching. At the time I thought it was a temporary stop on my road to literary riches and fame, but within the year it had transformed into a full-time gig teaching high school English. By the time Angelica found me, we had both changed. Angelica always gives herself a hard time for our breakup, but the truth was, I needed a little time to grow up."

Angelica squinted, as if trying to see into the past. "He *was* different. There was no doubt about that. He was…more concrete somehow?" She gave a little shrug, and a little smile. "I thought maybe he'd been through the ringer with another woman, but he's fairly mum on that front. Regardless, we were clearly better together the second time around."

Nathaniel glanced at Zack, but if his brother made the connection between Angelica's hypothesizing and their long-ago conversation in Jack-in-the-Box, he gave no sign of it. *Thank heavens,* Nathaniel thought. Though at the same time he felt a twinge of frustration. *Am I the only one who remembers Winter?* Once or twice, Nathaniel had come to the brink of sharing the story of Winter with his wife, but it was too weird, too far-fetched, too gut-wrenchingly raw, to broach. He couldn't decide which outcome would have frustrated him more: Angelica disbelieving him and thinking him a loon, or Angelica believing him but failing to grasp the intensity of his experience.

In the end, he simply kept the memory of Winter York to himself.

"I think the two of you are adorable," Ariel decided, beaming. She raised the martini glass. "Here's hoping Zack and I are so lucky. Cheers."

Four glasses gathered. Clinked. Nathaniel took a sip of his cocktail, a sidecar. The slight burn reminded him of his bladder. It dawned on him that a trip to the toilet would be a good excuse to clear his head.

"Excuse me," he said, rising from the table. "I'll be right back."

He went through the motions in the men's room. His mind a maelstrom. *Survivor's guilt,* he told himself, reaffirming an old self-diagnosis. But that wasn't exactly right. After all, he had seen Winter three years ago at the Trader Joe's in the University Area. Plus, he kept up with the *Savage Moon* book series closely enough to know that Nova Norcross was still alive, which meant, in all likelihood, that Winter York walked the earth as well.

But even if she wasn't dead, she still haunted him. *Are you okay?* he asked her in his mind. Then: *How could you be?* And, more selfishly: *Do you think about me as much as I think about you?* Looking in the bathroom mirror, he half-expected to see Winter's apparition appear before him. He thought he caught a glimpse of her, the memory shadow in his mind's-eye half-forming in the glass. *Are you still in danger? Did I betray you by walking away?* He turned off the faucet. Stood up straight. The memory shadow dematerialized into nothingness as he mouthed the last question out loud.

"Did we know each other long enough to actually be in love?"

A stab of…was it guilt? And, if so, what type? Guilt because he still had feelings for Winter? Or guilt because he had abandoned her to a terrible fate? *It's not the former,* he assured himself. He knew what he had with Angelica. Whatever this lingering turmoil of emotions surrounding Winter represented, it did not detract from the love he had for his wife. But if it was the latter, what did it matter? What, after all these years of doing nothing, could he possibly do now?

He ripped a paper towel from the dispenser to dry his hands. *Stop,* he told himself. *You knew that being in NoDa was going to make things worse. You are just reacting to your surroundings. Things will return to normal as soon as tonight's over.* He threw the paper towel in the trash receptacle. *They always do.*

*

When he returned to the booth, Ariel wasn't there. He slid into the black leather without giving it a thought, supposing she had gone to the restroom. But the off-kilter mood at the table cued him in that it was something different.

"What's up?" he asked. "Where's Ariel?"

Angelica displayed saucer-pan-wide eyes. "You won't believe this, but while you were in the restroom, the fantasy author Ariel mentioned earlier walked in. She went over to say hello."

Nathaniel turned in the heavy soup manner indigenous to nightmares. Across the restaurant, Ariel was talking to James Breach. James, clad in black pants and a blood-red button-up shirt, wore the engaged expression of an older man happy to be the object of a young woman's attention. Now in his late fifties, James looked little like the fading pretty-boy pugilist Nathaniel had wrestled to the ground a decade prior. Time and affluence had fattened him up, giving him the appearance of an early late-stages Brando. But there was a cleverness in his eyes, and a cunning in his hand, which was inching across the table, preparing to reach out for Ariel's own.

No! Nathaniel nearly screamed. Without thinking, he launched himself to his feet and hustled across the restaurant. His approaching presence distracted the author long enough for Nathaniel to cut in front of Ariel and use his body as a shield.

Befuddled expressions all around. Nathaniel was trying to think of a way to explain himself when the author reached out and grabbed hold of Nathaniel's wrist. "Excuse me," James snarled. "I don't know who you think you are, but I was in the middle of a pleasant conversation with...Ariel, was it?" The author discarded Nathaniel's wrist with a sudden distaste and extend his hand toward Ariel, trying for a last-gasp handshake.

Nathaniel waylaid the author's hand once more. "You might not know who I am, but I know you who are. It's why I don't want you shaking hands with my friend."

James laughed with feigned disdain. "Oh. You're one of the whackos, huh?" The author did his best to make eye contact with Ariel. "If this troglodyte is indeed your friend, my apologies. He seems to be of the mind-set that beautiful young women can't make their own decisions as to whether or not it's safe to shake my hand."

Nathaniel glanced at Ariel, being careful to keep his body juxtaposed between her and James. She looked more uncertain than anything else. "It's okay," she said. "I didn't come over here to shake your hand. I just wanted to tell you how much I like your books." She screwed on a *keep-*

the-peace smile and searched for something innocuous to say to break the tension. "My overprotective friend is actually a writer too. Fantasy, like you."

"He is, is he?" James gave Nathaniel a thorough once-over. "You do look familiar. Perhaps we've met?"

Don't jog his memory. "You've never heard of me, I'm sure."

"Try me."

"I'm self-published."

"Ah." James permitted a self-satisfied silence to have its say. "I suppose we can't all achieve the level of fame where nutjobs go to great lengths to cockblock our handshakes."

Nathaniel didn't respond. His heart was racing like a greyhound. The first inklings of what was in store for him now that he had made contact with James Breach began to settle in. Fighting off the fear, he stayed fixed on the task at hand: keeping James away from Ariel.

To his relief, Ariel cooperated. "Okay, I'm heading back to my table. It was nice meeting you," she said to James. "I can't wait to read the final book in the series." Nathaniel didn't have a clue whether his future sister-in-law was angry with him, but, for the moment, that was the least of his concerns. When she walked away, he started to follow on her heels, but before he could take a step, James Breach grabbed his wrist once more.

Nathaniel faced the *Savage Moon* sorcerer. The writer's lips peeled back in a hyena sneer. "If what you claim to believe is actually true, you're in quite a bit of trouble, aren't you?" The writer's grin turned jack-o-lantern. "Sweet dreams, friend."

Rage and fear flooded Nathaniel's body. He considered bludgeoning James with his fists right then and there. After all, he knew better than anyone that what the writer was suggesting was true. And if Nathaniel was doomed to be a dead man by the morrow, why not go ahead and beat the shit out of James Breach tonight?

The *Savage Moon* writer must have sensed Nathaniel's train of thought, because he released Nathaniel's wrist, broke off eye contact, and hunched into a slightly defensive posture. The change dulled Nathaniel's anger long enough for him to notice that an unnatural quiet had fallen. Half of the restaurant was looking their way. The pause gave Nathaniel sufficient time to envision Angelica watching him beat up an old man. Logic told him to throw a punch, but a lifetime of refraining from attacking old men in restaurants stayed his fists. Without a word, he returned to the table.

*

The remainder of the evening was a blur. Zack, who thought the idea of a writer with magical powers was hilarious, couldn't stop laughing; he clearly had no recollection of their conversation eleven years earlier. Ariel didn't appear upset at Nathaniel for what he had done, but she was also clearly no longer at ease. As for Angelica, she spent the remainder of the meal giving Nathaniel side-eyes that augured a much deeper conversation once they were alone.

Throughout, James Breach stole glance after surreptitious glance at their table. Plotting the night's writing, perhaps. Or, worse, connecting tonight's events to a long-ago time and place.

Nathaniel supposed that he would know soon enough.

When the check arrived, Nathaniel paid in full. James Breach had left ten minutes earlier. Outside, after awkward good-byes with Zack and Ariel, Nathaniel and Angelica retraced the steps to their car, allowing Nathaniel to once again relive the Winter York walking tour. They passed a busker on the corner crooning "Jolene." Nathaniel superimposed "High and Dry" over the top, dropped a fiver in the open guitar case.

As soon as they were clear of the crowds, Angelica asked the begging question.

"What was *that* all about?"

He stopped in the middle of the sidewalk. The ghosts of the past, present, and future all converged on the spot, offering him the chance to confess the missing segment of his life. But when he looked up at Angelica with her no-nonsense eyes, the words wouldn't come.

High above, the moon glimmered like a coin in a moonlit fountain.

"I overreacted," he heard himself say. "In my defense, James Breach is a known creep. I've read enough about him to know that for a fact. Enough to know that I didn't want him anywhere near Ariel. But yeah...I overreacted."

An image flashed in Nathaniel's mind: Angelica, waking up and rolling over, finding him dead in the bed. The accompanying thought: *that's going to happen no matter what.*

Angelica had him pinned with an uncertain stare. "You know the stories about that writer are fabricated nonsense, right?" She strained her eyes, looking for his soul. "Right?"

The ghosts of NoDa danced all around him. High on his deltoid, he could feel the moon tattoo burning in negative space.

"Right," he replied.

*

He considered his options. Resisting sleep for a week. Hunting down James Breach. Releasing a Kennedy Marks's-style exposé on social media and daring the writer to kill him in the aftermath. The latter seemed the sanest course, but, thinking it through, he realized that going public might influence the writer to come after his family. The second option—killing James in cold blood—was beyond him. That left trying to stay awake all week, but in the deepest core of his truest self he knew that he wouldn't take that route. A gnawing voice whispered the God's-honest: *This is the tab for a bill long past due. It's time to pay up.*

He tried hard to change his own mind. Putting his daughter to sleep appeared to do the trick. He grew nauseous when he kissed her on the forehead, the image of a world without him reframed as a world where Isabelle didn't have a father. *You'll stay awake seven straight days for her, damn it.* By the time he parted Isabelle's room, he was convinced that he had sloughed off the go-to-sleep madness.

He upheld the illusion during his bedtime routine by masterplanning stay-awake strategies. While brushing his teeth: *start drinking late-night coffee.* While taking a hot shower: *take cold showers.* While slipping into the boxers and T-shirt that served as his PJs: *bring your iPhone to bed.* But when Angelica leaned over to kiss him goodnight, he had done none of the aforementioned. *Tomorrow,* he swore. *Tonight, I'll tough it out. Tomorrow I'll prepare.*

Angelica lingered when she leaned in for their nightly kiss, running a hand through his hair. His already tenderized heart swore a new oath. *For Isabelle. And for Angelica.* There was the suggestion of sex in the kiss, but it was secondary, behind the need for closeness, comfort. He returned the kiss and held her close. She segued to his chest, and there rested her head, content. In the ensuing stillness he thought he sensed a question forming in the hollow of her throat, but, in the end, silence won out. Five minutes passed. At last, she squeezed him, turned over, and turned out the light.

He confronted the darkness with resolve. Hatched a rough plan. *When Angelica falls asleep, I'll make my way downstairs and drink a cup of coffee. Then it's television till morning.* He cycled the last half hour in his head over and over again on a loop, replaying the moments with his wife and child. *Stay awake. Stay awake. Stay awake.* He felt keyed up, but steady. In control. He patrolled the slumbering corridors of his mind with a bright light, keeping close watch for the sandman. But the king of sleep was nowhere to be seen.

He relaxed.

Then...a slip. A memory-feeling: the long-repressed desire for a cigarette. At first, he thought it an innocuous nothing, a blip, but in an instant Winter was attached to the cigarette's end, the enigmatic girl standing in front of the mall, and he was falling, giving in, remembering. The memory snuck into that nebulous dreamspace where memory-images go to mutate...but he was awake, awake, still okay, on the verge of going downstairs, completely in control; never mind Winter York with her burgeoning wings beckoning him to fly, the cigarette's ember end the sun toward which they ascended, James Breach's pen-tendrils reaching, the arcing horizon to the east, the sun slipping past as they hurtled onward, over a sea where an octopus slipped into the abyss, and there the black-blue sky, I'm-sorry-I, a moon like a cauldron, double-double-toil-and-trouble, slipping into—

*

The world tasted like falling stars, like prophets' tea, like apocalypse soup. Nathaniel was running away from a wrecked car that he had used to flee a wrecked city, something evil on his tail. High in the sky, a wicked moon brewed and brewed. *Where am I going?* he thought, but the part of him that was inside the dream simply ran, with no specific destination in mind. *James is writing this scene simply to kill me,* he realized. Cackling sounds closed in. He picked out a pocket of trees on the side of the highway and barreled toward them. *No,* he thought, *bad idea,* but he wasn't in control. Inside the copse of trees, a clearing. He stopped there to rest. But there is no rest for the weary, and there they converged on him.

Members of the moonbringer cult.

The five facing him crackled with a strange kinetic power, a power derived from the witch's brew of a savage moon lording high above. They spread out and encircled him, exuding bloodlust. Making hand motions, they drew him in, spiders concocting a spur-of-the-moment web. He was in over his head. And then they had him—though with what he wasn't sure—he only knew that invisible forces were strangling him, burning his body, picking him up from the ground. He understood that he was a rag doll, an object of torture, allowed to exist in this world purely for their amusement.

Seconds passed. Maybe minutes. Perhaps hours. Pain wracked his body, but, in those moments when he wasn't in its grip, he could see the world around him with a startling lucidity. It was a world frayed at the edges, a world where the god of moons and the moonbringer cult had nearly solidified their control. Shadows swept through the skies, pouring purple-black into the firmament. Nathaniel would think "What?" only to have the word disassembled by another shot of agony. *Kill me and be done with it,* he pleaded to no one, but no one heard. Occasionally, riotous laughter from the moonbringers pierced the veil of pain. During one such interlude, he screamed for mercy. To his astonishment, it was granted.

He was lying on the ground. When he looked up, the hyena faces of the moonbringers had switched their attentions to something—or somethings—new. He followed their eyes. To Nathaniel's left: a damaged monster of a man, the ends of his limbs alight with flame. *I know him,* Nathaniel thought. But, try as he might, he couldn't recall the man's name. Whoever the man was, he appeared diminished, but also latent with an incredible power, like a collapsing star. The members of the moonbringer cult looked at the man with a strange and faltering reverence, like animals in a pack wondering if it was at last time to take down the alpha.

Nathaniel adjusted his gaze to the right. His heart stopped. It was her. Winter York, posing as Nova Norcross. She stood on a mossy clearing between two white oaks, wings unfurled in all their breathtaking glory.

She looked mythic. Powerful. Determined. *More Nova than Winter,* he thought, and underneath that thought he experienced the intuitive awareness that the Nova Norcross before him was the Nova Norcross of James Breach's imagination, made fully manifest.

"Why are you here?" the man asked Nova. His voice was humorless, threatening, and tinged with fear.

The five moonbringers stood back, ceding the moment to Nova Norcross.

"For the same reason as you," Nova responded. "The god of moons sent me." She looked eager. In the miasmic moonlight, Nathaniel noticed a gleaming at her throat. A crescent-moon pendant.

Monster man snorted. "This is a setup. The god of moons said he wants a sacrifice, but why is this dumb schmuck special? I don't even know who the fuck *this* guy is." He made a dismissive motion in Nathaniel's direction.

"Neither do I," Nova said without looking Nathaniel's way. "But the god of moons wants him dead." She smiled. "And since he sent the two of us to do the same job, what really matters is which one of fulfills his will." Her smile grew wider. "The other one, it would seem, is expendable."

Monster man snorted again. This snort made him look like a bull. His shoulders rippled with the vestiges of a diminished vitality. He looked angry, the way a cornered animal looks angry. "Fuck you, Nova. You think because you're wearing that necklace, the god of moons favors you?

You're one of us now. And among *us,* there's no one the god of moons favors more than *me.*"

She responded with a razor blade laugh. Then she began circling, left to right, her wings rising and falling with every step. "That's a lie you tell yourself because you can't accept what's changed. The god of moons favors me now. Not you."

The man erupted. "I'll destroy you the same as I destroyed your friends!"

Her eyes alit with mischief. She bared her teeth. "Time to find out."

And then they clashed. She: violent poetry, slicing through the air, sword gleaming. He: rough and tumble, ready, heady, rolling out of harm's way with fire in his fists. They were sizing each other up, Nathaniel realized, while also holding something in reserve. The dance progressed in a series of swift movements, until, in the tumult of a quick-fire tangle, both landed blows. She came away with scorched feathers on her right wing, while he came away smarting from a slash that left his torso bright red and gaping.

They paused to reassess. The moment lingered, until, like simultaneous lightning strikes, decisions were made. Lips moved: summoning, sorcery, incantations. The world turned a gloaming green as high above, the moon overheated with magic. They grew, both of them, not into giants but into magnified versions of their already fearsome selves, suffused with supernatural power.

In the foreground, an apparition. A laughing bald-headed man appeared, flipping a coin high into the air.

They crashed into each other as the coin crashed to earth. This time, high sorcery was involved. The man, standing firm, transformed into a raging pillar of fire; he looked poised to immolate anything he came into contact with. Nova, conversely, swooped down on the man at the forefront of a celestial army: multiple spirits joined her in flight, a cutting rush of figures, some masculine, some feminine, all intent on the flame. At the moment of contact, a strange sort of logjam occurred. From Nathaniel's vantage, it looked as if the spirits cut in front of Nova at the last moment, and, using their ephemeral powers, weakened the flame. *They're the spirits of Nova's former allies,* Nathaniel realized. Then, in an instant, it was over: Nova emerged from the inferno with her bloody sword held high in triumph, while, behind her, the pillar turned to blackened ash.

For a perfect second the pillar of ash wore a face. Recognition washed over Nathaniel like a flood. *Kol Jones, as Burden Monks.* The cinders scattered on the nighttime breeze like a flock of soot-black starlings, and Kol Jones was no more.

Nova stood still, relishing the aftermath. *It's an important moment in the series,* Nathaniel understood, but even so he couldn't help but question if the moment wasn't equally meaningful to Winter. A terrible thought dawned on him. *My God, all these years she's not only had to deal with James, but with that psycho too.* But now…Kol Jones was dead. Nathaniel couldn't even imagine the chain of events that had led to this moment. The drip-dripping of guilt intensified in his soul.

"It's you...It's really you." Nathaniel realized, to his surprise, that he was speaking. "Nova Norcross. The girl with wings. The moonbringers' bane. Please...please...save me."

She turned on him with a cold fury. "*Save* you? No. That's not why I'm here."

Nathaniel tried to find the Winter inside with his eyes. Nova Norcross was a moonbringer now, that was obvious, but Nathaniel couldn't help but hope that the Winter York he had fallen in love with would somehow recognize and rescue him from this nightmare. Her gaze fell on him in a hush. He thought he saw a distant look of recognition in her eyes, but it was difficult to know for sure.

The cackling recommenced, a moonbringers' symphony. Nathaniel could see that more moonbringers had arrived. In the eerie moonlight, they resembled a clamor of rooks.

"Why *are* you here?" the writer-god made Nathaniel ask.

She moved closer, taking precise, perfect steps, her body framed by her glorious wings.

"To prove my loyalty to the god of moons. First by killing Burden Monks. Then by killing you." She glanced up at the Sorcery Moon. "Sacrifices keep the savage moons alive."

He tried to shout his real name. Convince her of who he was. But when he opened his mouth, all that came out was, "You don't even know who I am."

She made a cutting motion with her sword. "I don't need to."

Nathaniel could feel the cold chill of death creeping up on him. *This is how it ends.* He attempted to turn his thoughts toward memories of his life in the waking world, but James Breach's magic was too strong: Nathaniel's entire existence narrowed to Nova Norcross and the instrument of death in her hand. He felt his will surrendering. *This is fitting. This is how it should end.* He tried to find Winter with his eyes. He wanted her to know that he didn't blame her. He wanted her to know that, if anything, he was thankful for the years she had given him. For the life that he had lived while she was trapped in this atemporal hell.

She met his gaze. He could tell that she knew who he was. James Breach's dreamscape, as powerful as it was, couldn't stop the outside world from bleeding in entirely. She tried to say something, but her lips were stayed by the author's hand. At last, she wrangled the words.

"The god of moons demands a proper sacrifice. Turn and face the moon."

Like a puppet, he turned. As he turned, he wondered if the words Nova Norcross had spoken were her own; he wondered, if in James Breach's dreamworld, there was such a thing as free will independent of the author. But even as his thoughts rambled, his eyes searched skyward, guided toward the moon by the author's hand.

Only: there were two moons to choose from. A noxious, bubbling, witch's brew of a moon. And a Shadow Moon, a figment encased in negative space.

Which one? he wondered, waiting on the author to direct his gaze.

After a moment of waiting, it seemed the choice was his own.

Behind him, he could hear Winter's sword sweeping through air, reaching backwards in preparation for the death blow.

Nathaniel closed his eyes around the Shadow Moon.

II

Winter awoke with a mournful word on her lips.

"Nathaniel."

Stray tears ran down her cheeks. She knew that she had killed Nathaniel, but the illogical circumstances surrounding his appearance in the *Savage Moon* dreamscape seemed dreamlike itself, a nesting doll of illusory horror. Where had he come from? How had James Breach found him? Surely it wasn't a coincidence that Nathaniel had appeared on the same night that she and James had orchestrated the death of Kol Jones? She bit the inside of her cheek, drawing blood. "Fuck you," she rage-murmured at the absent author.

More tears, salty and hot. She wiped her cheeks with the back of her hand. As pointless as it was, she couldn't help but replay the dream in her mind. There she was, fresh from victory, elated and relieved that Kol Jones/Burden Monks was at long last dead...but then, slowly turning, there Nathaniel stood, the only boy she had ever loved. But how? Where had James found him? Had he been holding Nathaniel in reserve all these years? She tried to follow the thread of her ignorance back to its source, but even in the deepest, darkest corners of her subconscious mind she found no trace of Nathaniel in her dealings with James. Nathaniel had been safe. Out of the picture. Her only connection to him was in her daydreams, those personal bastions where she stored the sacred moments of her life. A place where James couldn't hurt him. Until last night—

She punched the bed. Screamed. In the aftermath, her hyperventilating breath triggered the sensation of wings rising and falling on her back. Usually when she tried to recreate *Savage Moon* sensations in the waking world, she couldn't summon them, but this time the feeling was so real that she almost believed that if she reached over her shoulders, she would touch feathers. The feeling gave her a sense of vertigo. The *Savage Moon* universe and the real world were colliding, blending, amalgamating. In truth, this had been the case for some time, but now Winter no longer felt capable of keeping the overlapping realms distinct. Examples abounded. Kol Jones, left for dead on a dog park path. Burden Monks, battle-scarred but alive, bargaining with the god of moons. Winter, meeting in secret with James Breach, their needs oddly aligned. Winter's cousin, Rachel, standing amidst the moonbringers, calling the next day to say that she had had the strangest dream. The knowledge that Winter was being strung along in both worlds by a master manipulator. And last night...a sense of triumph when she ran Kol Jones/Burden Monks through with the sword, blood-ash dripping from the end of the blade, the lingering threat at long last erased; only to find herself moments later severing her long-lost love's head from his body, the deed done in the light of a ghastly, ghost-green moon.

It was James's sick way of sending me a message. His way of letting me know that even though Kol is dead, I'm not the one in control. Like she could ever forget. But for James to dredge back up Nathaniel, and force her to murder him? It was demented. It wasn't that she didn't think James capable of terrible evil, but in all the years since their reunion, the author's every move, no matter how wicked, had been rational, purposeful. But the only purpose she could see in James having her murder Nathaniel would be to break her spirit, or to send her spiraling into madness. And why would he want that now, when Kol Jones had at last been dealt with and the book series was so close to the end?

What does any masochist want? To see someone suffer.

She picked up the burner phone from the bedside table. The one James insisted she use to contact him, the one that would be switched out for a different burner phone before long. Through the fog of grief, she pulled up the text thread between her and James. Fingers flying, she unloaded a stream of raw invective.

You unredeemable, sociopathic, sick fuck. How could you? You swore to me that you would never hurt him. You swore. His safety was the only thing I ever asked of you, the only thing you ever promised me. You do what you think you have to do, but know this—

Winter's flying fingers were interrupted by the buzz of an incoming text. A message from James Breach appeared on the screen like a summoned specter. She startled, eyes blinking in surprise.

C. 11:00 a.m. Something's changed.

It was the *Something's changed* that threw Winter. James was a parsimonious texter, preferring to avoid subtext that hinted at reality. The extra words suggested that reality had intruded upon James's life in such a way that he had no choice but to allude to it. It also reflected a disassociation from the previous night's events that was jarring even for James.

She considered what she had typed. Thought better of it. Her thumb locked onto the backspace, erasing everything.

I'll wait till 11:00, she thought. *I'll wait until I see James. Then I'll, I'll...*

Winter's train of thought surrendered to the avalanche of her grief. She sat on the corner of her bed and cried.

*

C was, for lack of a better descriptor, one of Winter's favorite places to meet James. An antiques market called The Depot, the space was sufficiently large that there was enough space to carry on a private conversation, but no so large that James could pretend that his behavior would go unnoticed. Their usual spot was in a booth where wicker chairs were sold, in the market's southwest corner. Shelves filled with knickknacks and ceramic dishware lined the stall. On the wall in the center of the shelving, a rustic Coca-Cola sign looped its way to meaning, becoming, in its formation, nostalgic capitalism.

James was rocking on one of the chairs when Winter arrived. To her disgust, he was wearing a trilby, the same pretentious affectation preferred by the god of moons. She steeled her mind as she approached. *Don't give yourself away. Be patient.* Inside, she was a tempest of emotions, primed to explode, but she knew from past experience that acting on murderous rage only strengthened the author's hand. Furthermore, something about her understanding of what had occurred last night was incomplete. She needed to let James talk. She needed to give him the opportunity to tell her what had happened.

He stopped rocking when he saw her approaching. Graced her with a god's-honest, genuine smile. Then, standing, he removed the trilby from his head, and gave Winter a brief flourish of a bow.

"My muse. You were magnificent last night. An avenging angel to make other avenging angels jealous. I stand, as always, in awe."

She ground her back teeth in lieu of responding. All morning she had been grieving the loss of Nathaniel, but, for a brief moment, her present sorrow was spliced with previous pains: the losses of Jessalyn, Obadiah, and Kennedy Marks. *And who do I have in my tally? Kol Jones.* But Kol Jones had been a win for James in the end too, hadn't he? *Every death is a win for James. He's killed Nathaniel, and pretty soon he'll kill me, and then, at long last, my nightmare will be over.*

James continued, "Oh, what a night! What a night!" The author's eyes were alit with joy. "One problem solved, and another one…illuminated. That's the only word for it, isn't it? All these years, never knowing where the inspiration came from, never knowing where it went, and then, as if in a dream, it reappears!"

Winter was confused. "What reappeared?"

"The Shadow Moon, of course! Did it not look different to you? It has seemed flat to me for so long, a shadow of a shadow…but last night! Last night it illuminated again, the same way it did all those years ago when you first came back to me! And now I see the series laid out before me like a dream."

Winter wondered if she was hearing James correctly. "The Shadow Moon?"

"Yes! The Shadow Moon! It has something to do with you. I can't quite put my finger on what the connection is, but it doesn't matter, I've got the feeling, I've got the thread, all I need to do now is write, write, write! And with you, my muse, guiding the way...victory is in grasp!"

The Shadow Moon? Winter let herself slip back into the dream, back into the pain, back into the moment when Nova Norcross's sword parted Nathaniel Pilot's head from his body, and...yes...she had looked up, into the sky, her eyes drawn to that secondary celestial body, that figment, that orb encased in negative space—

She gasped.

James looked at her like a predator becoming aware of movement in the bushes. "You know what the connection is, don't you?"

She didn't respond. Her thoughts were spinning. She thought she knew what the connection was, but she had no idea what it entailed—she didn't even know if it meant that Nathaniel was alive. What she suspected was that James had subconsciously connected Nathaniel to Nathaniel's moon tattoo without realizing that he had done so, and that somehow, someway, James had come back into contact with Nathaniel without understanding who he was, or what his connection was to the Shadow Moon. At least that's what her intuition told her, though of course she might be wrong; it was conjecture, after all, and—

"Nova. Tell me."

She gave him a look of the purest hate. His willingness to call her by that name, to be so indifferent of her personhood that he would choose to address her as Nova even when he wanted something from her...it spoke to the deep rot at the core of their relationship, and she wouldn't indulge it.

He considered her silence. When at last he spoke, he sounded plaintive, and earnest. "I wish you could yourself as I see you. I wish you could bear witness to Nova Norcross's transcendent glory night after night, and then, in the light of day, encounter the sad and angry Winter York, the version of yourself that you claim to prefer. I wish I could give you the gift of accepting life as it is. Of accepting the wonder that is Nova Norcross."

Winter spat her reply through gritted teeth. "Nova Norcross isn't real."

"Really? Is that what you think? My dear, Nova Norcross lives in the minds of millions of readers. She is known all over the world! Whereas Winter York...well, you know as well as I do that Winter York lives a life of the loneliest solitude, trapped in an existence where every friendship she makes ultimately turns to ash. So tell me...who is more real, in truth? Nova? Or Winter?"

When Winter didn't respond, James took the liberty of interpreting her expression.

"Suit yourself. Be Winter. Only be careful where Winter leads you. You've already ventured down that path once. I trust you won't go there again."

He had her there. From the moment she had pulled the trigger of the 9mm and watched Kol Jones fall to the forest floor, she had known that she couldn't resort to real-world violence without losing her soul. In the tense bargaining sessions that brought her and James back together as they tried to deal with the fallout from Kol's shooting and subsequent stunted survival, this had been the principal point: their battles, going forward, would be fought in the *Savage Moon* universe, a realm where, James occasionally reminded her, she had nearly bested him. She didn't trust that James would uphold his end of the bargain, but, as had been the case for Winter's entire adult life, she had to use whatever tools were at her disposal to gain leverage in her relationship with the author. He still held the upper hand, of course. But then again, he always had.

"Do I look like I'm on the verge of shooting you in a public place?"

He manufactured an at-ease grin. "No. You do not. And for your sake, I hope you never do."

A restive silence fell over the matter. She knew that James had taken measures to protect himself since the incident with Kol; she assumed that he had a concealed weapon on him now. Winter, of course, was the wild card. She had resorted to desperate measures once, and, so long as she was trapped in the *Savage Moon* world, there was no guarantee that she would not do so again.

James adjusted the trilby, looking like an actor in a period piece toying with his costume in-between takes. "I fear we've ventured off track. Your connection to the Shadow Moon. Tell me what it is."

She studied him. Did he truly not know? Or was he manipulating her for his own sick gratification, knowing damn well that Nathaniel Pilot was the connection? During their time together she had taken the measure of him a million times. Enough that she felt she could trust her instincts.

And her instincts told her that his ignorance was sincere.

"I think that the Shadow Moon is connected to Nova Norcross's sense of power."

Winter did not know where the lie had come from, only that it felt inspired the instant she spoke it into existence.

James studied her. "Go on."

"Years ago, when you wrote Nova Norcross back into being for the first time since college, I felt a surge of power. It was"—she tried to look shamefaced—"thrilling. To be Nova again. To be powerful again." She paused. Took a deep breath. Tried to set the stage for a convincing lie. "During that time, I was obsessed with the moon. I wanted, after my earlier experience in the *Savage Moon* world, to make the moon my own. I was entranced by its powers. By its connection to the divine feminine. When I reentered your world, I brought that connection with me. I've long hypothesized that the Shadow Moon is a moon of my own making. A moon to rival yours."

She loved the solidity of the lie. The way it filled Nathaniel's empty space like cement pouring into cracks.

James brought a finger to his bottom lip. After a moment he brought that same finger forward, an interrogative gesture. "Then why did the Shadow Moon fade one week after you returned?"

She gave James an icy glare. "Why do you think, James? You've taken everything from me. The moon went with the rest."

"What was different about last night?"

"Last night, you gave me my power back. Winter's power, not Nova's. Because of that, Kol Jones is gone. And the Shadow Moon shines once more."

The author's finger backtracked to his chin. A smile like a quartered apple formed on his face. "You've never mentioned this to me before. And unlike the ivy spiraling up your neck, there is no subliminal symbol connected to you to key me in to the Shadow Moon's existence." His eyes searched up and to the left, signaling that he was scouring the far corners of his brain. "For something in my writing life to come alive, I have to *touch* it. Or at least be aware of it. That's always been the case. I can't think of a single exception."

The perfect response flew like an arrow from Winter's tongue. "Your subconscious mind remembers all sorts of things that your conscious mind misses, James. I thought we had established that with the ivy."

James looked both unsettled and peeved. "I was aware of your ivy tattoo."

She gave him a dark, ironically sweet grin, making sure to keep the new secrets free from her face. "Were you? There was a moment by the roadside when it didn't seem that way."

A plague of doubt spread across the author's face. What Winter wouldn't have given to have seen James in his writing chair on that fateful day. Had he been in a fugue-like state when he wrote the scene? Had his fingers struggled to find the keyboard as the life force fled from his body? When he had called down the thunder and lightning, had that been the desperate act of a dying man-god?

217

How close, exactly, had she come to killing him?

James's face flickered with a sort of angry admiration. "A moment, yes. No doubt it was gratifying for you. I've experienced a million such similar moments. Moments when I've held your life in the palm of my hand and thought: Should I end it now?"

They held each other like combative lovers in the space of the ensuing silence. Seconds collapsed like dying stars. She tried to help him see the vision in her mind's-eye, the one of the moon god gasping for air as shoots of ivy wrapped around his throat.

All at once James stopped staring at her, and the tension shattered like glass. "But let's not ruin an otherwise glorious day," he said, looking away. "Back to the subject of the Shadow Moon. Let's say, for the moment, that I choose to believe you. Let's say, for the moment, that the Shadow Moon is a gift you've given me. Do you intend on taking it back?"

Keep playing the game. "I...I don't know if that's possible," Winter answered honestly. "Have I always believed that the Shadow Moon was connected to my sense of power in the *Savage Moon* universe? Yes. Do I know that for a fact? No. But if the Shadow Moon is as important to the series as you say it is, I would advise that you refrain from doing anything that would jeopardize Nova Norcross's—and, of course, Winter York's—well-being. Otherwise, the Shadow Moon might go"—she snapped her fingers—"poof."

James's gears were grinding. He wore the expression of a dead-eyed sea creature searching for the weak spot on a crustacean's carapace. "My, isn't your reasoning convenient?" He tilted his head in thought. "It's surprising, isn't it, that the Shadow Moon shone for a week all those years ago, when you murdered your octopus friend the first day that I touched you? It seems that your newfound sense of power would have dissipated then."

Obadiah. Winter choked down her rising anger, and focused instead on the flashbang explanation that formed in her mind. "Maybe that's where your touch factors in. The weeklong time period is how long you channel whatever you've intuited about a person after you've touched them. The Shadow Moon didn't go away for a week because you didn't touch me until a week later."

"That's logical," James answered. He arched his eyebrows. "Since I saw you yesterday, I suppose that means I have at least six days of the Shadow Moon remaining."

Inspiration struck. Winter shot out her hand, grazing James's wrist. He jerked back from her in alarm. She laughed out loud in wicked delight. It felt good, after all these years, to flip the tables on him. "I suppose that depends on how well this conversation went." The author scowled. Winter continued laughing. "Careful, James. Don't upset your golden goose."

James composed himself under the guise of a grin. "Let's hope that you're right, and the Shadow Moon shows up again tonight. If not, who knows what a blocked writer might do?" Happy to have had the last word, the author reached up and adjusted the smoke-gray trilby, turned on his heels, and walked away.

Winter took an oceanic breath. The depth and breadth of her on-the-spot lies shocked her. It had been a solid performance, imbued with the perfect amount of doubt to make it believable. Winter worried, however, that no matter how convinced James had seemed, he harbored theories he hadn't divulged. *He remembered Obadiah from all those years ago. Surely, he remembers Nathaniel too?* Perhaps somewhere in James's unshared thoughts he *had* drawn the connection to Nathaniel. Perhaps—and this was the most disturbing possibility of all—James already knew that Nathaniel was the connection to the Shadow Moon, and he was toying with Winter for his own wicked amusement.

But there was nothing to be done about her worries. What Winter needed to do now was act. And act quickly. If Nathaniel was indeed still alive, she needed to confirm it for herself. At the current moment, he existed in a Schrodingerian space. There was no going forward until she could either grieve his death properly, or—and this possibility made her feel faint with its potentialities—she found him and decided what to do with the knowledge that he was the Shadow Moon.

*

The neighborhood, Winding Woods, was tucked behind a strip mall, existing in one of those surreal enclaves that characterize the outer reaches of the Queen City, odd little worlds where middle-aged developments combat the helter-skelter unpredictability of urban sprawl. *Woods* was an imprecise moniker; the twisting streets were lined with Bradford pears, and a skinny circle of aged oaks and poplars enclosed the community in a sylvan embrace, but that was the extent of the neighborhood's arboreality. The house Nathaniel purportedly lived in, 7112 Rosewater Lane, sat on one of the few straight-arrow stretches of the neighborhood. Winter parked a few houses down facing Nathaniel's, concealing her car in the meager shade of a Bradford pear. Then she tried to decide what to do.

Finding where Nathaniel lived had been surprisingly simple. An online search of Nathaniel's name led Winter to a website where she paid a small fee to unlock a wealth of information on every Nathaniel Pilot who lived within a two-hundred-square-mile area. Her Nathaniel jumped to the front. A couple of quick social media stops confirmed that she had her man. Nothing on Nathaniel's handful of social media accounts suggested that he had died within the past twenty-four hours. And now that she was sitting outside of the home address that she had procured from the website, she instinctively knew that she was in the right place. It was like she was visiting the alternate universe that she had envisioned for Nathaniel when she helped him escape the clutches of James Breach years ago.

She wasn't there for long before a woman emerged from the house. Winter immediately recognized the woman from Nathaniel's Facebook photos. Angelica. A strange jumble of emotions roiled Winter's insides as, for the second time that day, she noted that Angelica looked nothing like her. If Winter's looks reflected the aesthetic of her name, Angelica's resembled a blazing summer day. Angelica's hair was an eruption from a golden volcano, and she was volleyball-player tall, a fact reinforced by the way she strode to the mailbox with an athletic grace. Seeing Angelica,

221

Winter had the impression of watching a bizzaro-world version of herself, living the life that Winter might have led. Winter laughed at the thought, a bitter little chortle. The laugh settled something in her. Calmed her down. A thought popped into her head, seemingly put there by a shoulder-sitting angel.

Do you mean to steal from her the peace you never had?

Winter brushed aside the imagined cherub, and tried to focus on the evidence presented by the here and now. It was tough to know for certain from watching a woman walk to the mailbox, but, to Winter's eyes, Angelica didn't look like a woman whose husband had died the previous night. But seeing wasn't the same as knowing. And, coming this far, Winter had to know.

You're not taking anything from her. And you don't owe her anything. You don't owe HIM anything. In fact, he owes you. For the life you've given him. So do it. Approach the house. Ask to see Nathaniel. Say that you're an old friend. It's true, isn't it? And if he's home, let him decide what happens next. He'll understand. How couldn't he?

She reached for the Hyundai's door handle, her heart pounding like a big bass drum. Stepped outside. The wind was kicking down the street like a playful donkey. She started toward Nathaniel's home, but after only a couple of steps she heard the distinctive whirring of a garage door climbing its mechanical mountain. Glancing up, she saw that the opening garage door belonged to 7112 Rosewater Lane. She stopped in her tracks.

Nathaniel stepped outside the garage. Still alive. He gathered his wife, who was returning from her trip to the mailbox, in a too-tender embrace, an embrace that intimated his awareness of how close he had come to death in the last twenty-four hours, an embrace that implied his understanding that he was not out of the woods. Angelica hugged him back, but Winter thought that she looked confused. The impression was reinforced when Angelica pulled back from Nathaniel and looked at him like she was trying to make sense of his actions. Words were exchanged. Then they hugged again, once more—he with a little less tender affection, she with a little more—and let go.

Watching them filled Winter with discomfort. It was too much an invasion of privacy, an invasion of the real. *He's alive. He's fine. It's enough to know. Now leave him alone.* Although Winter knew it was guilt-stricken-panic speaking, she listened. High overhead, a hawk *ki*-yed, breaking Winter from her trance, stirring her to move. Within seconds she was back in the Hyundai, turning over the engine, pressing the accelerator, keeping her eyes straight ahead, her eyes straight ahead…

Until she passed the house. Weakness made her glance at the man standing in the middle of the driveway.

They caught each other's eyes.

*

She sped away crying. Needing a distraction, she turned on the car stereo. The Avett Brothers CD in the player she found wanting. She switched it out for Lorde, the soundtrack to her *Savage Moon* sadness. She skipped ahead to track four, "Ribs," a nesting doll of a song, "Lover's Spit" aching on the inside. Somewhere in the intersection of Lorde's musical melancholy she recaptured a sense of the place and time where she and Nathaniel had momentarily existed.

A shining light on the dashboard demanded her attention: the universal tank and nozzle. Ahead, she saw a gas station. She pulled into the BP and turned down the volume on the stereo, a humdrum sequence that shifted her disposition to the here and now. Glancing at the rearview mirror, she saw a blue Mazda 2 pull in behind her. The glance was reflexive, nothing more. She coasted to a stop at tank #5. "Ribs" faded to nothing. "Buzzcut Season" burgeoned. She turned off the ignition. Stepped outside.

Unscrewing the gas cap, her eyes caught the blue Mazda parked in front of the store. Her gaze slid to the man standing beside the driver's door, staring at her.

Nathaniel.

III

Death was desperately wanting to say good-bye, only to find the god damning you to die disobliging. Death was the hot bite of cold steel. Death was the distance from the moon to the earth. Death was the waiting. The wondering.

Life was waking in your own bed. Nathaniel immediately brought his hand to his neck, searching for the cut, trying to remember the pain. But even at the moment of his death the pain had been faint, a burn over and gone in an instant, exchanged for a satellite existence. Now it was even less.

"You slept like a corpse."

Angelica was standing over him, dressed. Downstairs, cartoons blared out a symphony of juvenilia.

"Hey...um...I..." Tears welled in his eyes. He looked up at Angelica. In the emotion of waking to find himself alive, he had forgotten how to talk to his wife.

She looked at him with perspective anew. "What's wrong? Are you okay?"

"Um..." He sat up. Took a deep breath. His freshly awake vulnerability tempted him to tell her everything, but with every passing second the reality of what that conversation would be like solidified in his mind. His tears dried. "I had a dream. A...nightmare. It was really vivid." He forced out a little laugh. "I haven't had one that intense in a long time."

"What was it about?"

Nathaniel smiled. Angelica's customary bluntness was another reminder that he was back in the real word. "It doesn't matter. I'm just glad that I'm awake." He reached up and held her hand. "And that I have you."

She returned his smile, but her expression was more confused than caring. "All right." Suspicion suddenly colored her face. *She's remembering last night. She's curious if my dream was connected to what happened in the restaurant.* For a moment she looked as if she was going to ask him, but, at the last second, she changed her mind. "So… I'm going to get a move on with the day. You take all the time you need."

He waited until she had left, and then he collapsed on the mattress, his mind racing to retrieve the dream. It wasn't difficult. A *Savage Moon* dream was like a regular dream on steroids. The dream scenes were burned into the retina of his mind's-eye. Remembering, it turned out, was as simple as looking. Surprisingly, he found himself fast-forwarding past the trauma with Winter to his time as the moon. *The Shadow Moon,* he corrected himself. Nathaniel had long assumed that he was the link to the series's most conspicuous loose thread, but there was a difference between assuming and knowing. *James Breach has been searching for me all this time. The question is…does he know that I'm the connection?* It was impossible to tell from the dream. Like eleven years before, dreaming as the Shadow Moon was like dreaming from a pristine, crystal-clear remove. Except…for the pull. Eleven years earlier, he had come to life as an idea, with no direction. Now, his creator had a pressing question.

What is your purpose?

*

He stumbled through the morning, hampered by the heavy fog of distraction. For years he had followed the progress of James Breach's *Savage Moon* series, trying to stay knowledgeable enough to know the general arc without falling down the rabbit hole of obsession. Once or twice he had dipped his toes too far into the water, only to emerge hours later at the other end of a marathon internet session, his thoughts hopelessly and helplessly trying to connect the girl he had once known to the thousands of internet fan theories that populated the virtual world, but in the end he always pulled back to find himself keeping tabs at a middle distance, informed enough to know about the rumors surrounding the series, but not so enmeshed that he lost days worrying about Winter.

But now that he was back in the *Savage Moon* universe, now that he was certain that the Shadow Moon was integral to the end, he couldn't help but grasp at everything he didn't understand.

As the day moved along, the mental flailing wore on him. That and Isabelle's *please-daddy* demands; that and Angelica's ever-perceptive eyes. *What's the point in thinking about it? There's nothing I can do. For myself or Winter.* He supposed that the most likely scenario was that this week would be much like the one eleven years ago: he would experience dream after dream sitting suspended in the sky, while James Breach wrote the *Savage Moon* world around him. Beyond that, it was out of his control.

In the meantime, he had a flesh and blood family to take care of.

By the early afternoon, he had resolved to treat the coming week like any other. At the end of it, he would either be alive or dead, but he wouldn't be insane from the worrying of it. As far as his thoughts on Winter were concerned, she had managed without his assistance for the last decade-plus, and, as he didn't have the first clue how he might intervene to help her, that was how it would remain. He had rescued Ariel from the clutches of James Breach because he had known how to do so. Rescuing Winter was, as it had always been, beyond him.

He thought it important to let Angelica know that he was not wrapped up in the *Savage Moon* world. Not by telling her, of course, but by looking at her, touching her, communicating via the unspoken that he was here, and present. The impulse came on him suddenly: he abandoned a midafternoon snack of salted peanuts to follow his wife outside, where she had gone to check the mail. The garage being the closest route to the dining room, he took it, and caught his wife up in an embrace halfway down the drive.

She felt like home in his arms. "Hey."

"Hey right back at you." Angelica wasn't one for pointless worrying, but the faint lines on her forehead suggested that his preciousness concerned her. "What's this all about?"

"Nothing. I'm glad that you're my wife. I'm glad that we have each other. That we share a life together. That's all."

She pulled back and looked at him. "Same as yesterday, same as today, same as tomorrow."

He couldn't think of the right response, so he smiled. The smile melted into another hug, only this time the intensity was on Angelica's end. "Is Isabelle still asleep?" she asked when they separated. Nathaniel could tell that she was still concerned, but also ready to move on from whatever was bothering him.

"I think so. Yeah."

"All right." She gave his arm a quick caress. "I'm going back inside to check."

A car was driving down their street. Small, white, civic-minded. Angelica brushed past him, returning to their day-to-day life, but Nathaniel paused, drawn to the car. Watching it roll toward him, he had the impression that he was recalling the forgotten tail end of a dream.

A woman was at the wheel. She looked at Nathaniel. Her face asked a decade-plus-old question.

Time collapsed into the present.

The car drove past.

He didn't know how he knew that it was Winter. He only knew that he did.

He rushed back inside the house and grabbed the car keys from the key bowl. "I'll be back. I need to run a quick errand," he shouted into the house.

Angelica's "okay" sent him out the door.

*

Seeing Winter emerge from the car at the gas station made Nathaniel think of a falling star. Usually, she existed for him as a celestial body hanging from the heavens, bright but stationary, too distant to truly be known. But all at once she was burning across the frame. He watched her approach with a reverent awe. Her hair, still cosmic black, looked like a waterfall poured from the night sky. She wore faded denim and a simple black scoop-neck shirt. He expected her expression to be hard, unforgiving, keeping with the theme of the woman who had told him *Don't. Ever. Fucking. Contact. Me. Again.* (and had more recently given him the brush-off at Trader Joe's). But, to his surprise, she wore liquid diamonds in her eyes, and a look on her face that could only be described as grateful.

"You're alive. I—" She paused. For a moment she looked like she had gotten ahead of herself, and had only now remembered her role; but then something in her broke, some dam of restraint, and she hugged him.

He hugged her back. The BP parking lot transformed into a sacred space, as a decade's worth of unspoken words, thoughts, and repressed worries found release.

They separated. Stared at each other. He thought that she looked like Winter; meaning both the girl he had once known and the season. He had always believed that winter's beauty deepened further into the season, when the memory of fall and the promise of spring were stripped away and there was nothing to do but accept the day-in, day-out reality of what winter entailed. This was what he thought when he looked at her: that the embattled woman before him was a wonder to behold, and, as much as he wished he might have spared her the pain of the last eleven years, it contributed to her spellbinding presence.

"I'm sorry. For everything that you've been through." He looked down. "I'm sure I don't know the half of it."

She sniffled. Wiped away a tear. "It's been a lot," she admitted. "And then, last night, when you appeared in the dream, when he made me…" Her face burned with a sudden rage. "I thought you were dead. I was sure of it." A distant-satellite smile found its way to her face. "But you're not. You're okay. At least…for today."

Her concern moved him. "You came to my house. You found where I live." He meant it as a statement of gratitude, of wonder, but she misinterpreted him.

"I didn't mean for you to see me. You have a life, a family, a…a wife. The last thing I would ever want to do is disturb that." Her face flash-fried with guilt. "But I had to know for sure. I had to see you with my own eyes."

"It's okay." He grinned in spite of himself. "If it makes you feel better, I thought I was dead too."

She pinned him with her striated-green eyes. "But you're not. Because you're the—"

"—Shadow Moon," they said together.

Like a wind sweeping in a new weather front, the words *Shadow Moon* changed the conversation. She continued holding him with her stare, looking, strangely, both intense and off-balance. "Do you dream as the Shadow Moon?"

"Yes."

Winter gave her lip a short-lived bite. Her eyes jumped to the pondering realm for a second, only to quickly return and lay claim to Nathaniel's own. "Show it to me."

He knew exactly what she wanted to see.

Nathaniel rolled up his sleeve. With her fingertip, Winter traced the inky, blue-black curve that gave the moon its shape. Her closeness caused him to break off eye contact, but his gaze resettled on her neck, where he saw the ivy tattoo twisting around the trellis of her spine. It enthralled him the same way it had eleven years ago. The thought crossed his mind that something about it had changed, although, for the life of him, he couldn't discern what it was.

"When did James run into you? And what happened?" Winter asked, withdrawing her hand.

"Last night. We were at a restaurant in NoDa. James was there, and before I knew what was happening, my brother's fiancée recognized him and walked over to introduce herself. I had to intervene. James didn't respond kindly when I stopped him from laying a hand on her. In the ensuing exchange, he made sure to lay a hand on me. I was certain I was a dead man." Nathaniel took a deep breath. "And... I don't know... I guess a part of me felt like it was just comeuppance. I told myself I would stay awake for the entire week if need be. But then, when I lay down, I couldn't...or didn't...fight it. I fell right to sleep."

Winter looked unsurprised. "Don't beat yourself up. It's tougher than it seems. I stopped fighting it a long time ago."

The memory of last night's somnolent undertow returned. Nathaniel had supposed that he had simply surrendered, but now, looking back, he saw how larger forces might have been at play. He continued, "And then I was dreaming, and everything that happened...happened. When it seemed that you...or Nova, I mean...meant to kill me"—the look of guilt on Winter's face was genuine, and heartbreaking—"I looked up at the Shadow Moon. And then"—he snapped his fingers—"just like that, I *was* the Shadow Moon."

She nodded. Eyes glistening. "Did the experience feel the same as it did last time?"

He thought back. "Yes and no. Last time it didn't happen in an instant, and it didn't happen the first night. It wasn't until you and I were...separated...that James dreamed me to life as the Shadow Moon."

"What is it like? Being the Shadow Moon?"

"It's..." He found himself grasping for the words. "...I'm not really sure how to describe it. It's like I'm part of the Savage Moon universe, but at a remove. It's like I'm whole, but not fully formed. It's like..." the right words came to him, "...it's like James Breach still hasn't decided what he wants to do with me."

Winter's eyes clouded with worry. "I met with James today. This morning. All he could talk about was the Shadow Moon, and how he felt like it was the key to the series. He was so excited that he cut me off before I could rage at him. I was upset...I couldn't believe that he had found you, that he had had me kill you. But then, when he started talking, it dawned on me that he hadn't made the connection." She shook her head. "In truth, I barely made the connection myself. The Shadow Moon had been dormant for so long, it wasn't until James started talking about it that I realized it was connected to your reappearance. That was when it dawned on me that there was a chance James didn't know who you were. That was when it dawned on me that there as a chance that you might still be alive."

She exhaled. When she spoke again, her voice was quieter. "This is all conjecture, of course. He might know exactly who you are. He could be stringing us both along." Her expression searched his. "What do you think? Do you think he recognized you?"

"I don't think so. But once he has time to reflect? Who knows?"

Out on the road, a driving dispute roused hands to car horns. The sound caused a bubble to pop: all at once the myriad noises of the workaday existence came rushing back in. *What am I doing here?* Nathaniel thought, glancing at the gas station's come-and-go clientele. He stole a look at Winter. She was looking at the ground, her eyes darting like minnows. *How could I possibly help her?*

"When you fall asleep tonight, you should reach for the god of moons."

Nathaniel's body fired off an electric shock. She had provided the answer to his unspoken question. "Reach for him? What do you mean? How?"

The look Winter gave him was level. Stone-cold sober. Nova Norcross intense. "It's possible to act on James's subconscious. Especially if he writes you into the book as something other than yourself. I know it from personal experience. There was a time when James kept writing scenes with ivy into the books, because of my ivy tattoo. Every time he included ivy in the book, I was the one in control. Or at least it felt that way. If he honestly doesn't know that you're the inspiration for the Shadow Moon, your power in the dreamworld might be...immeasurable."

Nathaniel's eyes grew wide. "You're talking about the scene in *Lightning Moon* where Nova nearly strangles the god of moons to death with ivy. You think James almost died when he was writing that scene?"

Winter pursed her lips. Dark secrets troubled her eyes. "Maybe. It felt to me like he was dying in the dream. And then, afterward, our relationship changed. It became...heightened...somehow." A scarlet shadow of shame crossed her face. "He was unnerved by what had occurred, but, in all honesty, I think he was inspired by it too. He saw the character of Nova differently after that. Everything since has been building to what you saw last night."

"The death of Kol Jones? Or you as a"—he gave an involuntary swallow—"bad guy?"

Once the words were out, Nathaniel realized he had referred to Kol Jones by his real name, and not by his *Savage Moon* character name, Burden Monks. Winter's distant stare told him what he already assumed: it didn't matter. Both *Kol* and *Burden* were dead. "All of it." She looked lost all of a sudden, adrift on a sea of internal emotions. "I'm sorry. This is difficult for me. You and I have this connection, but in truth, I don't really...know you." Her expression apologized for the cut. "That's not to say that I haven't held the memory of you close, but..." She faltered.

Nathaniel reached a hand toward Winter but didn't quite touch her. "It's okay. Really. I get it. You don't owe me anything." He hesitated. "I'm the one who owes you."

There it was. The heart of the matter. He watched as Winter weighed his words like Anubis, measuring them against the feather of truth. He was tempted to double down, to restate, to insist, but when he revisited the words, a sudden vertigo overtook him, and he kept quiet. The relative charm of his everyday existence suddenly stood in bright contrast to Winter's blighted existence, and he couldn't help but wish for a return to—how had Winter put it?—his life, his family, his wife. He glanced at Winter and saw from her stare that she was testing him. *Go ahead,* her eyes challenged him. *Take it back.* She almost looked like she wanted him to.

But he held his tongue. He was here. He had said what he had wanted to say for eleven years. And now that he had said it, he was going to keep his word.

She accepted his silence. "If James realizes that you are the Shadow Moon, it could mean your death." A pause. "You know what happened to Obadiah."

The inflection of Winter's voice implied a statement, not a question. Nathaniel nodded.

Winter looked away. "Kelly Anne told me that you stopped by the shop after Obadiah died. So, you know that when James connects a tattoo to a person, he can use that knowledge to kill them." She focused in on him again. "If James knows or figures out that you are the Shadow Moon, there is nothing I can do to protect you."

He replayed in his mind what it was like to be the Shadow Moon. The latent power was enormous. The thought of turning it against James, or having James turn it against him, frightened him.

But it didn't change his mind. "I owe you. And you need me." He tried to make a joke. "Going our separate ways clearly didn't work. Let me help you finish this. Let me help you escape…him."

To Nathaniel's surprise, Winter's expression turned unspeakably sad. But a resolute smile quickly took its place. "Okay. We'll try." She gathered herself. "First steps first. Tonight, when you become the Shadow Moon, reach out to the god of moons and see if you can influence his actions. See if you can bind him to your will."

He didn't know exactly what she was asking of him, but he nodded his head with a fervor. When at last his chin stilled, he was left staring at her in the space of an ill-defined quiet, a quiet tied to the tenuous, temporal present. It was a moment, Nathaniel knew, that would soon go up in smoke; a moment that, in its remembering, would take on a weight far greater than what the present's glass-fragile equilibrium was able to bear. Words like *I wanted* and *If only* and *I've always loved you* tugged at his lips, but they were all wrong. *This is it,* he realized. *This is all we get.* Winter fashioned a soft, melancholic smile for him, a smile stitched out of all the words that could not be said. He made one for her in turn.

"I'm going to give you my number," she said, breaking the spell. "After tonight, once you've tested yourself against him in the dream, you can call me. If you want. If you don't, I'll understand." She listed ten digits starting with 704. He punched them into his phone under the contact initials W.Y. "I'm asking too much of you," she said, almost as an afterthought.

"No," Nathaniel replied. "The problem is that you haven't asked enough."

She gave her head a small shake. "You can't say that. You don't know." Her gaze returned to the cosmos of her inner thoughts. "Saving you was one of the best things I ever did."

He thought that she was on the verge of saying more, but when he opened his mouth to respond, the right words wouldn't come.

She laid a fleeting hand on his wrist. "Go," she said. "Go home.

"We'll see each other in our dreams."

*

The remainder of the day sped by. Nathaniel went through the motions at home. When the sun went down, Nathaniel prepared for battle, imagining, in his mind, how he would wake in the dream as the Shadow Moon and bring the Savage Moon universe to heel. Perhaps it was adrenaline, but he felt almost numb to the fear. By all rights he should have died the previous night. But he hadn't, and now the opportunity to flip the tables on James Breach outweighed any trepidation he felt. *I am the Shadow Moon. I am the Shadow Moon,* he repeated to himself over and over again.

The day collapsed into night.

Once in bed, sleep came like a carnivore, devouring him. On the opposite end of the gullet, he sat sterling in the sky, perfectly formed and positively pointless. *What am I?* he wondered, considering, for the first time during his incarnation as the Shadow Moon, the nature of his existence. Outwardly, all was the same as it had been the previous night. Below was the Earth, and bedlam: the moonbringer cult propagated chaos in all four corners of the globe, and Nova Norcross, formerly the cult's most formidable adversary, now flew at its helm. Next to the Shadow Moon and higher in the firmament was a noxious brew of a moon, the savage incarnation of the moment, colored green, purple, and black, and redolent of magic. And last was himself. When he tried to turn his vision inward, he found it impossible. He only had the sense that he was half-formed. Incomplete.

He focused on staying in a meditative state. Trying to see the dream within the dream. *Winter told you to reach for the god of moons,* he remembered, but, now that he was here, it didn't seem like the most pressing issue. What good would it do to communicate with the god of moons if he had nothing to share with him? He stayed within his dream self, the *he* he could not see, until, in a burst of insight and self-actualization, Nathaniel understood his purpose.

And with that understanding, he materialized.

His form filled the sky. He was a spheroid, light and bright, cut from the cloth of the darkness surrounding him. What color there was on his surface gave him form without giving him excessive definition. And like a shadow is darkness in the daytime light, he was light in the darkness, coasting across the sky.

As if summoned, the god of moons appeared. Or was it James Breach? The being/character/person simultaneously hovered in the sky and in

Nathaniel's shadow-moon mind. The instant the god of moons was present, Nathaniel was overwhelmed by the tension humming between the two of them, like electricity crackling on the wire. *Reach for him,* Nathaniel told himself, but the thought was ridiculous, because the connection between them was already like a current.

Why did you return? the god of moons asked.

Nathaniel held nothing back. He knew what his purpose was, and he shared it fully.

The god of moons smiled. It was a hellish scimitar of a smile; a smile made for monsters; a smile that was like a lung-emptying squeeze. Then the god of moons's smile ballooned into an open mouth large enough to swallow the Shadow Moon whole. For a second it seemed to Nathaniel that the god of moons would do just that. But instead, words tumbled out, like demons from the gates of hell.

IV

Winter awoke feeling cold with evil.

Slowly, lethargically, she rolled over and released the bedside window shade. Outside, the morning sun was stretching into day. *I should go for a run,* she told herself, but instead she rolled back over and pulled the covers up tight around her chin. For years, Winter's morning run had served as a purgative of sorts, a way to exorcise the demons of the night. But on this particular morning the night sat in her stomach like a stone, weighing her down. *He's changing me,* she thought. She gave an angry little laugh, and then a little gasp. *No,* she realized, *he's changing Nova Norcross.*

The sharp edges of last night's dream cut at her psyche like broken glass. She had fallen asleep with the intention of keeping her attentions focused on changes in the Shadow Moon, but, instead, she had been forced to live inside the skin of a murdering moonbringer cultist. *I didn't agree to this,* she protested, then gave another caustic little chuckle. Hers was a prisoner's complaint about deteriorating living conditions. No one—least of all the warden—cared.

Still, she continued revisiting the dream. *What is his end game?* she wondered. She had long speculated that the series was drawing to a close, but, chained as she was to Nova Norcross's limited perspective, it was difficult to gauge exactly when that would be. Last night's events had thrown her for a loop. The end, it seemed, was either much closer than she had anticipated, or much further off.

Ember Gray. The new girl's *Savage Moon* name flew into Winter's mind like one of the daggers Ember had hurled at Nova Norcross last night. Since Kennedy's death, Winter had made it a point of principle not to spend waking hours ruminating on James's new characters, but, as this one appeared to be supplanting Nova Norcross's role as the heroine, it was difficult not to. *She's the new me. That's clear enough. And I'm, I'm...* Blunt reality smacked Winter in the face like a bucket of cold water.

I'm the new Burden Monks.

Winter forced herself to get up. The remembered dream crashed over her in waves. Pacing around the bedroom, she recalled standing at the head of the moonbringer cult. Invoking the powers of the Sorcery Moon. Promising, to the fevered acolytes, that they were standing on the precipice of an eternal night, an era that Nova Norcross would usher into being. She went further back in her mind, to earlier in the dream when she had jousted with Ember Gray, a slinky, fire-headed, emerald-eyed wonder. Comprehension doused her with another bucket of cold. *She's not only the new Nova Norcross. She's James's new muse as well.* Winter stopped pacing. She tried imagining, for a moment, Ember's real-world counterpart: a woman making her way through life, red-headed and young, and now, a woman enslaved to the whims of a capricious writer-god.

And what is it to you? The dark, disturbing humor that over the years had wrapped itself like tentacles around Winter's core self gave a little squeeze. She smiled wickedly at the dream-memory of Ember Gray giving chase to Nova Norcross. One character good, one newly evil, both of their moral temperaments beholden to the vicissitudes of James Breach's pen. "You're in the game now, honey," she said out loud to a woman she had never met. Her use of Kennedy's parlance worked like a spell in reverse, causing her dark humor ward to collapse. A fog bank of sadness moved in, and she found herself struggling, as she had so many times before, to find her way through the moral morass that was her life.

She tried to get a move on with the day. Turning on her cell phone, she checked to see if Nathaniel had called. Nothing yet. She wondered once more if she shouldn't have pressed him for his number in turn, but the thought of further infringing on his life only added to her nausea. *If he calls, he calls. If he doesn't...* She revisited the dream, trying desperately to remember if she had noticed anything different about the Shadow Moon. But, besides the recollection of a vague peripheral brightness, no memories were jogged.

Feeling her thoughts snagging on the emotional minefield that was yesterday's reunion, she focused her energy on preparing the morning meal. She considered making an omelet, but, in the end, settled on a bottom-of-the-bag bagel with dairy-free cream cheese and a quartered orange. She ate sitting at a kitchen island covered in a distasteful maple Formica laminate. Looking around the apartment, she noted, and not for the first time, how at odds her living space was with her personal vision of what a home should feel like. There were odd splashes of individuality on display—the most notable being a blue-and-maroon expressionist landscape that hung in the living room like a tantrum of personality—but, on the whole, the apartment looked more like an exercise in absence of character than a reflection of Winter's person. *And why is that?* an inner voice taunted. Oh, she knew exactly why. It was because the chief effort of her existence was to contract Winter York to a degree that Nova Norcross could do no harm.

And how is that working out for you?

She dropped her chin as if trying to avoid the piercing gaze of an interrogator. All the effort accomplished was to bring an image of Nathaniel to her mind's-eye. A forbidden thought bullied its way into existence. *Nathaniel should have been mine.* Guilt instantly pricked her conscience. She had meant it yesterday when she told Nathaniel that the last thing she wanted to do was disturb his life with his wife and child. But that didn't mean that in the gnawing pit of her soul she didn't desire the life they might have led together; the fairy tale existence that, had her timeline not been interrupted by James Breach's demonism, might have been theirs to make.

Her thoughts skipped back to that long-ago night in NoDa. To the last house where she had stamped her personality. *I was myself there,* she thought, remembering the lovely, languid way she had entertained the boy from the bookstore in the house with the white wood paneling; the playful repartee between them; the Rushdie reading and the striptease; the effortlessness of falling in love. *Falling in love.* She had always known in her heart of hearts that that was what it was. For a time, she had tried to convince herself that the magic of that night was an embellishment after the fact, created by the drama of the circumstances, and that, had they not bonded over an evening rife with danger, lust, and alcohol, they would have soon gone their separate ways. But that was bullshit. What they had had was real.

Then why did you do what you did yesterday? Winter stared at the empty plate of bagel crumbs and orange peel like it was a magic mirror that might reveal the inner workings of her heart. For years, Nathaniel's hard-won safety was the one solace that Winter had taken from her *Savage Moon* ordeal. But yesterday, only moments after discovering that he was safe, Winter had made a suggestion that placed him in mortal peril. A selfish suggestion.

'When you fall asleep, you should reach for the god of moons.'

Why?

Why did you say that?

The bagel crumbs and orange peel revealed their mystic meaning. *Because you know the price of winning a battle in this brutal war.*

She jerked away from the plate, thinking, for a horror-filled second, that she had seen Kol Jones's skull in its cloudy reflection. Angry at herself for flinching, she defiantly stared at the plate anew, daring Kol to haunt her. "I'm not at all sorry that you're dead," she spat, icing the plate with spittle. She continued staring, daring Kol to return.

A minute passed before she began to feel like a madwoman. She put the plate down and stood up in a huff. *Where's my phone?* A quick scan of the room revealed that it was in its usual spot, riding a smudgy wave of fingerprints on the glass ocean of the coffee table. She plucked it up and sat down on the dated, piebald couch. Determined tears traced rivulets of suppressed emotion down her cheeks. *Call, damn you,* she said, staring at the time on the screen, wishing that it would turn into ten digits. But if the boy she had once loved had information to share with her, he wasn't ready to do it yet.

Please, Nathaniel. Call. I need to talk to someone. I need to talk to you.

She felt her willpower breaking. She was used to solitude, to keeping her own company, but yesterday's gas station encounter had broken something open in her. She desperately needed human contact. She considered picking up a book, but the damage done by James Breach's pen had left psychic scars that prevented books from being a place of refuge. Before she could reason out her actions, she dropped her cell phone and returned to the bedroom to grab her other phone. The burner phone. Her fingers typed out a message to the one person on the planet who had been a constant in her life these past eleven years. The one person she knew would be available to her.

11:00. E.

＊

James Breach was waiting for her in the gazebo adjoined to the pond. Hands resting on khaki-clad knees, trilby on his head. He looked, as he had for years, like an actor physically ill-suited for the role of the god of moons, but one determined to win the part. He was substantially slimmer than he had been at the outset of the series, but, because the weight loss had accrued on a linebacker frame, the end result was that he looked misshapen, like an alien stuffed into a casing of human skin. He wore a crisp black jacket over a pristine white polo. Seeing Winter approach, James stood and smoothed out his pants, and smiled his hangman's smile.

Winter assumed, as she had since the incident with Kol, that he was carrying a gun.

Up in the sky, clouds shuffled along on a conveyor belt of wind. The temperature rose and fell depending on whether a cloud was covering the sun. The same breeze played at the pond water like fluttering hands, and made gooseflesh of the exposed skin on Winter's arms and upper back.

"I can't tell you how happy it made me when I saw your text."

James spoke before Winter had fully crossed the wooden walkway. She waited to answer until she was standing next to him inside the gazebo. "Why is that?"

"We have come so far, you and I. Do you know there was a time in our relationship when I took you for granted? But no longer. After what happened with Kol, and after what you attempted with the ivy, you showed me the truth of who you are. Ever since, I feel that our relationship has been more...collaborative. It was necessary now, I believe, for me to feel what you had felt for so long. Like you might"—he paused, and looked deep into her eyes—"kill me. Out of that...let's call it creative tension...new possibilities emerged. Possibilities that made moments like this possible." He paused. "I know why you're here. And as my creative partner, you have a right to know: What comes next?"

What we have isn't a partnership, she thought. But she didn't say it. "Okay, then. Tell me. What comes next?"

James readied a noose on the gallows of his lips. "I suppose that depends on you." He motioned to the gazebo bench. "Let's sit down, shall we?"

She took a seat. James sat down beside her, and, to her surprise, removed the hat. The short, sandy-blond hair atop his head looked like a wheat field after the reaping. Seeing it relaxed Winter. His blond hair was much less unnerving than the god of moon's bald pate.

"What did you think of Ember Gray?" He pronounced the name in a way that made it clear he had practiced saying it hundreds of times.

Winter gritted her teeth. She didn't know if she was protective of the girl or jealous of her. "She isn't Nova Norcross, but she has a certain flair." The truth kept coming. "I can see why you chose her."

James nodded, pleased. "You and I both know that no one can replace you. But for the series to move forward, a new protagonist had to be introduced."

For the series to move forward. James's words should have made Winter apoplectic with rage, but she merely felt resigned. "The series isn't ending?" She gathered her strength. "What do you mean to do with me?"

James beamed. "I loved how you said 'me' just then. As if there were no difference between the woman sitting before me and the wondrous creation that is Nova Norcross." He hurried on before she could protest. "I was thinking…I've been thinking for some time, actually…that Nova Norcross might become the goddess of moons." He paused. "We will rule the *Savage Moon* universe together."

The shock of his suggestion stunned her. She didn't know what to say. He took her silence as permission to continue. "You are not who you were, Winter York. You haven't been since you fired that gun at Kol." He leaned forward so that his arms rested on his knees. For a horrible, spellbinding second, she not only thought that he was going to reach out and touch her, she almost wanted him to. "You made a choice. A choice that I respect. You chose to fight. To survive." His voice turned tender. "I know that what you want more than anything else is to defeat me. And I'm sorry that's the one thing I cannot let you do. But what I can offer you instead is the chance to flourish. To thrive. You need only do what you took the first step toward doing when we worked together to set aside Burden Monks." He showed her his eggshell teeth. "Embrace, at long last, your full potential as Nova Norcross."

Winter tried to wrap her mind around what he was suggesting. To some degree, she knew that he was right. She *had* changed since she made the decision to ally with James against Kol. She had changed so much, in fact, that there were moments when she worried that she had gone too far. Moments when she worried that she had passed the point of no return.

James looked like he knew what she was thinking. Desperate to throw him off the scent, Winter forced herself to scoff. "Don't pretend that you've been on my side this whole time. We both know that you were leveraging Kol and I against each other. The only reason I'm alive and he's dead is because you decided mine was the more compelling storyline."

James shrugged and presented his wrists as if for handcuffs. "I'm a writer. It's what I do."

Winter looked away. She revisited, for the thousandth time, the fallout from her decision to shoot Kol. Kol, who had been crippled in body by the gunshot but not in mind. And what a vengeful mind it was. Days after the shooting, Winter had received a letter detailing the many unconscionable acts he intended to commit against her the moment circumstances allowed it. *The only reason I lied to the police, bitch, is because I wouldn't dare do anything that might jeopardize my opportunity to exact revenge against you personally,* read one of the tamer parts of the letter. It was a horrific time: Kennedy was dead and Winter was certain her life would soon come to an end. The only question was whether Kol or James would commit the act. But, to her surprise, James built a text message bridge to her, implying, over and over again, that they could find a way forward. She was convinced it was a ruse to get her to drop her guard, but, when James made it clear that he wouldn't hesitate to follow through on his longstanding threat to hurt her loved ones if she didn't meet him before the week was up, she met him in a public space. There he persuaded her that their interests were aligned: she had done him a favor by crippling a man who had become an unpredictable liability, and, in turn, he would protect her against any recriminations Kol might want to take. James made good on his promise by stringing Kol along, promising the henchman that he could have his vengeance against Winter in the *Savage Moon* dreamworld, while at the same time securing assurances that he wouldn't do anything rash until then. Winter knew that James was playing the both of them to his advantage, but she also genuinely believed that James preferred her storyline over Kol's.

Two nights ago, he had at long last proven her right.

The wind quickened once more. It played the lattice straps on Winter's open-back top like a spirited harpist.

Out on the pond, geese toy-boated across the water.

"And if I decide that I want nothing to do with being your partner? Nothing to do with being the *goddess of moons*? What happens then?"

James reached out and touched her on the arm. "Then there is nothing left for us to do but go our separate ways."

Winter's breath caught in her throat. She wasn't sure if it was from fear, or relief. She had no doubt that 'go our separate ways' was James's way of saying that he would kill her off in the dreamworld, but, nevertheless, the thought of everything coming to an end made Winter feel an unbearable lightness of being.

James continued, "Tonight, you have a choice to make. In as Nova Norcross. Or out as Winter York." His smile segued into a sigh. "I understand if you want out. Truly, I do. And I promise: if you do want out, I will accommodate you." He paused. "But that's not what I want. What I want…is to share the world I've created with the person who helped me build it." He squeezed her arm. Smiled a secret smile. "We both know that's what you want too. It's the reason you brought me the Shadow Moon."

Winter weighed her response on the scales of silence. Was he trying to trick her? She didn't know what to say. She only knew that a response was needed, a placeholder to maintain the delicate equilibrium between them. Feeling time ticking away, she offered him the confidence of her eyes until the words came to her.

"It's like you can read my mind."

He laughed an unsettling laugh. "For both of our sakes, let's hope so."

The wind kicked up again. It was high enough to howl, and howl it did, yipping and yelling and whipping and wailing and grabbing at James's trilby. In the blink of an eye the wind sent the hat tumbling over the gazebo railing and into the pond.

"Damn it to hell." James rose, flustered, and stepped onto the short bridge that connected the gazebo to the shore. He looked as if he was going to kneel and paw at the water, but, upon seeing the trilby move farther out of reach, he simply stood and watched it drift away.

Now, Winter thought. She stood and strode past him. She felt his eyes settle on her back as she walked away, alighting on the twisting ivy spire.

"Nova," he said.

She kept walking.

"Winter," he called again.

She put a hiccup in her step, but didn't stop.

He laughed. A god-of-moons's cachinnation. When at last he stopped laughing, he called after her. "Tonight."

And then again.

"Tonight."

*

She spent the rest of her day staring at her cell phone. Hoping that the boy she had loved long ago would save her, if not from James Breach, then at least from herself.

But the phone never rang.

V

James Breach had a ritual, before he wrote, of going outside and staring at the moon. He would rise at the witching hour, brew a cup of premium Stumptown coffee on the Keurig, and step out onto the Juliet balcony connected to the master bedroom doors of his French country home. Then he would scan the sky. New moons and cloudy nights were always a disappointment, although that didn't necessarily mean they were a harbinger of writer's block. He was a professional, after all, and could, using the powers bestowed upon him by the supernatural force that favored his talents, push through. But seeing the silvery satellite—whether gibbous or crescent, waxing or waning, half or whole—always stirred him to the creative act, so that the moment his coffee cup was emptied, he went inside to write.

Tonight, on this most augural of nights, the moon was waxing gibbous. *Fitting,* he thought, for it reminded him of the Shadow Moon, whose form, even when clear in his mind's-eye, remained smudged at the edges. *Tonight, I must will it to full,* he told himself. A draught of fear fluttered his insides as he considered the possibility that the Shadow Moon would not accede to his wishes. He elected not to fight the sensation, and instead allowed it to fill him up, like cold air from an open window pouring into a room.

It is a risk that you must take.

Tonight, you must risk everything.

He sipped on the coffee slowly. It was nice out, cool and temperate, the wild winds from earlier in the day having resolved their fury. He remembered for a moment his lost trilby—now likely bobbing near the pond's banks—but he quickly pushed the thought aside. He chose instead, as he often did, to imagine the *Savage Moon* universe overlaid on top of this one. The way a conventional writer might. First, he imagined the savage moon of the moment—the Sorcery Moon—high in the sky, bubbling and brewing. Then he imagined Nova Norcross's winged silhouette against the moon's ghastly green light, and then he imagined his newest heroine, Ember Gray, running around on terra firma, tracking Nova's flight path. Hovering nearby was the Shadow Moon. He imagined the *Savage Moon* universe as it was in his head, when his hands were not on the keyboard.

After a moment, he noticed that his eyes were closed. He opened them and laughed.

His imaginings had nothing on the real thing.

He stepped back inside. His office was located on the opposite end of the house upstairs. He made his way there with a priestly precision of movement, making every step a part of the writing sacrament. Though his fingers had yet to touch the keys, he could feel his body readying itself for the alternate reality, transitioning to a state that was much closer to the writing experience than his trivial imaginings on the Juliet balcony. Leaving the master bedroom behind, he made his way down an L-shaped hallway that overlooked the living areas downstairs, his fingers trailing on the gallery balustrade. The sepulchral quiet of the house his only accompaniment. At the end of the hallway, he turned left into a miserly box of a room.

He had never intended to use the room as a permanent writing space. The previous owners had utilized the room as an upstairs nursery, but, when James purchased the house, he set up his computer and desk in the room, thinking it would serve until he could overhaul the downstairs office. But the overhaul never happened. Something about the compression of the room…worked. It wasn't that he had had difficulty transitioning to the dream state in previous writing spaces; it was only that, in this particular room, the experience seemed deeper, more enveloping.

Once inside the room, he turned on the desk-side lamp with the drum shade. Its soft light painted the room with a muted brightness. Next, he coaxed the computer from its sleeping state with a fingertip brush of the touchpad. The computer groaned in response, a mechanical, whooshing complaint, but it came to life all the same, adding a coat of blue light to the soft yellow. Then he sat down on his Herman Miller office chair, and, with a few clicks of the mouse, summoned the work in progress to the screen. Upon scrolling to the present page, he removed his hands from the hardware.

He glanced at the digital clock in the computer's lower right-hand corner.

12:41.

James Breach took a long, deep breath. His thoughts snapped back to that magic moment close to a decade and a half ago when it had all begun, when his grasping writerly mind plunged into a dream of his own making, a dream so visceral and real that reality paled in comparison, a dream that, upon the leaving of it, he found he could revisit again and again. The mystery of his newfound magic was compounded by his befuddlement at the source of it. How, after years of writing, had this occurred? The answer came first in drips and drops, then by intuition, as he thought about the two young women in his creative writing class who had inspired him to write the book in the first place.

His powers, his magic, his godlike ability to fashion a living, breathing dreamworld, came from touching others and plunging them into the dreamworld with him. Regardless of whether they wanted to go or not.

He resumed his normal breathing pattern. Whatever vestiges of guilt he had once felt for destroying the lives of others had long disappeared. Being a writer meant you either played god, or you did not.

And he had made his choice long ago.

He raised his hands to the keyboard.

VI

Outside of Nathaniel's home office window, the dark of the night sky.

He looked despondently at the printer paper strewn on the desk before him. The laser-jet printouts of a madman. He had spent the day absorbed in the work, believing, in his soul of souls, that what he was doing might be of use in the dreamworld. But now that night had fallen, it seemed a fool's preoccupation, the futile flailing of a hack author. If his dream the night before had taught him anything, it was that the *Savage Moon* universe was James Breach's realm. *This,* he thought, gathering the papers into his hands, *was an exercise in desperation.*

The idea had seized upon him in the morning. Upon awakening from his nightlong tete-a-tete with the god of moons, Nathaniel knew beyond a shadow of a doubt that his dreamworld powers were unequal to James Breach's. If there was to be any hope of imposing his will on the god of moons inside the dreamworld, he needed to bolster his psychic reserves. To that end, he decided to spend the day writing versions of James Breach's story that ended with the Shadow Moon freeing Nova Norcross from the god of moons's grip. *If you write it into being, you can will it into being.* But now that his imagination was spent, his plan seemed naïve. *If anyone manipulates anyone,* he thought, *it will be the god of moons manipulating me.*

Nathaniel tried to gulp down his fear. But his mind kept returning to the god of moons's vision for Nova Norcross. More than anything, Nathaniel wanted to be the catalyst for Winter's salvation, but based on what the god of moons had shared with him, Nathaniel knew there was a better chance that he would be the catalyst for her undoing.

He glanced at the digital clock on the computer. 9:32. *I should call Winter,* he thought for the thousandth time that day. But every conversation he pictured included admitting the truth: namely that nothing about his encounter with the god of moons had given him hope that he could alter James Breach's designs. And if he was destined to fail Winter, he saw no point in distressing her about it beforehand.

A knock on the door. Angelica poked her head inside the office, the cascade of her blonde hair sweeping around her shoulder. Her expression was a mixture of curiosity and feigned unconcern. "You know that you've been in here the entire day, right? Did inspiration strike? Or should I contact the looney bin?"

The sight of his wife caused his heart to ache. *What the fuck am I doing?* he thought. *Why the fuck am I risking my life for a woman that I barely know?* "I'm leaning toward the looney bin," he fake-laughed, shaking the papers at her.

Angelica raised her eyebrows and gave a little shrug. "Do you want me to take a look at it?"

He considered his wife with a dopey, plastic grin, a mask to hide the roiling, riotous emotions tearing at his insides. "No," he replied. He felt his will hardening even as he rejected her offer, his resolve growing canyon-deep. He had only two options before him, and, of the two, seeing it through to the end was the only one that he could live with. "It's not where it needs to be yet," he said.

Angelica looked at him with a *come-back-to-me* smile. But as had been the case ever since the dawn of their second life together, she determined to let him return to her at his own speed. "Okay. You do what you need to do. I'm going to bed." And with her smile still haunting him, she disappeared, and Nathaniel was alone again.

Nathaniel took a deep breath. Closed his eyes. Cleared his mind. After a few moments the threads of the story came together once more in his mind's-eye, filaments of fiction forming into something greater than its disparate parts.

He turned to his computer once more. *Write it into being,* he thought. *Then will it to life.*

VII

The drifting began shortly after he started typing. The best James could describe it was like he was sitting on a raft on the shore of the beach, and his keystrokes were the waves that carried him away. In the early phases he had to row against the current, but it wasn't long before he was afloat in deeper waters, adrift in the dream.

And what a dream it was. Picking up where he had left off the previous night, he brought Ember Gray into focus. His new *Savage Moon* queen, with her hair like a crown of hellfire. He tugged at the line of her consciousness and found her, as expected, asleep. The *he* that was *he* inside the dream smiled at the ease with which his newfound muse assented to slumber. *Jordana Fawkes is her real name,* his waking mind reminded him, but he pushed the thought aside. As far as James was concerned, only Ember Gray existed now. Far off he could feel his fingers flying. And as they flew, so did Ember. She tore through the many twisting paths of an amusement park at night, frantically searching for Nova Norcross and the moonbringer cult, trying desperately to stop the onetime superheroine from joining her powers to the moon god. But instead, beneath the swooping curve of a giga coaster track, Ember discovered members of the moonbringer cult lying for her in wait.

They fell on her with a nightmarish fury.

James waited until the fighting was in full force, and then he cut away from the scene. His plan was to return to Ember at the novel's end: she would emerge from the fracas bruised and battered but still alive, the only ray of light in an otherwise dark ending. It would not be the ending that the readers expected—James had implied for some time that this would be the last book in the series—but he knew it was an ending that the readers would accept. Readers pretended to want happy, hopeful endings, but James understood that what they really wanted was an excuse to continue reveling in the darkness.

It's time, James thought. He was always "present" in the *Savage Moon* dreamworld, but more often than not his presence was metaphysical, abstract. It was only when he changed into the god of moons that he could live out the experiences.

Becoming the deity was as simple a matter as typing in one world, and materializing in another: in the span of a slipping second, James was alive inside of the dreamworld, transformed into the character-god otherwise known as the god of moons. Once settled in his deific skin, James scanned the dark-lit horizon. Licked his lips. Dreamed of her arrival. The dream turned into words on the page, words that brought Nova Norcross to him.

His muse silver-slashed across the sky, a human lightning bolt.

James quietly reveled in his victory. A small part of him had worried that she would refuse to fall asleep. That he would be forced to bully her into slumber. But here she was. As planned.

They stared at each other across the celestial plain, sharing the ineffable now.

In a faraway world, James stopped typing.

This, he thought, *is my reason for being.*

Satisfied, he turned his gaze skyward, and commanded her to do the same. High above, the two moons paraded their respective majesties. The Sorcery Moon, like every savage moon before it, was an instrument of design, created to elicit a specific response from any who laid eyes on it: namely, fear. Conversely, the Shadow Moon was a cipher, an entity that asked a question instead of answering it. After years of circling each other in the sky, the two satellites were close enough to kiss.

"Nova Norcross," the god of moons purred. "My lovely. My sweet. I'm so glad you came."

She fingered the moon pendant encircling her neck, playing the part of the willful servant. But she didn't look at him. Instead, her eyes stayed fixed on the two moons. "There's going to be an eclipse."

"Yes," he responded. "Yes, there is."

Nova Norcross dropped her gaze and gave him a no-nonsense stare. "What does the eclipse mean?"

His soul swelled with joy. "It means that a window is opening. It means that you, my most cherished servant, may choose to join me in the pantheon of gods."

"Join you?"

"Yes. Join me. Become the goddess of moons. Rule alongside me." He glanced skyward, where the Shadow Moon took its first bite of the Sorcery Moon. "When the eclipse is total, all you have to do is take my hand and surrender your name."

She gave him a strange look, but said nothing.

He smiled in response. They both knew that Nova wasn't the name he had in mind. "It's time for you to leave your old life behind. It's time for you to become who you have always been destined to be."

In the sky above, the empty white sphere devoured the ghastly green one.

The god of moons threw his head back and surrendered to the encroaching void.

Control slipped from his fingers. In an instant, the dreamworld was up for grabs. *This is what it feels like to be one of my characters,* he thought. For a moment he felt pure: like any god worth his salt, he had come to live among his creation as his creation. Turning over power to the Shadow Moon was a risk, but one he felt prepared to take. If Winter was the source of its inspiration, he could manage the fallout. After all, he had done it before with the ivy tattoo.

And if she wasn't...well, he had his own theories as to the origin of the Shadow Moon.

Nova stepped toward him across space and time. *My Nova.* James's brain stumbled on a tripwire and for a brief moment he was back in the lecture hall where he had first seen her years ago, the lovely, nameless young woman who had catalyzed the creation of this remarkable universe of the mind, but then he righted himself to find her taking his hand, closing the circle. "Your name," he requested. He leaned in close. "Your real name." He would change it to Nova when he edited the book, but, in this moment, that wasn't the name he wanted.

He waited for "Winter" to fall from her lips. Of her own free will. Of her own accord.

But when he looked at her, she appeared lost in the ocean of her mind. It was unsettling. Nova Norcross had for so long been a creature of his design, bound to his whims and desires, but now, for the first time in the series, she was free to make her own decision. Looking at her, it was clear that she was struggling with the choice. *She will do what I've suggested. It's the only rational decision.* But the longer he looked at her, the less certain he felt. He thought that he had presented the choice in such a way that it wasn't a choice at all: either she joined with him in this world, or she departed the other one. And yet there she stood across from him, operating in a space where he had no purchase: the vast and unknowable realm of her private thoughts.

He felt a tingling of fear.

At last, she surfaced, and took a small breath. Craning her neck, she cast a long and meaningful look at the Shadow Moon. Then her eyes hardened with resolve. "I choose to take your name instead.

"James Breach."

VIII

Nathaniel slipped into bed shortly before midnight, the newly written pages swimming in his head. With his right hand he reached out and touched Angelica on the small of her back. As expected, she was already lost to slumber. Sighing, Nathaniel closed his eyes and readied himself to enter an alternate reality.

A little less than an hour later he awoke inside of a beautiful nightmare. Far below he could see his long-lost love flying above a world in shambles, leading a parade of madness; while closer to Earth, her newfound foil performed complex feats of derring-do, dancing for a master off-screen. Nathaniel, conversely, simply existed. Existing as the Shadow Moon felt akin to being a god on high, except that, if he paid close enough attention, he could feel the faint pull of the puppet master's strings.

Above and behind him, the Sorcery Moon. Glowing. Brewing. Bubbling. Stewing.

Nathaniel leaned his lunar body in an intercepting direction. The equivalent of asking James Breach a question.

Not yet, came the reply. *Soon.*

An instant later, the god of moons appeared. The puppet master, stepping on stage. Like an angel or a demon, James Breach's dreamworld avatar hovered in the sorcerous sky, drawing the entirety of the *Savage Moon* universe toward him like gravity.

One object flew faster than the rest. From the far horizon, Nathaniel's long-lost love rocketed to the god of moon's side. *Winter.* Supposedly she was Nova Norcross here in the dreamworld, but Nathaniel knew that was an illusion, a trick the god of moon's played on himself.

In reality, she was always and only Winter York.

Nathaniel watched from his perch in the heavens as the god of moons and Nova Norcross began to talk. He listened as the god of moons told himself lies, the biggest of all being that he could have the one thing he had always been denied.

Winter York's surrender.

But the god of moons was determined to believe. And therein Nathaniel saw his opening.

Now, Nathaniel thought. *Will it to life.* Taking hold of the puppet strings, he tugged back ever so gently, and whispered a lie of his own into the god of moons' ears. *She will give herself to you. Freely. If only you will give up control and give her the opportunity.*

The god of moons heard what he wanted to hear. Seconds later, the Shadow Moon reached its long-appointed destination.

The eclipse had begun.

The weight of the Sorcery Moon's shadow was tremendous. It was, after all, the symbolic source of the god of moons' power. But Nathaniel bore it on his back with the burgeoning belief that his vision of an ending might win out.

In the sky below, Winter capitalized on the newly open window of free will to extract a long-awaited revenge.

IX

Nova grabbed hold of his body. He didn't fight back. Her wings, like feathered pistons, drove them toward the earth, the soft flush of her feathers batting against his face. It was a heaven, a hell, an exhilaration, a disappointment. *Why can't you see what the two of us might be together?* He had tried so hard for so long to build a bridge between them, only for her to choose once again to go to war against him.

But this time there would be no coming back.

This time he would end her.

And still they fell. He told himself that he would resist her in a second, but doing so meant that the dream of Nova Norcross was over, and he wasn't ready for that. Over her shoulder, he could see the Shadow Moon. Its empty white form draped over the Sorcery Moon like a magician's cape. Seeing it, he felt perplexed. Befuddled. Was he missing something? Far away, he could feel his fingers typing, ever typing, always typing, only for once the cord wasn't connected and he couldn't make them stop.

Something was wrong.

He tried to throw her off him, for naught. Panic coursed through his veins. He had known that he was taking a risk in allowing the eclipse to occur, but based on the connection he had made with the Shadow Moon the night before, he felt confident he could quickly right any deviation from the intended storyline.

It appeared that he was wrong.

Someone that he wasn't consciously aware of had control of the story.

Nova slammed him into the ground. Impact drove the air from his lungs, causing a stampede of pain. His wits scattered to the wind. Nova grabbed him by the collar and began dragging him along the ground, but his mind wasn't with her, it was scrambling after the Judas moon high above. The imposter. *We had an understanding,* he ineffectually thought. With an animal desperateness, he labored to mount a defense. He grasped after the secondary satellite, but the hardwired connection he had established the night before was no longer there. Quickly, he tried to deduce where he had gone wrong, but nothing added up. He reached after Winter. She was still there, but his subconscious mind was under the influence of another.

Nova hauled him toward the edge of a forest. He knew what was coming. The ivy. Nova spoke, and the shoots of green came to life like a monstrous snake stirred from its den, moving toward him, wrapping him up. His brain was a fog, but the prospect of death pierced the veil. There was a small part of his mind where he still had agency, and it was there where he retraced his steps from the past week, trying to ignore the tendrils of ivy squeezing his life force away. The Shadow Moon, he understood, was writing the book through him. He had thought that he had the Shadow Moon under his thumb, had thought, after communing with it yesterday, that it was nothing more than a manifestation of either his or Winter's subconscious desires, but now he understood that it was a separate entity entirely. *Quick! Remember!* But there was so little yield from the previous week, only Nova and Ember, and when he reached out to their real-world counterparts, there was no change, no difference.

Who else could it be?

Who else?

A dagger-sharp memory. *The man from the restaurant.* The only person outside of Winter, Kol, and Jordana that James had made physical contact with this week. But it didn't make sense. The man from the restaurant was dead: James had seen his head sliced off firsthand, making him one of one-hundred forty-two formerly alive persons that James had seen off the planet through the means of his mind. This particular death had been one of James's favorites: James had been on the verge of snaring much prettier prey before the S.O.B.'s cockblocking tactics; plus, Nova had been the one to administer the deathblow, cementing her place in the god of moons's retinue. That fellow was *dead* dead. But reality suggested the opposite: the mere thought of the man caused the ivy's boa-constrictor grip to lessen. High above, the Shadow Moon at last slipped off the surface of the sorcery moon, allowing green to bleed through.

In response, Nova doubled her efforts. Her ivy tattoo didn't have the hold it once did on James's subconscious mind, but its imprint was still strong, an imprint that, combined with the efforts of the Shadow Moon, she used to considerable effect. She stood over him, working through the ivy, conjuring magic that normally belonged only to him.

His lungs were like a squeezed balloon, ready to pop.

The man from the restaurant! James forced himself to focus. High above, the Shadow Moon continued sliding, losing its grip. James continued fighting, thrashing against the ivy, trying to free his avatar's form from the throttling vine. He was making real headway now, enough that he could see the worry in Nova's eyes. He kept his thoughts fixed on the man from the restaurant, searching for the connection, scuttling backward through the memory years to when the Shadow Moon first appeared. And then, like a key sliding into a lock, he saw the young man that he had spared. Winter's one-night love affair. A flash of a tattoo as they grappled with each other in Winter's NoDa abode.

The dormant image of the Shadow Moon, once again brought to life.

And with the image, a name.

Nathaniel.

Nathaniel Pilot.

He poured all of his strength into pushing Nathaniel away.

The eclipse ended in a frenzy of shredded vines. The god of moons pushed himself up off the ground and looked to the sky, where the Sorcery Moon reigned once more. Once again, he had won. Once again, he had prevailed.

Now it was time for revenge.

The god of moons recalibrated his stare and took in Nova Norcross. The familiar scimitar-smile carved open his face.

"Tsk, tsk, Nova. That was a mist—"

He buckled at the knees. He felt woozy. Confused. He checked Nova's expression for an explanation, but her countenance befuddled him: she wore the mask of an avenging angel, a mask he had made her wear many times before, although in that drifting, darkening moment he didn't have a clue whether her choice of expression was hers or his.

He found that he could not hold her gaze.

His chin dropped.

In the light of the ghastly green-black Sorcery Moon, he saw that his suit was covered in blood.

Falling to the ground, his last vision was of the shredded vines.

They were covered in thorns.

X

He was certain that he had failed her.

For the longest time, he had no idea what was happening below him. It was all that he could do to hold fast to the Sorcery Moon; all that he could do to evade the god of moon's panicked, grasping mind; all that he could do to bear up under the tremendous weight of ushering a world that wasn't his into oblivion. He kept hoping that at any moment he would wake up, and that, by virtue of his waking, James Breach would be dead and the *Savage Moon* dreamworld would have collapsed.

But instead, the dream persisted. The Sorcery Moon slipped from his grip. And James Breach, frantically following the breadcrumb trail of memory, found Nathaniel hiding eleven years down the line.

The eclipse ended instead of the dream. Nathaniel, bereft of his powers, stared down from the heavens and saw a spine-chilling, soul-sucking sight. The god of moons was advancing on Winter with a vengeful intent. Nathaniel looked on with paralytic horror, expecting at any moment to see Winter struck down before his eyes.

But after a couple of steps, James Breach's dreamworld avatar slowed, stumbled, and collapsed to the ground.

It was only then that Nathaniel noticed that the god of moon's suit was soaked in blood.

Time stood still. Nathaniel tried to reason through what had happened, but he didn't have enough context to make sense of it, nor did he understand why the dreamworld hadn't vanished the instant its creator died. Or maybe it had? Each time he thought to look for something in the dreamworld it was already gone: the Sorcery Moon disappeared at the approach of his gaze, as did the members of the moonbringer cult, as did the hellscape below, as did the corpse of the god of moons. *I must be awake, or wakening,* Nathaniel thought. But then his eyes alit upon a dreamworld vision, the only fantasy remaining.

Nova Norcross.

Or rather, Winter York.

The universe narrowed to Winter. She took flight on mythic, midnight-colored wings, cutting through the vanishing tableau like she had long been the only entity inside of the universe that was real. Up, up, up she flew, ascending toward a moon transforming into a man. As Nathaniel watched her approach, he could no longer tell if he was in James Breach's dreamworld or a different realm entirely. But then Winter was before him, and he decided that he didn't care.

She wore a smile made of eleven-year-old memories. Her wings retracted, and with them the last vestiges of Nova Norcross. Nathaniel studied her face with an intimate slowness, indulging in the simple pleasure of seeing Winter for who she truly was. His eyes slipped from her face to her neck, and there he saw the twining ivy twisting away from her spine, reaching for her visage like it was sunlight. Understanding that he was missing something, his eyes lingered on the tattoo, until at last the difference dawned on him: thorns had been added to the ivy, small blades of suffering. Insight multiplied upon insight. *James must have seen the thorns without consciously realizing that Winter had changed her tattoo. She used them as a secret weapon*. Processing this, he looked at her with newfound wonder; but when she returned his gaze, he understood that she didn't want to be the object of his adoration.

She wanted, if only for a moment, to share his love.

He tried to communicate to her something that was lasting and real. But the dream was starting to slip. Whatever realm they were in, it was, like every other realm where their paths had crossed, a passing place. It was so thin, in fact, that Nathaniel could see through the membrane of reality to his waking life; for a moment he thought he was falling through, waking up, losing, for once and for all, his connection to Winter York.

But then she reached for his hand. Her skin was soft and cool, reminiscent of an autumn morning years ago. With her touch, their connection strengthened once more. He looked at her, and saw that she was looking into the soul of him.

He listened hard to what she had to say.

"Don't. Ever. Fucking. Forget Me."

He laughed a reflexive laugh, and she followed in turn. Then the tears began to flow. He wanted to say something similarly distinct and personal in return, but the dream was already dissolving again, their time together determined to take its leave.

Winter held the dream together by stepping forward and kissing him. The taste of forever was on her lips. It triggered a movie reel of memories: their shared past ran through Nathaniel's mind in perfect clarity, starting with Winter standing outside of the mall and then progressing rapidly, tattoos and a pizza parlor and a Rushdie reading followed by the slow nightmare of everything that followed. Throughout, waves of emotion pounded the shores of Nathaniel's being: love and heartache and melancholy mixed with horror and hopelessness, the surf pounding and pounding with unremitting force, until all at once Nathaniel's mind came hurtling into the perfect present, where all had been redeemed.

At which point Nathaniel opened his eyes and realized with a start that he was awake.

Epilogue

It was late evening when Winter entered the Tattered Cover Bookstore in Denver, Colorado. It didn't take her long to find what she was looking for: the final book in James Breach's *Savage Moon* series stood on one of the display tables near the front of the store, screaming for attention with its peacocking cover. She considered the design with a studied detachment. The four moons from the final book paraded across the nighttime sky. The rotting, maggot-filled, red-and-ghostly-white Corpse Moon. The mammoth, silver-and-blue streaked Colossus Moon. The brewing, bubbling, green-purple-and-black Sorcery Moon. And last, looking like a dream within a dream, the cloud-cut Shadow Moon.

She picked up the book. With her right thumb, Winter traced the contours of the Shadow Moon. Her thoughts were starting down a familiar path when a voice jarred her from her reverie.

"Aren't you excited to finally read it? Especially with all the gossip surrounding the author's death?"

Winter turned to find a brunette-haired woman perhaps ten years her junior, staring at her with a co-conspirator's smile. Winter gave a polite smile in return, returned the book to the display stand, and took a small step back. "Um. I'm not sure. I've had mixed feelings actually." She raised conflicted eyebrows at the woman. "I might even skip this one."

The woman looked at Winter like she was insane. "But you've read the others, right? How could you skip the finale?"

The answer was so simple that Winter was filled with a sudden joy. She gave a short, sharp, two-punch laugh. "You know, I think that after all this time, I finally realized that the series just isn't for me."

She left the befuddled woman standing at the book display, and retreated into the bowels of the bookstore. For weeks she had been dreading the release of the final book in the series, believing, in her haunted heart, that with the book's release James Breach would somehow find a way to upend her life even from the grave. But now that the day was here, now that she had touched the book and no harm had come to her, she understood, once and for all, that she was finally and truly free.

She soon found herself in the fiction section. She lingered among the books, her eyes alighting on the spines like songbirds trying out different branches. There had once been a time when idling in a bookstore was one of her greatest pleasures, but her sojourns to the Savage Moon dreamworld put a pall on that activity; she couldn't help but associate them with her own imprisonment. But now...now she felt like she could fall in love with bookstores all over again.

Slowly, she made her way through the alphabet. Once, she pulled a book from the shelves with a large crow on the cover. She stared at it for a time without processing the title or the author. Her only thought: *Kennedy.* When she had drunk her fill, she touched two fingers to her lips and transferred the kiss to the crow, and then reshelved the book with loving care.

Feeling a burden lifted, she continued down the line, stopping now and then whenever a title or a cover drew her interest. She had two books in hand for purchase when, near the end of the Rs, she discovered a tidy string of novels written by Salman Rushdie. Nestled between two hardcovers were a handful of the author's paperbacks, among them *Shalimar the Clown*.

She pulled the book from the shelf. The frayed rope on the cover brought a tear to her eye. She had lost her original copy—the one she had taken from Nathaniel in exchange for a Camel Light—during an apartment move a couple of years after her "second beginning" with James. The circumstances surrounding the loss of the book were difficult to recall with clarity, but, as best she could remember, she had left it behind at the old apartment in the hopes that she might more easily move on from the boy she had once loved if there wasn't always a book at her place reminding her of his existence.

Now, she felt differently. She no longer wanted to move on: she wanted to cherish, to remember. *I'll buy it,* she thought. *Better, I'll finally read it.* A smile of the sweetest sorrow filled her face as she thought about that long ago night at her place in NoDa, when she had performed a playful striptease for her newfound crush in exchange for the pleasure of being read to. A part of her wanted to hold fast to that memory and that memory only, but it was soon replaced, as it always was, by the image she had of Nathaniel now, a man who was both a husband and a father.

I'll buy the book. But I have to give up something else in return.

She placed the books in her hand—*Shalimar the Clown* included—on the bookshelf. Then she took her cell phone from her pocket. Her heart felt fluttery and her hands felt weak, but, with a few simple touches, she called to the screen the dead-of-night text message exchange she had shared with Nathaniel seven months prior.

Nathaniel: **This is Nathaniel. Are you okay? Are you alive?**

Winter: **Yes. It worked. It really worked. It's over.**

Nathaniel: (1/2) **Oh thank God. I know what I experienced, and I think I know what you experienced, but I still wanted to make sure that you were okay. The end of the dream…**

Nathaniel: (2/2) **I thought we were in the same place, but I wasn't sure if it was real or if I was dreaming a dream of my own making.**

Winter: **It was real. We were both there. You heard what I said to you, right?**

Nathaniel: **Yes.**

Winter: **That's all I ask. Everything else between us has to remain unsaid.**

Nathaniel: **I know. And I promise. I never will.**

There were so many times that night and so many times since when she had been tempted to continue the conversation, so many times when she had stared at the text message conversation and sensed that Nathaniel was struggling with the same choice on the other end; but in the end, months and months passed and it became clear they had surrendered their relationship to a lovely, bittersweet limbo. Now the only thing left to do was to honor the beauty of that decision forever.

She swiped left, erasing the text message conversation. Then she went into her contacts, and erased Nathaniel's name from there as well.

She took a deep breath and smiled. Then she picked the books back off the shelf and made her way to the register.

When she stepped outside the bookstore, the Denver night had grown cold and crisp. High above, a waxing moon showcased its celestial colors, painting the city with a splendid, silvery light. Winter, making her way to her vehicle, didn't notice it. It wasn't until she was in her car and driving west that she caught the moon's reflection in the rearview mirror, flashing like a trout in a river of stars. She glanced at it for only a moment, and then redirected her gaze toward her future.